Taken by SURPRISE

by

Kenna White

Bella
BOOKS

2011

Bella Books, Inc.
P.O. Box 10543
Tallahassee, FL 32302

Printed in the United States of America on acid-free paper
First published 2011

Editor: Katherine V. Forrest
Cover Designer: Judy Fellows

ISBN 13: 978-1-59493-268-7

Other Bella Books by Kenna White

Beautiful Journey

Beneath the Willow

Body Language

Braggin Rights

Comfortable Distance

Romancing the Zone

Shared Winds

Skin Deep

Yours for the Asking.

Dedication

This book is dedicated to all those volunteers who rolled up their sleeves, stepped over the debris and rushed to the aid of those who lost so much to the May 22nd tornado that ravaged Joplin, Missouri, my hometown. We can't imagine surviving the endless days of devastation without your donations, support and hard work. Just when we thought it was too much to bear, a shoulder and a smile were there to carry us through. I am forever grateful.

It is also dedicated to Karen for her friendship and honesty. And to Marvita for her passion, patience and her sincerity. Like the air that I breathe, I can't imagine this past year without them.

Acknowledgments

A big hug and thank you to my readers for their kind words of encouragement that keep me motivated. And to Hannah, Pam, Lee, Denise, Kat, Loretta and all my other pillars of support. I wish you soft breezes and gentle journeys.

About The Author

Kenna White lives in a small town nestled in southern Missouri where she enjoys her writing, traveling, making dollhouse miniatures and life's simpler pleasures. After living from the Rocky Mountains to New England, she is once again back where bare feet, faded jeans and lazy streams fill her life.

Chapter 1

Leigh Insley stood over the box of chains, hugging her leather jacket over her chest as the wind-whipped snow swirled around her. The sub-freezing temperatures burned her lungs and made her nipples ache but she had no choice. Surely all her years of college and her one hundred forty-seven IQ meant she could install snow chains. She pulled her cell phone from her pocket and pressed the eight on her speed dial. Maybe Maureen would know. She knew everything else.

"Maureen? Is that you?" she said to the coughing voice on the other end of the line.

"Yes." The woman sneezed then coughed again.

"Your cold sounds worse. What are you doing at the office? Go home. Rest."

"I'd feel even worse if I was home. Mary's coughing and

sneezing all over the house." Maureen sniffled then blew her nose. "Is the view in Aspen breathtaking?"

"I wouldn't know. I'm not there yet." Leigh flapped her knees together, hoping to warm them under the thin fabric of her dress slacks. "Do you know how to install snow chains?"

"Snow chains? Is it snowing? It's beautiful here in Denver."

"It's been snowing since Glenwood Springs. I thought I could get to Aspen before it got too deep but it's impossible to get any traction through this stuff."

"I'm surprised you got a cell. I heard cell coverage in the mountains is impossible."

"It comes and goes. Don't be surprised if the call drops. But do you know how to install these things? There are no instructions in the box. Just greasy heavy chains."

"I'm sorry but I have no idea. Mary does that stuff. Do you want me to ask someone in the office if they know how? Perry's here. Let me get him."

"No, not Perry. I doubt he knows what a tire chain is for. He's from Florida."

"Pull into a gas station and have a mechanic do it. Or call Triple A."

"I'm stuck on the side of the road and couldn't get through to Triple A." Leigh shivered then stomped her feet to warm them. Why had she worn a business suit and dress boots into the mountains? It might be her signature professional attire but a fleece-lined jogging suit would have been smarter. And her stylish whiskey-colored leather driving gloves might match her jacket but they were all but useless against the frigid temperatures.

"Glenda wants to know if you will be back for the meeting with the zoning commission on the twelfth."

"I told her yes but I'm not going to the table without resolution on the variance. Have Jeannie check on that." A car passed, its snow chains ca-chunking against the pavement and a swirl of snow enveloping Leigh in its wake. "And tell Bev not to sign anything on the Calhoun merger until all parties have reviewed and signed off on the changes. I don't want any surprises this time." Leigh turned her back to the blast of snow off the back of a passing truck.

"Bev has been stuck in the U.K. since Monday. Some kind of transit strike. They can't get to the airport."

"They?"

"Yes, Bev and Lisa. The taxi drivers won't cross the picket lines. Bev is so mad she's ready to strangle someone." Maureen went silent.

"Lisa who?"

"Oh, honey, I'm sorry. I shouldn't have said anything."

"Who, Maureen?" Leigh asked solemnly. If her instincts and the rumors around the office were right, Bev had a new girlfriend.

"Lisa Hinson."

"Oh." The perky brunette from the governor's office who helped on a case last year. She was probably the reason Bev volunteered to work such long hours on that one. "How long have they..."

The call dropped before Leigh could finish her question. She thought about replacing the call but decided she didn't need to know how long Bev and Lisa had been dating.

Bev Richards was gorgeous. She was also a knowledgeable and successful lawyer, dedicated to her work; the qualities Leigh found most appealing four years ago when Bev joined the law firm. Within a year they had gone from discussing cases across the conference table to discussing them over a glass of wine by a crackling fireplace. Bev was ten years Leigh's junior, and her professional persona attracted Leigh like a kid to a toy store. Leigh's only mistake was in confessing her attraction to Bev to her secretary. But Maureen, beyond muttering about affairs in the office, had shown surprising restraint in not mentioning it to anyone else in the firm. A long-time loyal employee, Maureen could be trusted. Even when the relationship with Bev faded, Maureen refrained from *I told you so*. She somehow sensed the heartache was still there just below the surface and delivered silent sympathy with the cup of coffee she brought to Leigh's desk each morning.

Another truck slowed and honked. Leigh waved it around her then climbed back in her car and turned on the engine to warm up. She was too cold to wrestle with the chains and since she had no clue how to attach them, defrosting her nipples and knees sounded like a better idea. She turned the heater on high and cupped her hands around the vent on the dashboard.

"God, I look like the abominable snow monster," she mumbled after a glance in the mirror. She brushed the snow from her hair and tried to push some shape back into her hair. As a child, her hair was blonde with adorable naturally curly ringlets. At forty-eight it was dishwater blonde with a hint of premature gray at the temples and lazy squiggles of curl that frizzed in the rain.

Within fifteen minutes snow covered over the windows, blocking her view but it was useless to apply the wipers. She wasn't going anywhere. The last ten miles had been taken at a crawl, her tires slipping and spinning on the slick pavement. After a few more minutes with the heater she'd take another look at the chains. How hard could it be?

Just as the feeling was returning to her fingers and toes, her driver's side door flew open, a pair of grease-stained jeans and a brown plaid flannel shirt all Leigh could see through a blast of blowing snow. The stench of diesel fuel and tobacco smoke invaded the car and her nostrils.

"Hey! What are you doing? Get out of here," Leigh shrieked, grabbing for the door handle and shoving back at the flannelled body. One of the denim-covered legs blocked the door from closing. The blowing snow stung Leigh's eyes and temporarily blinded her.

"What are you doing, lady? Trying to commit suicide?" the voice bellowed from somewhere in the blizzard. "You're in the middle of the freaking road, lady!"

"I'm up against the guardrail. There's plenty of room to get by. Now move."

"This isn't a parking lot."

Leigh continued pulling at the door handle, repeatedly whacking the intruder in the leg with the car door. A gloved hand took hold of Leigh's wrist and squeezed. "Look, mister," Leigh said, snatching her arm away. "I don't know what you want but if you don't let go of my door I'm going to call the police."

The gloved hand unhooked a cell phone from the waistband of the jeans and tossed it on Leigh's lap.

"The number is nine-one-one. Tell the dispatcher Margo said you're two miles south of the Quigley turnout, southbound." The figure squatted next to the car and scowled into the open door.

Through the swirling snow Leigh could see brown eyes framed by dark eyebrows and high cheekbones. From the smell and the clothes, Leigh expected this to be a burly man with a toothpick in his mouth and a two-day old beard. But in spite of the thermal underwear visible at the neck of the tattered flannel shirt, this was, in fact, a woman. She appeared to be somewhere in her forties. She had a stocking cap on her head with a few curls poking out at the temples. Her face was speckled with soot but it didn't hide a deep scowling crease between her eyebrows. "If you get a cell, let me know. I haven't been able to get one for over an hour."

"You're not a man," was all Leigh could say as she stared at her brown eyes.

"No. Not the last time I looked, I'm not." She reached over Leigh's legs and turned off the ignition.

"I'm using the heater, thank you very much." Leigh gave her an irate scowl and turned it back on.

"Haven't you ever heard of carbon monoxide poisoning?" She turned it off again and pulled the key out of the ignition. "Don't you know you have to keep the tailpipe clear or the exhaust will back up in the car and kill you?"

"Yes, I know that. I'm not stupid. When the snow gets deeper I'll clear it away." Leigh pushed the woman back as she began to choke at her overwhelming stench.

"Did you get out and look to see if it was clear?" She nodded toward the back of the car.

"I know how deep it is. My exhaust pipe is not covered."

The woman muttered something that sounded like *skinny bitch* as she reached in and grabbed Leigh by the arm.

"What are you doing?" Leigh asked as she was dragged from the car.

"I hate you snooty rich-bitch snow bunny socialites who sit

around the ski lodge in your Fifth Avenue fur-trimmed parkas, sip cocktails and act like you own the place. You play the innocent damsel in distress so you don't have to take responsibility for anything."

"Who the hell do you think you are? Let go of my arm or I'll have you arrested for assault. And I certainly am no rich-bitch snow bunny. I am perfectly capable of taking care of myself." Leigh tried to pull away but couldn't break the woman's grip.

"Show me where the exhaust pipe is, lady," she demanded, escorting her to the back of the car.

Leigh felt a flush of embarrassment when she noticed snow had drifted up over the rear bumper, covering the license plate and halfway up the trunk of her white Lexus sedan.

"What happened? I don't understand. I could see it fifteen minutes ago." Leigh began frantically pawing at the snow.

"Fifteen minutes in these mountains is long enough for drifts to cover an entire car."

The blowing snow and frigid temperatures didn't seem to bother this grizzled mountain woman. She crossed her arms and watched Leigh burrowing down through the snow like a dog digging for a bone. "You're going to get frostbite, lady." She had a stubborn set to her jaw that Leigh found infuriating.

"First of all, my name isn't lady. And secondly I happen to be wearing gloves." She waved her hands then went back to digging. This woman with her frayed flannel and trucker stench wasn't going to intimidate her.

"Yeah, I see your gloves. I bet they're wet through, aren't they?"

"How would you know?" When Leigh tossed a look over her shoulder, she caught the woman staring at her ass.

Eyes off the merchandise, Paul Bunyan. I'm not your style.

"Leather driving gloves are useless in the mountains," Margo said, raising her gaze.

She was right. Leigh's fingers were nearly numb from the cold. She shook her hands and patted them together to warm them before going back to digging for the exhaust pipe. It wasn't until that moment that she noticed the huge snowplow parked several yards away, its motor still running, lights flashing and the blade raised like a giant guillotine ready to slice through whatever got in its way.

"Are you driving that?"

Margo turned and stared at the truck then proudly declared, "Yes, as a matter of fact, I am. What's wrong with that?"

"Nothing. I just didn't expect..."

"You didn't expect a woman to be driving a snowplow, right?" She gave Leigh's body another scan.

"I'm just surprised to see a snowplow, that's all."

"I've got to get to work. You better get those snow chains on before it gets too deep." She began retracing her tracks through the snow toward the snowplow.

"Have you ever installed tire chains before?" Leigh asked nonchalantly, trying not to sound incompetent.

"Many times. Why? Don't you know how to put them on?" She started back for Leigh's car.

"Oh, sure. No problem." Leigh didn't know why she said that.

"You've never installed snow chains before, have you?" Margo gave a patronizing chuckle.

"Sure I have." Leigh moved closer to the rear tire like a mother hen protecting her chicks.

"You have not. At least not these chains on this car."

"How would you possibly know?"

"First of all, your car is front wheel drive, not rear. They won't do you any good back there. And these are chains for fourteen-inch wheels." She pushed her toe against the label on the end of the box. "Your Lexus has seventeen's."

"Sure they'll fit. They were in the trunk."

"I'm telling you, lady, they are the wrong size."

Leigh turned her head sideways to read the tire markings in the light from the snowplow's headlights.

"Right here." Margo rubbed her gloved thumb across the sidewall.

"Can't you adjust the links or something?"

"No, they aren't one size fits all. They are made to hug the tire and offer traction. Not dangle like earrings. You should have checked them before you headed into the mountains in the winter."

"Well, I wouldn't need them if you snowplow drivers did a better job of keeping the highway clear, now would I? What do you do? Wait till it's six inches deep before starting to plow?"

"No, actually, we wait until it's ass deep on a grizzly bear before we start. That's how we measure it," Margo said sarcastically. "Seems like a pricey car like this would have a pair of chains that fit."

"I thought it did." Leigh didn't like looking stupid and especially in front of this Rocky Mountain hillbilly. But she also knew this woman and her repugnant aroma might be her only chance for rescue. "Cell service should be available in town, shouldn't it?"

"Should be."

"Could you call Triple A and give them my location?" she asked as politely as she could, considering whom she was asking.

Margo crossed her flannelled arms and shook her head adamantly.

"Well, that's pretty heartless. It's not as if I'm asking you to tow my car. Just call and tell them where I am so they can send a tow truck. I'll give you the toll-free number."

Margo continued to shake her head.

"I'll pay you. How much would you charge to make a phone call for me?"

"I'll be glad to take your money but that isn't going to get you a tow. Not tonight. The tow services have been tied up with stranded county and utility vehicles all afternoon. And I doubt they'd come out when technically you are illegal. The chain-up signs have been flashing since noon."

"You mean I can't get my car towed to Aspen at all?"

"Oh, it'll be towed. The highway patrol will take care of that."

"The highway patrol has a towing service?" Leigh brightened.

"Not the way you want. They'll tow your car to the impound yard, charge you storage and give you a ticket for ignoring the chain-up law, illegal parking and for blocking traffic. You're talking five or six hundred dollars, easy."

"Six hundred dollars to tow my car?"

"Maybe more. And if someone hits your car you could be liable for that too."

"A parked car is not liable. Parking ticket, yes. But it is not a moving violation, therefore not the proximate cause of the damage. Liability falls to the driver of the moving vehicle."

"Are you sure?" Margo challenged.

"I'm sure. At least that's the scuttlebutt around the fireplace at the ski lodge." Leigh had no intention of admitting she was a lawyer. This woman didn't need to know anything about her personal life. Leigh folded her collar up against her chin and held it there. "How long do you think it will be before the highway patrol comes along?"

"I have no idea. Are you planning on waiting here with your car?"

"I thought I would, yes."

"Have you got a full tank of gas so you can run your heater? It's going to be a long cold night. And remember, you can't fall asleep. You'll have to clear the snow away from the exhaust every ten minutes or so. You might want to keep a window cracked just in case. You should leave your flashers on too."

Leigh watched as Margo headed back to the snowplow. She had a decision to make and make fast. Should she remain with her car, soon to be completely covered with snow, or ask for a ride? Which was safer? She had always heard staying with the car in a disaster was the right thing to do but she had also heard freezing to death wasn't a nice way to go. She didn't even like to apply a cold compress. And with less than a quarter tank of gas, she'd be frozen stiff by midnight. But did she really want to be trapped in the cab of a snowplow on a snowy night with this foul smelling and sarcastic woman?

"What would you charge for a ride into Aspen?" Leigh called just as Margo was about to climb in.

"I'm not supposed to pick up hitchhikers. They might be dangerous."

She's going to make me beg. I just know it.

"I'm not exactly a hitchhiker. I'm a stranded motorist."

"Stranded motorist without forethought."

"Okay. Yes. Without forethought." *She's enjoying this, the jackass.*

"Stranded motorist without a survival plan."

Leigh looked up and down the highway one more time, hoping for someone else, anyone else she could coax a ride out of but there wasn't a headlight in sight and it would be completely dark soon.

"Well, come on, if you're coming." Margo swung the door open then looked back at Leigh. "I've got thirty miles to plow before midnight. I need to get moving before this road gets away from me."

Leigh collected her purse, tote bag and briefcase. She scribbled a note and left it under the wiper for the highway patrol to see then turned on the flashers, locked the car and headed for the passenger's side of the snowplow.

"You have to get in on this side," Margo called. "The passenger door lock is stuck. Can't get it open." She climbed down and held the door as Leigh struggled with her belongings up the three steps into the high cab. Leigh felt a strong arm boost her up as she teetered on the top step, about to lose her balance.

"Thank you," Leigh said, sliding in across the filthy seat.

"No problem."

The floorboard was littered with discarded foam coffee cups, a smashed doughnut box, greasy rags and empty cigarette packs. A black plastic lunch box with a broken latch was wedged between the seat and a floor gearshift. An assortment of hand tools, candy wrappers and aerosol cans lined the dashboard.

"You can rake that stuff out of the way," Margo said, settling into the driver's seat and latching her seatbelt. She ground through the gears, found one she liked and released the clutch. The big truck lurched forward.

"Where's the seatbelt on this side?" Leigh carefully picked through the trash tucked into the back of the seat cushion.

"There isn't one on that side. Got ripped out, I guess." She flipped a lever to lower the blade and began scraping the pavement even before Leigh got settled.

"Wow. Kind of a rough ride, isn't it?" Leigh grabbed her tote bag with one hand and her purse with the other to keep them from sliding into the garbage pit on the floor.

"Yeah, it's a kidney buster all right. I have to pee about every thirty minutes." She shifted gears, constantly checking her mirrors and the edge of the road. "It's the oldest truck in the fleet. They only bring the old ones out when we get slammed like this. It's none of my business but where are you going to spend the night?"

"At my cabin on White River Road."

"Whoa. How far up?"

"A mile or so."

"White River Road won't be plowed yet."

"Isn't that what this big truck is for, plowing?"

"Not this one. I don't have the maneuverability and traction for hilly roads like that."

"I'll pay you a hundred dollars to take me to my cabin."

Margo burst out laughing and said, "I was wondering how long it would be before you said something like that. There's probably two feet of snow on White River Road. That's rugged terrain up there. I can't get this up there."

"I made it last year in the snow. Of course it wasn't in this car."

"Let me guess, an SUV with all-wheel drive."

"Yes, it was." Leigh heaved a disgruntled sigh. "How far is the nearest hotel?"

"Aspen but I doubt you find any rooms available. This storm took a lot of people by surprise. It stranded a bunch of tourists who didn't listen to the weather forecast. You might not find a room anywhere this side of Glenwood Springs."

Margo sorted through the junk on the dashboard and pulled out a half-eaten roll of Lifesavers. "Want one?" she asked, flipping one up with her thumb.

"No, thank you." Leigh wondered how long they had been there and what the fuzzy stuff was stuck to the wrapper.

Margo popped the Lifesaver in her mouth then tossed the roll back onto the dash where it rolled under the litter.

Leigh pulled out her cell phone and tried to make a call.

"Still no cell?" Margo held the red Lifesaver between her lips like a tiny tongue.

"No."

Keep your food in your mouth, why don't you? That's gross.

Margo kept a watchful eye on the road as the plow sliced through the deepening snow. It was a painfully slow process, one that had Leigh second-guessing her decision to accept a ride to town. The longer she sat cooped up in this rolling trash heap, the more the contents of her stomach threatened to come up.

"Do you mind if I crack a window?" she asked as her eyes began to water.

"Go ahead."

Leigh lowered the window a few inches and stuck her face through the opening. Breathing the cold air and blowing snow was better than tossing her cookies onto her shoes.

"Are you car sick?" Margo downshifted around a curve, swerving to miss a roadside marker. "Shit. When did they put that sign there?"

"No, I'm not car sick." She took another deep breath then raised the window so it was only open a crack. "Pardon me for asking, but doesn't the stench in here bother you? Or don't you smell it?"

"Smell what? If you mean the cigarette smoke, that belongs to the other guy who drives this truck. I don't smoke." She swerved again then scowled into the rearview mirror.

"Never mind." Leigh leaned her head toward the window, occasionally taking a cleansing breath of fresh air. She tried her phone again. "Oh, thank goodness," she gasped in relief as her cell came to life. She opened a Web access page and searched for a hotel room in Aspen. She didn't care how much it cost. Anything would do.

"Any vacancies?" Margo asked, looking over at what she was doing.

"It's still searching." Leigh couldn't hide her disappointment.

"No, huh?"

"Not that I can find. You'd think there would be something." She did the search again but again nothing showed up. "Damn, I just lost the signal."

"I know a place you can probably stay if you don't mind that it's not a five-star hotel. It's not fancy but it'll be clean. It's a little further than I'm supposed to go but what the heck. I need a bathroom and another cup of coffee anyway."

"At this point, I don't think the star rating makes much difference. Is it very far?"

"We should be there by ten o'clock." Margo used her sleeve to wipe the condensation from the windshield.

"I didn't realize plowing snow was such a slow methodical process. This is like watching an old person climb stairs."

"You try pushing two tons of snow at a time and see how fast you go."

"I just meant."

"I know what you meant." Margo gave her a smirk then went back to the business of slicing a path through the white night.

Leigh rode along in silence, listening to the drone of the engine and the metal blade scraping the pavement. The snowplow was the only vehicle on the road and it had been almost an hour since they passed another pair of headlights. Except for the nearly impassable road and the inconvenience of being stuck on the side of the road, the snow-covered night was gorgeous. Leigh closed her eyes and imagined sitting in her cabin by a crackling fire with the mountain serenity outside. Something else crept into her thoughts, something she was powerless to stop. Why had Bev taken Lisa to London? Had they been seeing each other last year as Leigh tried her best to save their relationship? Had they been sleeping together while Leigh attended countless meetings and dinners?

"Hey," Margo said, giving her shoulder a gentle nudge. "Are you all right?"

Leigh opened her eyes and blinked back to reality.

"Are you okay? You look like you were having a bad dream." Margo downshifted and rounded a corner.

"No, I wasn't sleeping."

Margo chuckled and said, "You sure were doing a lot of snoring for someone who wasn't sleeping."

"I wasn't sleeping and I don't snore," Leigh said, collecting her dignity.

"Oh, right. I forgot. You women don't snore."

"*We* women?"

"Yeah." Margo pulled to the curb and raised the blade. "Wait here. I'll be right back." She left the engine running as she opened the door and climbed down.

They had entered the outskirts of Aspen where only a few modest homes lined the darkened street. Margo crossed to a small stone bungalow. The house was dark. Even the porch light was out. She stood on the porch, hunching against the blowing snow as she knocked repeatedly. Finally a light came on and the door opened. She stepped inside then reappeared a minute later and trotted back to the truck.

"All set," she said, reaching in and grabbing Leigh's tote bag. "I've got a place for you to stay."

"I thought you meant a hotel," Leigh said, tugging on the strap to reclaim her bag.

"Wendy said you can sleep on the couch. Watch your step. The snow is deep here."

"I'm not sleeping on anyone's couch."

"Look, lady. I'm already behind schedule because of you. In exactly one minute I'm turning this rig around and heading back for Wingo. If you don't want to stay here, use Wendy's phone, call someone to take you someplace else but I don't have time for this crap."

"How am I supposed to get someone to come out in this? The snow is a foot deep."

"And my job is to clear it, not taxi you around looking for a place to spend the night." Margo slung the tote over her shoulder and glared up at her. "Now come on. Wendy's waiting. She wants to go back to bed."

"I don't know these people."

"Wendy Baldwin has lived in Aspen all her life. She's sixty-four, single and babysits for a living. She doesn't smoke or do drugs except for arthritis and high blood pressure medicine. She only drinks on Christmas and her birthday. She has a one-eyed cat named Herbert and is kind enough to offer her couch to wayward travelers who don't install chains before heading out in a blizzard."

"I can just guess what you said to her about me."

"For cripes sake. Look, my dinner was a bologna sandwich. The defroster in this piece of crap truck only works when it feels like it, the spring in the seat has been stabbing me in the ass for forty miles and I'm not supposed to pick up stranded motorists. The hotel district is that way about five miles. So what's it going to be? Wendy's or the sidewalk?"

"You may know this person but I don't."

"Do you only stay at hotels where you know the owner?"

She had a point. It was all a matter of trust. And right now, at ten fifteen on a snowy night in Aspen, Colorado, did Leigh trust this Margo person enough to accept a night's lodging with someone she recommended.

"You didn't know me when you climbed into my truck. What's wrong? Wendy's house not fancy enough for you?" She looked over at the bungalow. "I'd take Wendy's couch over a king-sized bed with room service any day."

"I'm not a snob, you know," she said, climbing down and following in Margo's footsteps.

"Could have fooled me."

A short squarish woman peeked around the edge of the door, holding a yellow bathrobe closed at the neck. Her hair was short, mostly white and disheveled. Crust had formed in the corner of her eyes telling Leigh she had already been asleep.

"Come in, come in," she demanded. "You're letting the heat out."

"Wendy, this is Leigh." Margo stepped aside for Leigh to enter.

"Hello, Leah." She pulled Margo out of the way and closed the door.

"It's Leigh," Leigh said, extending a hand to the woman but she didn't seem to notice. "Hello, Wendy."

"Stomp your feet on the rug, both of you."

"I can't stay. I've got to get back to work." Margo set Leigh's tote bag on a nearby chair.

"You're not leaving until you reach down the comforter from the shelf. So just troddle your little hiney right back there and get it." Wendy turned Margo by the shoulders and pointed her toward the hall. "Pull down a pillow and the pink flowered sheets, too."

Margo muttered something as she disappeared down the hall. She returned carrying an armload of bedding.

"Not that comforter. The one on the top shelf," Wendy complained.

"This was on the top shelf." She dumped the load on the couch.

Leigh stood by the door, watching and listening as Wendy and Margo bickered about the comforter and Margo's need to get back on the road. In spite of the squabbling and occasional profanity, there was an unmistakable connection between the two women.

"Then just go on," Wendy finally said, shooing her toward the door. "Go play with your truck. We don't need you. And don't slam the door. You knocked a plate off the shelf last week."

"You're sure a bossy bitch this evening," Margo said as she grabbed the doorknob.

"Damn right I am. My knee is killing me and the garbage disposal backed up all over the kitchen floor. Now get out of here."

As soon as Margo was out the door, Wendy turned to Leigh and smiled. "Now let's get you settled, honey." She unfolded a sheet with a snap and floated it over the couch, tucking and smoothing it neatly. "Where are you from, Leah?"

"Denver." Leigh saw no reason to correct her name again. She obviously wasn't listening.

"What are you doing in Aspen? Skiing?"

"Business." Leigh draped her coat over her tote bag in the chair and went to help with the bedding.

"What kind of business? Are you one of those travel agents who schedule bus trips to ski resorts?"

"No. I'm not a travel agent. Let me finish this." Leigh took the comforter.

"Would you?" Wendy caught herself as if her knee was about to give out. "The bathroom is down the hall. Towels are in the cabinet under the sink. Let me know if you're going to take a shower in the morning."

A shower must cost more, Leigh thought. "I'll be up early. I have a conference call scheduled for seven thirty," she said, slipping the pillow into the pillowcase.

"I've always wondered how they do that. Everyone talking at once. Well, don't mind me. Sometimes I'm up and in my sewing room by six. I need to get the hem in Dallas Sopple's drapes before noon." She headed down the hall. "Good night and sweet dreams, Leah."

"Good night and thank you for allowing me to stay with you."

"You're welcome, honey. Turn off the light when you're through."

Leigh heard the door close at the end of the hall. She was left in the living room lit by one low-watt table lamp. She made a quick trip to the bathroom then slipped out of her slacks and blouse. She'd have to sleep in her bra and panties since she didn't pack any pajamas. She'd planned on spending the night in her own cabin in her own bedroom where she kept extra clothes. She snapped off the light and snuggled down beneath the comforter. She was almost asleep when she remembered there was at least one stranger down the hall, a woman who, for all Leigh knew, could be Jack the Ripper's mother. She retrieved her blouse from the chair and slipped it back on, as if that would protect her.

Why do I let myself be talked into these things?

Chapter 2

Leigh had slept surprisingly well. The comforter was warm and smelled like vanilla and lemons. Fabric softener sheets, no doubt. Her normal early morning routine included a few texts and emails before she stepped in the shower. The house was quiet when she opened her laptop and checked for available Wi-fi reception without success. Thankfully she had cell service and checked her messages that way. Maureen left a text message that the conference call had been canceled, something about inflated stock dividends. Leigh would check on it later. She texted a reply then headed for the bathroom with her toiletry bag for a quick shower.

Wendy was a good housekeeper. The black and white checkerboard tiled floor and walls were spotless. The towels were neatly stacked and there was no hair in the drain. Leigh wasn't above reporting a sloppy housecleaner to the front desk even in a five-star hotel. Showering in a tub with someone else's dirt ring was unacceptable.

Leigh had finished rinsing the shampoo from her hair and squirted on a generous glob of conditioner when she noticed a small face peeking at her from the edge of the shower curtain.

"What are you doing in here?" she shrieked and grabbed for the shower curtain to cover herself from the child's view.

"Hi. Can I go potty?" the little girl asked desperately as she held herself. She was dressed in pink flannel pajamas and fuzzy slippers twice too big for her. Her hair was a rat's nest of tangles.

"Couldn't you wait? I'll be out shortly." Leigh looked over at the doorknob. "I thought I locked the door. How did you get in here?"

"The lock doesn't work. I gotta go." She began the potty dance, hopping on one foot then the other.

"Couldn't you wait five minutes?"

"No."

"All right, I guess. You may use the toilet."

"Thanks." She instantly pulled down her pants and took a seat, modesty taking a backseat to urgency.

Leigh pulled the shower curtain closed and rinsed her hair, giving the child privacy. She assumed she would leave when she was finished, allowing Leigh to complete her shower in peace. But the little face reappeared.

"Can I flush?" she asked, obviously relieved and happy.

Leigh didn't know the first thing about raising children but assumed bathroom training included operating the equipment. "Yes. By all means, flush."

"Okay." She disappeared.

Leigh heard the toilet flush and instantly knew why she had asked for permission. The water temperature changed from pleasantly warm to blasting Leigh with scalding water. She screamed and jumped out of the tub, sliding across the tiled floor. The child stood watching as if she were the star attraction in a freak show. Leigh grabbed a towel and hugged it to her chest as she closed her eyes and agonized over the pain.

"That's funny," the child said, giggling at Leigh's contortions.

"Yes, very funny," Leigh said through gritted teeth. "You just gave me third-degree burns but I'm sure it is very funny."

"You said I could flush."

"I know I did. And now I have learned something new." Leigh now knew why Wendy told her to announce any plans for a shower.

"What's your name?"

"Leigh," she said, slowing regaining her senses. "Do you think I could have some privacy?"

"My name is Lindsey. My birthday was Wednesday and I'm six." She picked through the contents of Leigh's cosmetic bag, examining each item. "Is this lipstick?"

"Yes. Why don't you go out so I can finish my shower and get dressed?" Leigh reclaimed her cosmetics and waved her toward the door but Lindsey sat on the edge of the tub and watched.

"How come you are here?"

"Because my car was stuck on the highway and I couldn't drive it." Leigh took another towel from the stack for her hair but struggled to keep herself covered while she dried it.

"How did you get here then?"

"A woman gave me a ride. Wouldn't you like to go out?"

"No. I'm fine." She picked her nose. "Wendy makes the best pancakes. I love pancakes."

"That's nice." Leigh bent over to towel dry her hair. It was impossible to hold the other towel up for modesty and she knew Lindsey was staring at her wobbling breasts.

"How come your car got stuck? Did you run out of gas?"

"The snow was too deep for me to drive in it."

"Did you have snow chains on your tires? You're supposed to have snow chains on when it is snowing, you know."

"Yes, I know."

Damn, am I going to get a lecture from a six-year-old too?

"Lindsey, are you in there?" There was a knock at the door.

"Yes, she is."

"You come right out of there. I told you to leave that lady alone. Now come on. You need to get dressed."

"I'm helping," Lindsey replied.

"I'm sure you are doing something but it probably isn't helping," Wendy said.

"Uh-huh," she insisted.

"Send her out of there if she gets in the way, Leah."

"Maybe you should go get dressed like she said," Leigh added encouragingly.

"I'll be right back," she said, bolting out the door.

Leigh assumed that meant she had the bathroom to herself and closed the door. But Lindsey was back in less than a minute carrying an armload of clothes.

"We can get dressed together," Lindsey said gleefully.

"Isn't it a little crowded in here for that?"

"No. We've got room." Lindsey stripped out of her pajamas. Her little body was pale and petite. The blond hair hung halfway down her back and looked like it hadn't been combed in days. She had big blue eyes and rosy cherub cheeks. She seemed small for her age. But then Wendy was short. Perhaps this was her granddaughter.

Lindsey watched as Leigh dressed, mimicking her every move. She seemed fascinated with the lace-trimmed underwire bra Leigh pulled on and hooked. Lindsey pulled a cotton undershirt from her pile and slipped it over her head, tucking it in her panties.

"Lindsey?" Wendy called, tapping on the door. "Are you still in there? I told you come get dressed. The bus will be here in fifteen minutes and I still have to brush your hair."

"I'm getting dressed. Leigh is helping me."

"And I'm sure that wasn't her idea," she replied, her voice trailing off down the hall.

Lindsey pulled on jeans with sequins on the pockets and a Hannah Montana sweatshirt as Leigh dressed in the slacks and blouse she had worn yesterday. Lindsey stood at the sink, making an attempt at brushing her teeth while Leigh gathered her things and opened the door.

"Wait for me." Lindsey dropped the toothbrush in the cup and hurried after her.

"Come eat your breakfast, child," Wendy called from the

kitchen. Her hair was combed but she was dressed in the same yellow robe. "Sit down and eat your toast while I see if I can get a brush through that squirrel's nest."

"I'm helping Leigh," she said, following close on her heels.

"She'll have to survive without you. The bus will be here soon." She waved the child toward the kitchen table, holding a brush in her hand. "Sit down and hold still." She slid a plate of peanut buttered toast in front of her then started in on her hair. "I don't know why she doesn't just cut this mess and let you have short hair. It would be so much easier." She sank the brush into it and worked it through.

Leigh was busy repacking her tote bag and folding her bedding when her cell phone rang.

"Good morning, Maureen," she said, taking a seat at the end of the couch. She pulled her laptop onto her lap. "Yes, I got your email. What's the holdup?"

Leigh was absorbed with her call and didn't notice Lindsey standing next to her until she saw her reflection in the laptop screen. Leigh tried to concentrate but Lindsey crept closer, leaning against the arm of the couch.

"That property was zoned commercial long before anyone put a road through there. They'll need to get their ducks in a row then we can reapply for the permit." Leigh gave Lindsey a quick glance then turned her attention back to the file she had opened. "Yes, Colorado Springs has property available. Heck, even Aspen has building sites but the prime locations are hard to come by. They'll be sorry if they let this property slip through their fingers."

Lindsey leaned over the arm of the couch to study what Leigh was typing. Her feet came off the floor and she tipped over, obstructing Leigh's view.

"Oops," she giggled, pushing against the laptop to regain her balance and accidentally touching a key that deleted the last sentence Leigh typed.

"Wait, Maureen," Leigh said, frantically pushing Lindsey out of the way and retyping. "Say that again. I didn't hear you. No, no. Before that."

"Is that a real laptop?" Lindsey asked, seemingly unable to keep quiet another moment.

Leigh reached up and stroked Lindsey's face, hoping to coax her into silence.

"Fax those percentages to their offices, Maureen. He can't argue with facts." Leigh covered the phone and said, "Could you do something for me?"

"What?" Lindsey asked eagerly, leaning on the arm again, bobbing up and down like she was a teeter-totter.

"Lindsey, you come away from there. Leah is trying to work," Wendy called. "Don't bother her."

"What did you say, Maureen?" Leigh asked, covering her other ear so she could hear above Wendy's booming voice. "Hello?" The call had dropped. Leigh tried to replace it but couldn't get a cell. "Dammit."

"Uh-oh. You said a naughty word. You aren't supposed to say dammit." Lindsey whispered the curse word then put her hand over her mouth.

"Yes, I know," she said, grimacing with frustration as she continued to try the call.

"You have to put a quarter in the jar."

Leigh heaved a sigh and turned to her, realizing she wasn't going to get anything done until she gave Lindsey the attention she wanted.

"Why do I have to put a quarter in a jar?"

"Because Mommy said so. If you cuss, you have to pay the jar. She had to put two dollars in last week when she slammed her finger in the door."

"I don't think I have any change. I'll have to owe you."

Lindsey set her jaw and stared at Leigh. "Are you broke?"

"No, I'm not broke. I just don't normally carry change on me."

"Then you shouldn't cuss."

"I'm sorry." Leigh closed her laptop and slipped it in the case. "I'll try to remember that."

"Leah," Wendy called from the kitchen. "I forgot to tell you. Your car is out front. A tow truck dropped it off while you were in the shower."

"My car?" Leigh went to the window, the news almost too good to be true. "How did they know where to bring it?"

"Margo must have told them. I put your keys there by your purse."

"How did they get my keys? No, don't tell me. I don't want to know." Leigh assumed Margo had stopped by during the night and took her keys. At least she had her car back.

"Would you like some coffee? I've got toast and oatmeal for breakfast."

"No, thank you." She would love a cup of coffee and a leisurely start to her day but she had things to do, including checking on her cabin. She planned to air it out, stock the refrigerator and spend a few days relaxing before the realtor listed it. She also knew there would be a few details from the office she'd have to handle, contract revisions, communication with clients and appointments to schedule. Maureen was a dependable, efficient secretary but some things Leigh preferred to do herself. Yesterday's unexpected blizzard had pushed those plans back. A six-year-old hanging over her shoulder wasn't helping either. It may be slow going up the road to her cabin but the sooner she tried, the better she'd feel about it.

"How much do I owe for the night's stay and the shower?" Leigh asked, opening her wallet. Margo was right. It wasn't a top rated hotel and she didn't have a room with a bed but it was clean. And for that she was willing to pay.

"Nothing, honey." Wendy went back to the kitchen.

"I want to pay you. Sixty dollars? Eighty?" Leigh pulled out several twenties and followed Wendy into the kitchen, Lindsey right behind her.

"You don't owe me anything. Any friend of Margo's is a friend of mine."

"I'm not a friend of Margo's. I was stranded on the side of the road and she offered me a ride. That's all. Now, how much?" She took out another twenty and placed it on the kitchen table. "Is one hundred fair?"

"Wow. One hundred whole dollars?" Lindsey gasped, her eyes huge.

Wendy frowned disgustedly as she gathered the bills and stuffed them back in Leigh's wallet.

"I told you I don't need your money. The house is small and

nothing fancy but it's my home. I can open it to friends without expecting them to pay me." She seemed offended by Leigh's offer, not what she intended at all.

"Are you sure?"

"Yes, dearie. I am sure." Wendy went to the sink, turning her back on Leigh.

"Thank you. I appreciate your hospitality." That didn't seem to pacify Wendy's anger. Leigh came to the sink and touched her arm. "I didn't mean to insult you."

"That's okay. I wasn't insulted."

"I very much appreciate your opening your home to a complete stranger. It was very gracious of you."

"She owes the jar a quarter," Lindsey said.

"Never mind, Lindsey. She doesn't owe you a quarter."

"But Mommy said. If you cuss you have to pay."

"Tell you what," Leigh said, handing a dollar bill to Lindsey to be done with it. "I'll pay you a dollar. How's that?"

The child thought a moment then said, "That means you can say two more naughty words and not pay."

"Three more," Leigh corrected. "But I don't need to say anymore naughty words. You can keep the rest of it."

"What do you say?" Wendy insisted.

"Thank you."

"You're welcome." Leigh went to finish packing. In spite of Wendy's insistence that she didn't need the money, Leigh left fifty dollars on the end table before heading out to her car.

The ten inches of snow that blanketed the streets last night had been cleared. Leigh wondered if Margo had spent the entire night scraping the highways around Aspen.

Snow and bitter cold were hardly foreign to Aspen. It seemed to thrive on the adversity of winter. The streets were thick with traffic and pedestrians bundled against the cold. Leigh followed Main Street then wound up Smuggler's Mountain Road. It hadn't been completely plowed and by the time she reached the turnoff onto White River Road it was snow packed and slippery going. She followed the drive through the pine trees and stopped under a portico attached to a two-story timber-framed cabin.

Leigh had purchased the cabin as a refuge from work, but

adding Internet service, cable television and telephone as well as upgrading the kitchen and furniture had made it as much an office as a mountain retreat. The three-bedroom, two-bath home was nestled in a grove of aspen trees and Colorado blue spruce. It had a massive stone fireplace on the end, its chimney towering above the trees. Decks on both levels offered picturesque views across the valley and Aspen Mountain beyond, views even the hotels in town couldn't match. An outside wooden staircase led to the second-floor deck off the master bedroom, one of Leigh's favorite features. A door under the overhang led into a utility room and ski storage then up a half-flight of stairs to the kitchen, living room, dining room and two more bedrooms. The cabin could sleep eight but Leigh didn't have time to enjoy it herself. Making it available to a few select clients for weekend getaways was her way of justifying ownership and made it a business write-off. It had been six months since anyone used the cabin and she fully expected it to need a good cleaning before it could be listed.

She slung her tote bag and briefcase over her shoulder and headed for the door, looking forward to a clean change of clothes and a cup of hot coffee. Surely there was coffee in the pantry.

In spite of the protective portico, the wind had blown snow against the cabin halfway up the door, blocking her way. She swiped her foot at the drift, trying to clear the entrance. When she did, the door opened, allowing the snow to fall inside.

"Oh, shit," she gasped, jumping back. She knew she had locked the doorknob and engaged the dead bolt. She remembered checking and activating the security system, something she was very careful to do even when she went for a walk in the woods. "Hello?" she called, leaning around the doorjamb. Trying to suppress the fear in her voice she yelled, "Pizza delivery. Anyone home?"

She stepped over the snow and placed her bags on the washing machine then tiptoed up the stairs into the kitchen. The refrigerator door was open but the light was out. Empty beer cans and liquor bottles were strewn across the counters along with pizza boxes and chip bags. Half eaten slices of pizza littered the floor.

Leigh wasn't sure if she should run back out the way she came in or defend her property. Her heart was pounding as she took a butcher knife from the drawer and peeked around the corner into the living room. Dried muddy footprints led through the house and down the hall. The stale smell of cigarettes, marijuana, rotten food and liquor hung in the air. The cabin was cold as if the furnace wasn't working, even colder than it normally was when she put the furnace on vacation mode. It took Leigh a moment to overcome her shock and fear and notice the large screen television and the twin leather sofas were missing. So were the wine cabinet, stereo and DVD rack. She followed the footprints down the hall, holding the butcher knife over her head like a javelin, ready to spear anyone who crossed her path. She crept around the door into each bedroom only to see drawers emptied and mattresses overturned.

The upstairs master bedroom was worse. The king-size mattress was ripped and shredded as if the intruders had expected to find treasures sewn into the padding. The drawers were emptied, the clothes piled on the floor and stinking of urine. The computer desk had been ransacked and the wires ripped from the wall. The sliding door onto the deck was off the track, the glass broken. Snow had blown in, staining the carpet in a wide ring.

Leigh lowered the knife as tears rolled down her cheeks. She didn't know if she was more angry or frustrated. She didn't have time for this. Insurance would cover the damage but she had work to do. And where was she going to sleep while in Aspen? She certainly couldn't stay here. She suddenly wished she had never bought the cabin. Why hadn't she bought a vacation home in Florida or maybe the Bahamas?

While Leigh waited for the police to arrive she stepped out onto the deck and phoned her office.

"Maureen, this is Leigh. I've had a break-in at the cabin. Everything is trashed."

"A break-in?" Maureen gasped. "When?"

"From the dried mud and stale pizza, I'd guess a week or two, maybe more. It'll need repairs before it is habitable again."

"What can I do?"

"Nothing. I'll let you know when I have Internet access. I'll try and find a hotel in town with Wi-Fi. There is one thing you could do for me, if you could. Call Kathy Braden's office. Her number is in my Rolodex. Tell her I'll have to meet her in her office tomorrow afternoon. Twoish, if that's all right with her. I certainly can't entertain a realtor up here."

"Are you all right?" Maureen asked with concern.

"I'm fine." Leigh took a deep exasperated breath. "But the place is a mess. They took everything that wasn't nailed down and destroyed or peed on the rest."

"Do you need me to contact the insurance company?"

"No, I'll fax Linda the police report as soon as I get a copy. I want to get the ball rolling on the repairs." Leigh's eyes drifted across the valley. "I don't have time for this. I just wanted two weeks of peace and quiet before I sold the cabin. Was that too much to ask?"

"I'm so sorry, honey. I know you needed this too. You haven't had a vacation in two years, not since…" Her voice drifted off but Leigh knew what she was about to say. She hadn't taken a vacation since she and Bev had flown to Lake Tahoe two Christmases ago and even that was to attend a conference. It was on their way home at thirty-five thousand feet, that Bev announced she was moving out of their townhouse. Had she thought the rarified air and first-class travel accommodations would somehow soften the blow? It was Easter before Leigh could even think about booking an airline ticket without tears welling in her eyes. She still couldn't fly American Airlines.

"Maureen, have you heard from Bev? Was she able to get to the airport yet?" Leigh felt a chill of loneliness overtake her.

"Haven't heard," Maureen said quietly. "Leigh, I've got Expedia open. Gaylord Hotel, four-star, valet parking, room service, free Wi-Fi, two restaurants, lounge, twenty-four hour fitness center, within walking distance of downtown shops." Maureen gave a whistle. "Wow, must be high season."

"I'm sure. Are there any rooms available?"

"Yes, king non-smoking, town view. No rooms with a mountain view available."

"What's the number?"

"I just texted it to you. Did you get it?"

Leigh checked her screen. "Yes, got it. I'll give them a call. Thanks, Maureen. You're a peach. I have to go. The police are here to process the crime scene."

The police, two brusque and businesslike older men, took her statement and a list of stolen items. They dusted for fingerprints and in a more sympathetic manner helped her secure the premises for the night. Evidence indicated this was conducted by someone who knew how to bypass the security system. The officers suggested this was one of a string of break-ins and they had a good idea who was involved. With evidence gathered at the scene, especially fingerprints and body fluid samples from which DNA could be extracted, they expected an arrest soon.

"Is this your underwear drawer, ma'am?" the officer asked, pointing to one of the open dresser drawers.

"Yes." Leigh took a look then diverted her eyes. It was disgusting.

Using rubber gloves and a paper bags, he collected several articles of lingerie, soiled with a sticky substance. He bagged a pink satin robe, similarly soiled and stuck to the corner of the mattress. It was the robe Bev had given her for her birthday, the one that felt so good after a hot bath. She felt like she had been violated. But why had they done it? Leigh had no idea.

"Are you all right, ma'am?" one of the officers asked, studying Leigh apprehensively. "Ma'am?"

Leigh couldn't answer. She had a good idea what the sticky substance was and the sight of such a vile insult had stunned her. She felt her knees weaken. It was all she could do not to slide down the wall and wrap herself in self-pity. No, she wouldn't do that. She had no choice but to stay strong. There would be time for pity later. Leigh went out into the hall, bracing her hand against the wall as she regained her composure.

She had collected what she could from her ransacked bedroom but it wasn't much. She had no intention of washing out urine soaked lingerie and sweaters. She stopped at a strip mall on the way into town and purchased underwear, bra, slacks and a sweater. That would do for now. She still needed a heavier coat. Her leather jacket didn't offer much protection from the cold mountain wind and snow. But she was too tired and hungry to shop further. She needed a hot meal. If she had the energy to order it, a stiff drink wasn't out of the question either.

All that was left of the sunset was a faint glow by the time she pulled up to the valet parking attendant at the Gaylord Hotel. After checking in, she phoned her insurance agent. As a corporate attorney who handled everything from simple wills and trusts to complicated mergers and property investments, she knew how to run the gauntlet of insurance company agents. They would have preferred she stay at a less expensive hotel, one out on the highway perhaps. She reminded them that the hefty premium she paid for an upscale vacation home provided her like and kind coverage. They finally agreed, covering the cost of her hotel stay as well as repairs and replacements to the cabin. She also called the contractor who had done the remodel on the cabin. After all, he knew the cabin and she trusted him to do the repairs without gouging the insurance company.

The Gaylord was a classy, well-appointed hotel. But Leigh missed her cabin. She missed the security and comfort it provided. An aching melancholy washed over her as she stood at the window, staring out at downtown Aspen's shopping district, the streetlights glistening in the freshly falling snow. She clutched a cup of room service coffee in both hands as she watched the wind-driven snow splat against the window. It looked cold, too cold to go out shopping for a coat. She'd do that tomorrow. Tonight she just wanted a shower and a good night's sleep in a real bed.

Chapter 3

It had snowed off and on throughout the night, ending just before dawn. Aspen was covered with several inches of fresh powder glistening in the morning sun. An army of shop employees was on the sidewalks with shovels and snowblowers clearing the way for the day's customers.

Margo Tosch stomped her boots and tapped the shovel on the sidewalk before opening the door to the Polar Bear Apparel Shop. She carried the shovel through to the storeroom in the back of the store, unzipping her insulated coveralls along the way. The bell on the front door jingled.

"Is that you, Karen?" she shouted, wrestling her legs out of the coveralls.

"Yes. Good morning," a young woman replied, stomping her feet on the mat before heading to the storeroom.

"I need you to reboot the computer. It's acting weird." Margo hopped on her other foot as she struggled to untangle the leg opening.

"The virus scanner is running," she said, taking a quick look. "No wonder it's doing insane stuff. It's on full scan. Do you want me to cancel it?"

"NO! Let it finish." Margo hung the coveralls on a hook in the bathroom then checked her looks in the mirror. She combed her fingers through her hair, trying to undo what an hour of wearing a stocking cap had done.

She did not disapprove of the image in the mirror. She had an athletic body. She didn't have to work at it. It just happened. She had always been lean and well proportioned, even as a child. She had thick curly hair, flawless complexion and a small mole precisely centered on her right cheek, one that disappeared into a dimple when she smiled. The coveralls dispensed with, she was dressed in sleek black jeans and a cream colored cable-knit sweater.

"Why does it do that?" she asked, looking over Karen's shoulder as the monitor flashed warnings and messages across the screen.

"Do you really want me to explain what the firewall is doing to protect your system?" Karen went to fill a cup from the coffeemaker. She was thirty-one and seemed younger with her pale freckles, short strawberry blond hair and a row of piercings up both ears. She also had a tattoo of a dragonfly around her middle finger. Margo forgave Karen's semi-garish appearance and occasional adolescent behavior when it came to matters of the heart because she had an uncanny intelligence for anything technical. She was also punctual, loyal, dependable and had an amusingly giddy personality. "Don't touch that," she snapped as Margo was about to click the mouse.

"So long as the damn thing doesn't delete my inventory and account balances I'm happy." Margo squinted at the screen then went to the front window to watch the snowplow make a last pass down the street. She pushed back the sleeves of her sweater and stretched, exposing a few inches of pure white midriff and a small tattoo of a coiled snake in the small of her back. Her jeans sat on her hips with a silver and turquoise studded black belt. It matched the silver ring on her pinkie finger. Her rear was small, firm and nicely defined.

"Can you handle things for a while?" Margo asked, returning to the counter where Karen was activating her code into the cash register.

"Sure. Where are you going or should I ask?"

Margo rummaged under the counter for a package with a credit card receipt taped to it.

"Don't tell me you're actually going to meet that woman for breakfast," Karen said then groaned dramatically.

"What woman?"

"Don't give me that. You know exactly what woman I'm talking about. That New York bleach-blond over-the-hill Barbie doll, that's who."

"You're a snob, Karen. Mrs. Chambers is a very nice woman. She spent a lot of money in here. And, as I remember, she gave you a very generous tip."

"And she was flirting with you so hard I thought she was going to swallow her dentures."

"She was not flirting with me. She was just being polite." She looked at Karen's skeptical smirk then burst out laughing. "Okay, so she was a little gushy. The poor woman just lost her husband."

"She's ancient, Margo. She has to be at least seventy."

"Do you want a date with her?" she joked as she pulled on a quilted vest and tucked the package under her arm.

"God, no. She probably isn't even gay. Why not date someone who isn't straight?"

"I'm not dating her. I am just having coffee and a bagel with her. She invited me and I said yes. She doesn't have any family." Margo opened the front door of the shop and flipped on the open sign. "I'll be back."

Margo trotted across the street and headed around the corner to the St. Regis Hotel. The restaurant in the lobby was an upscale eatery catering to the rich and famous. The menu was leather-bound, the tablecloths were linen and Margo's jeans, although fashionable and well-fitting, got a scowl from the tuxedoed maître d'.

"Hello, dear," a woman said from a corner table, smiling up at her. She held out a dainty hand to Margo.

Her jewelry was tasteful but expensive as were her clothing, hairstyle and makeup. She wore a brown cashmere sweater and tan wool skirt, gold necklace and matching gold loop earrings. Her hair was platinum blond with not even a hint of roots showing. The two diamond rings on her left hand were the size of rings from a gumball machine, but Margo knew they were anything but fake. Stella Chambers sat at the table with a sophisticated yet reserved elegance.

"Hello, Mrs. Chambers." Margo took her hand and squeezed it then sat down, the maître d' waiting until she was settled before placing a napkin across her lap and handing her a menu.

"Oh, honey, call me Stella," she insisted then sipped orange juice from a stemmed goblet. "I'm so glad you could join me."

"Our quiche is fresh spinach, prosciutto and shitake mushrooms," the waiter announced. "Our soufflé is pan-seared Canadian bacon with white wine and lemon asparagus." He brought Margo a goblet of ice water before leaving.

"Your sweater came in." Margo set the package on the corner of the table. "I think you'll like the pearl detailing."

"Thank you, dear." She moved the package to the empty chair. "I need to talk with you about my new jacket. I just don't know if I like that color. It doesn't go with anything in my closet. Plum is such a hard color to work with these days." She added a few careful drops of cream to her coffee. "I'm afraid I'll have to exchange it for the black one. Black is so much easier to wear."

"I'm so sorry it didn't work out for you." Margo poured herself a cup of coffee from the carafe. "I'll be glad to exchange it whenever you have the time to stop by the shop. I assume you mean the merlot down jacket."

"Merlot?"

"Yes, that's the newest color. I thought it was plum too. But according to last month's Paris fashion magazine it's a much richer tone than plum. It has more character, more depth of color. It really pops next to something navy or gray." She scanned the menu, leaving Stella to ponder her revelation.

"Merlot. I hadn't noticed it was that color. But the lighting in these hotel rooms is so poor. You really can't tell what you have on. You know, I saw a pair of silver gray ski pants in your shop. They might be just the thing to go with that jacket. What do you think?"

"Silver gray? Absolutely. I think that's a great idea. Perhaps a black and silver belt?"

"Oh, I love it," Stella said with a girlish giggle. "I simply must have it for the dinner I'm attending tomorrow night. The dress is casual so I think it'll go, don't you? It'll be perfect. You are a dream, Margo." She reached across the table and gave Margo's cheek a pinch.

"I bet you'll be the hit of the dinner. You look so good in those colors."

"You think so?" Stella hung on Margo's every word.

"No doubt about it. When I get back to the shop I'll put those slacks back for you." She was laying it on thick but that's what Stella wanted and needed. Someone to pay her a compliment and make her feel important.

Margo had learned to read her clients. If they needed a little sugar to help their self-esteem, she could accommodate. Stella had the money to buy whatever she wanted. She came to the Polar Bear in search of something special in what she bought and for the attention she received. All through a leisurely breakfast she listened to Stella's stories and jokes, laughing at the appropriate spots and offering support and understanding at the tragic moments. Stella drank it in, reveling in the attention.

Margo slipped her credit card onto the check tray.

"You'll do no such thing," Stella insisted, reaching for the check. "I invited you to join me."

Margo intercepted her hand and held it fondly.

"Don't be silly. You are one of my favorite customers. It would be my pleasure to buy you breakfast."

"Thank you, dear. You are so kind to an old widow woman like me." Stella checked her lipstick in the compact and reapplied. "I hate to dine and run but I have an appointment for a facial and a massage. My sinuses are just killing me."

"Probably the altitude."

Margo walked her through the lobby and pushed the elevator button for her. "You take care, Stella. I'll see you later."

"I'll come over around one to try on those gray slacks. I can't wait to see how my merlot jacket will look with them." She gave Margo a hug and kissed her cheek then entered the elevator, smiling broadly. "Bye bye, dear."

Margo waited for the elevator door to close then headed back to the store, happy to have been of service.

Chapter 4

Aspen was known for upscale boutiques that specialized in everything from one-of-a-kind jewelry creations to Paris-chic winter apparel. There were bigger and better ski resorts when it came to the number of lifts and acres of groomed slopes but there were none better when it came to classy places to enjoy winter's beauty. The brick buildings had housed turn-of-the-century banks, hotels and businesses. Now they were home to some of the trendiest shops this side of Denver, one of the reasons Hollywood's elite could be found strolling the shopping district and eateries.

Leigh hurried down the sidewalk, hugging her jacket around her shivering body. The first item on today's agenda was to replace the winter coat the robbers had stolen from her closet. The shop in mid-block with the mannequin in the window dressed in ski apparel seemed like a good place to start and it was too cold to go much further.

"Hello and welcome to the Polar Bear," a young woman called, sticking her head around the curtain at the back of the store. "Be right with you."

Leigh scanned the store for winter coats. She knew what she wanted and didn't have much time to find it.

"Sorry to keep you waiting," the woman said, carrying an armload of sweaters to a rack near the window. "My name is Karen. Can I help you with something? Ski wear?"

"I'm looking for a winter coat."

"Downhill or cross-country?" She smiled expectantly.

"Neither. I don't ski." Leigh pulled off her gloves and went to work sorting through a nearby rack.

"What did you have in mind? Kapok? Thinsulate? Down? Did you want waist, hip or knee length? Dressy or casual?"

"Lots of choices," Leigh replied, moving to another rack. *At least she seems to know her merchandise. Maybe this won't take all day.*

Karen took a pink parka from the rack and held it up. It reminded Leigh of Pepto-Bismol.

"This one has a zip-out vest liner and elastic inner cuffs to keep snow out." When Leigh didn't brighten at the coat, Karen took another from the rack. "This one is hip length and rated for ten below. It comes in six colors but red, white and black are on back order."

"Looks like a sleeping bag," Leigh said, squeezing the puffy sleeve.

"Actually it's warmer than most sleeping bags. We've got some great new colors this year. Lime, raspberry cream, frosted peach."

"Sounds like flavors for smoothies." Leigh eyed a rack of down parkas, none of them fruit colored. "Ah, here we go."

"I know it's none of my business, but I have to ask. Why did you come to Aspen during the ski season if you don't ski? Don't get me wrong, I think it's great. Aspen is wonderful all year long. I love it. But winter here is a little harsh if you don't enjoy the ski season."

"I'm here on business." She flipped through the rack, giving special attention to the ones long enough to cover her rear.

"That one you're looking at comes in both hip and knee length. It's available in four colors; white, pink, navy and silver gray."

"Is this down filled?" Leigh checked the tag.

"No, it's fiberfill but very warm. Not as warm as down, but a good all-weather coat. It's water repellant too."

"I want down with cuff liners, preferably gray."

"This one is down," Karen replied, pulling one from a rack. "Subzero rated and it has a zip-off hood."

Leigh liked the style but the fake fur around the hood instantly reminded her of Margo's comment about fur-trimmed socialites.

"I don't care for the fur."

"No problem. It snaps off." She demonstrated. "Between you and me, I don't like it either. Even if it is synthetic fur, why do we have to pretend to kill animals to decorate our clothes? Try it on." She held it out for Leigh to try.

Leigh slipped it on and zipped it closed then checked the look in the mirror, satisfied she had found what she wanted. She didn't need to try on dozens of coats. This would do.

"I'll take it. I'd also like some gloves, heavy ones. My driving gloves just aren't warm enough."

Karen led the way to the display where Leigh tried on various styles. She settled on a pair of thick silver and white Thinsulate gloves. She also selected a wool hat and scarf set in white.

"Will there be anything else?" Karen asked, politely filling the time while they waited for Leigh's credit card to process. "The system has been really slow this morning. I'm sorry."

"Do you carry winter-weight pajamas?"

"I'm sorry, no. We don't carry pj's. We do have Thermasilk though."

"And what's that?"

"Silk long underwear. They're lightweight but very warm. It's what most skiers wear to cut down on bulk." Karen opened a package containing a long sleeved turtleneck top.

"Are they as warm as thermal underwear?" Leigh asked, stroking the soft fabric. She remembered Margo was wearing waffle weave thermal underwear under her flannel shirt and seemed to be toasty warm in spite of the blowing snow.

"Warmer, I think. You barely know you have them on. We sell a lot of these."

"They don't seem very heavy."

Leigh noticed a life-size poster on the wall behind the counter of a woman skier carving a graceful trail through the deep powder. "It looks so easy, doesn't it?"

"Yeah, I wish I could ski like that," Karen said, smiling up at the poster.

"Don't you ski?"

"Sure, but not like that. She's one of the best."

Leigh checked out the sweaters and fleece tops while Karen helped another customer shopping for thermal ski socks. The woman seemed to be in a hurry and paid with cash.

"How are we doing here?" Leigh asked, drumming her fingers on the counter.

"I'm really sorry. Sometimes it just takes awhile to come online." Karen squinted at the screen, frowning her frustration.

Leigh pulled her cell phone from her purse and answered it on the third ring.

"Hi, Maureen. How's your cold?"

"Better, maybe." She still sounded stuffy. "How's it going? Did you find a repairman to fix the damage?"

"Yes. The contractor who did the remodel a few years ago." Maureen had been Leigh's secretary long enough for her to know that wasn't the reason for Maureen's call, just her way of easing into the conversation. "What's up?"

"Things look good on the Smith merger. The contract came back this morning by messenger. I'll email it so you can take a look."

"Great. Anything else?" That wasn't the reason for the call either.

"Hi," a cheerful little voice called. Leigh felt a tug at her sleeve. Lindsey grinned up at her, her cheeks rosy pink.

"Hello," Leigh uttered, surprised to see her. And Wendy.

"Oh, hello, Leah," Wendy said as she hurried through the store to the counter.

"Is that a kid?" Maureen asked.

"Yes. I'm in a store shopping for a new coat."

"You should have said something. I can talk with you later. Give me a call when you have a few minutes."

"That's okay. What is it?"

"I'll give you the details later. It's just a piece of property in Aspen Helen Vick is curious about. Actually two pieces of property. The other one is in Colorado Springs near the Biltmore Hotel. But we've found the stats for that one. It's the one in Aspen we can't find anything on. She wants a comparison. But she won't expect an answer on it until she gets back from her cruise. We've got plenty of time."

This was the reason for the call. Helen Vick heard about property she hopes to buy for a bargain price and turn into upscale condos.

"Can you email me the info? I'll check it out."

"Sure. Talk with you later."

Leigh's semi-vacation had just taken another unexpected turn. But Helen had been a client for years and this was what she did, invest in prime locations for a quick and profitable turnaround. Helen could smell out an investment opportunity better than a Wall Street executive. Leigh closed her phone and stepped away from the child who was now zipping and unzipping insulated ski pants. Wendy was at the counter, talking with Karen about release forms and rescheduling an appointment.

"Don't mess with those, missy," Wendy said in Lindsey's direction. "You'll get the zippers stuck."

"No, I won't." Lindsey continued working the zippers. Wendy gave her a stern look and pointed a warning finger at her. Lindsey stopped but only after giving one last tug on a zipper. "What did you buy?" she asked Leigh.

"A coat." Leigh waited at the corner of the counter for Karen to finish processing her transaction.

"A pink one? I like the pink one in the window. When I get big I'm going to be a model."

"That's nice." Leigh cleared her throat and peered over the counter to hurry things along.

"When will she be back?" Wendy asked impatiently.

"I have no idea." Karen wrinkled her brow as she continued to punch keys on the keyboard. "What the fffff?" she muttered under her breath.

"Did the coat cost lots of money?" Lindsey asked, standing at Leigh's side like she belonged to her.

"Hush, Lindsey." Wendy reached over and tugged at the child's hood. "Don't be rude."

"Do you have any kids?" Lindsey asked.

"No." Leigh looked over at the screen, trying to see what the holdup was.

"How come?"

"Because I don't." Leigh wished she had enough cash on her to pay for her purchases. This was taking way too long. "Is it the card?"

"No, I don't think so. It's just taking a really long time to process."

"I have to go to the bathroom." Lindsey's eyes suddenly got big and she clamped her legs together.

"The door is unlocked." Karen nodded toward the storeroom but kept her eyes on the screen.

What is it with this kid and bathrooms?

"I think it's finally going through," Karen announced as the printer began spitting out the receipt.

Leigh scrawled her signature on the slip, gathered her purchases and snatched the receipt from Karen's hand as Lindsey groaned and made a dash for the back of the store.

"Thank you," Leigh said, heading for the door without waiting for a sack.

"Thanks for coming in. I'm really sorry about the wait. Come see us again," Karen called as the door closed.

Chapter 5

Leigh walked the contractor and the insurance claims adjuster through the cabin, pointing out the damage and what needed to be repaired. The noxious smell of urine and rotting food permeated the air. She hesitated at the bedroom door and looked back. She couldn't help remember her down comforter on a snowy night and wonder if she'd ever feel that warm and safe again. With a mixture of anger and sorrow, she turned the keys over to the contractor and headed back to town for a quick lunch then the meeting with Kathy Braden, the realtor who would eventually turn her cabin-getaway into nothing more than a pleasant memory.

The Gaylord Hotel's restaurant was as good a place as any for a salad and a cup of coffee while she looked through some texts on her phone. Maureen hadn't yet forwarded her the information on the property Helen was curious about but she was too efficient not to. Leigh had just taken a bite when she looked up and saw a dazzling redhead with sparkling green eyes striding toward her. She had a vivacious smile and her arms were spread wide for a hug.

"Leigh Insley!" the woman declared. She leaned down and wrapped Leigh in a hug, her fur-trimmed parka tickling Leigh's nose. It smelled of Chanel.

"Gwen?" Leigh covered her mouth as she hurriedly swallowed a bite of salad then looked up at her. "What are you doing in Aspen?"

"I heard you were here and the terrible news about your cabin. Are you all right, honey?" She gave a horrified scowl as if she expected Leigh to admit the details of being molested by a gang of looters.

"I'm fine. Upset, of course. But I wasn't home during the robbery. How are you? How long has it been? Two years."

Leigh had met Gwen Foley three years ago in Denver at a dedication ceremony for a new LGBT center and again six months later when she handled the sale of a strip mall for one of Leigh's clients. She was an energetic, intelligent and articulate woman. She was also one of the most successful real estate agents in the Denver area, representing only top-tier properties. Leigh admired her success and her drive.

Leigh pushed her salad aside and patted the chair next to her, saying, "Sit down and tell me what you've been up to."

"Didn't Kathy tell you?" Gwen slipped out of the jacket and draped it over the back of the chair. She sat down, adjusting the hem of her form-fitting sweater.

"Kathy Braden?"

"Yes. Oh, Lord. I assumed you knew I was handling your sale. This is so embarrassing, Leigh."

"When did you start working for Braden and Covey?"

"I moved to Aspen a little over a year ago. I love it here. The ambiance is almost palpable. Aspen has it all. Dining, shopping, nightlife. Could I have some coffee, miss?" she said to a passing waitress. "Black."

"How about some lunch? My treat."

"No, nothing for me. Just coffee. I'm on a diet. The food and the altitude in Aspen are fattening. I gained ten pounds the first month I moved up here."

Leigh couldn't help but think Gwen was the last person in Aspen to need a diet. She was somewhere in her mid-fifties and still had a narrow waist, nicely rounded hips and plentiful bustline. Her fur-topped boots accented well-proportioned legs. She was a walking ad for aging gracefully. She was as femme a lesbian as Leigh had ever met.

"So Kathy didn't tell you I'd be handling things because of her little mishap?"

"What little mishap? Is Kathy going to be all right?"

"Oh, sure, the poor thing. Her nephew was teaching her how to snowboard and she fell. Her boot didn't release from the binding and," Gwen held her hands out as if breaking a twig and made a cracking sound. She closed her eyes and shuddered. "I bet it hurt like a son-of-a-bitch."

"I bet." The thought of it sent a chill up Leigh's spine. No wonder she wasn't a winter athlete. "Are you sure she's going to be okay?"

"I think so. She called me last night and when she mentioned your name I couldn't believe it. Leigh Insley. What a stroke of luck. I've meant to call you a dozen times but you know how it is. There's always something going on. So what can I do for you, honey? Does this have anything to do with the robbery? You aren't selling your cabin because it got broken into are you?"

"No. It has nothing to do with that. I just don't have enough time for it. It's ridiculous of me to keep a vacation cabin when I'm lucky to find two weeks a year to get up here. I've allowed some of my clients to use it but that only leads to problems. I don't have time to clean and repair what they destroy."

"I understand completely. That's a long drive to clean bathrooms and change the linens. It's a shame though. I'm telling you, Leigh, there's nothing like a little time in the mountains to rejuvenate the soul." Gwen gave a dreamy sigh.

"That's why I bought it. But just getting up here to get it listed took a month of planning. Now with the break-in, there's all the more reason to sell."

"Do you want me to supervise the repairs? We offer property management for a very reasonable fee. We have handyman crews to fix about anything."

"No, I'm here. I'll stay until it's repaired and ready to put on the market."

"Then tell me about the cabin. What are we working with here? Mortgage? Contractor liens?"

"No. I own it. No mortgage. No liens. It was built twenty years ago but I had it remodeled after I bought it eight years ago. It's typical timber-framed construction. Three bedrooms, two bathrooms, a working fireplace in the living room and master suite. Stainless steel appliances and granite countertops. Four-and-a-half acres with a view of Aspen Mountain to the west. Lots of storage for skis and equipment although I never use it."

"Wow, I'm impressed. Sounds more like a home than a cabin."

"I suppose so," Leigh said, wiping her mouth with her napkin. She felt a surprising twinge of regret as she described the cabin she once loved. "As soon as the repairs are finished I'll let you know so we can arrange a tour. I told him I need this completed ASAP. He said the repairs are all cosmetic, carpeting, broken glass and things that shouldn't take too long. Nothing structural. I have some information I'll email you. Measurements, stats, basic contractual clauses to be included and the asking price."

"I'll take good care of you, Leigh." Gwen smiled warmly and placed a hand over Leigh's. "You don't have to worry about a thing."

"What's your commission, Gwen?"

"Six and three-quarter percent."

"Six and three quarters?" Leigh took the last sip of her coffee then looked over at her.

"I know, I know. The industry standard is six. But Braden and Covey provide some services those cut-rate agencies don't. Things like online virtual tours available 24/7. We only show our better property like yours to clients with preapproved credit. And of course we are MLS."

"I expected to pay a six percent commission, Gwen. Virtual tours aren't unusual and in today's mortgage mess, showing to only preapproved clients is just smart business practice. But I'll agree to your six and three-quarter although I have some contingencies. The listing contract and your exclusivity will exist for six months. I want to be notified when the property is shown and I reserve right of refusal on all offers. There will be no owner-financing. The price includes contents. Appliances, furniture, drapes, dishes, linens. Everything but the computer and my personal items."

She gave Gwen a serious gaze. "And Gwen, the asking price is not negotiable. The buyer must agree to all stipulated conditions in the contract. I'm having an inspector go through it after the repairs are finished. Everything will be in working order and up to code. I would encourage them to do the same." Leigh smiled softly. "I need an agent who knows the market and can handle things for me. I'm glad it's you, Gwen. I trust you won't allow one of your associates to waste my time with ridiculous low-ball offers."

"Absolutely not." Gwen shook her head vehemently. "That won't happen. I can promise you that. If you'll email me that information I'll draw up a contract. I'm anxious to take a look at the property and get to work on this. We'll have your cabin on the sold list before you know it."

The sound of that gave Leigh another chill. Gwen's confidence didn't diminish the rush of emotion Leigh felt over giving up the one place where she had found peace and solitude from her hectic life. How could a few acres and a pile of timbers have become so meaningful? How unlike her to put such weight on mere possessions.

"I've got to run, sweetheart," Gwen said, glancing at her watch. "I wish I could stay and visit but I've got a closing in fifteen minutes. Call me. I'm dying to see the cabin." She tucked a ten-dollar bill under the edge of the coffee cup then gave Leigh a kiss on the cheek before hurrying away like a commuter late for a train.

Leigh returned to her salad. But seeing Gwen again after two years had put a smile on her face. She was still a successful and gorgeous woman, worth a smile.

"Ms. Insley?" a voice called.

"Yes?" Leigh looked up from her salad. "Oh, hello again," she said in surprise.

It was Margo, looking bulky in a pair of insulated coveralls. She pulled off a glove and dipped her hand in her pocket.

"I need you to verify your address and provide picture ID," she said.

"Excuse me?"

"ID."

"I'm sorry but I don't show my ID indiscriminately."

"You might want to make an exception this time." Margo removed her stocking cap and ruffled her hair, several dark locks settling over her forehead like little springs.

"I don't think so," Leigh said and went back to her salad. She had no idea what this bizarre woman had in mind but she wasn't playing along.

Margo leaned down and whispered, "Six two six one."

"I beg your pardon? What is six two six one?" Leigh asked, leaning away from her. Today Margo smelled like strawberries and peppermint, much better than the diesel and tobacco smoke smell from the other night.

"The last four numbers of your Visa card."

"What?" She scowled up at her. "How do you know that?" Leigh's cynical side had been aroused. How did this woman know anything about her credit card or her personal business?

Margo placed her hand on the table palm down and slid it toward Leigh.

"I'm trusting you are Leigh Insley and your billing address is on Oak Harbor Avenue in Denver." She removed her hand to reveal Leigh's Visa card, the one she had used to buy the coat.

"Oh, my God," Leigh gasped and snatched it up. "How did you get this? You stole my Visa?" She glared up at Margo, holding the card to her chest like it was a long-lost child.

"I didn't steal your Visa, lame-o. You left it on the counter at the Polar Bear."

"How did you know that's where I left it?"

"Because that's where Karen found it. And why do I have it? Because Karen gave it to me. I could have reported it to the credit card company and sent it to you but I thought you might need it while you were here in Aspen. And why did I bother? Because I want my customers satisfied. And I want to apologize. Karen told me about the problem with the card terminal."

"Your customers?" was all Leigh could think to say. What could this truck-driving, diesel-smelling, flannel-wearing lumberjack possibly have to do with her two-hundred-dollar parka purchase? "You work at the Polar Bear?"

"Yes, when Karen lets me." She gave a quirky smile. "Ms. Insley, I own the Polar Bear."

"You own it?" Leigh asked skeptically.

"Yes."

"*You* own the Polar Bear Apparel Shop?"

"You make it sound ridiculous and I'm not sure I appreciate that."

"I thought you drove a snowplow for a living."

"I do a lot of things for a living. Don't you?"

"Actually, no. I do one thing."

"Lucky you. I don't drive a snowplow regularly. I was filling in. A couple of the drivers were out with the flu. They were short-handed the other night."

"They just pull people off the street to drive those huge trucks?" Leigh scoffed. "No wonder the highway was impassable."

"The highway was impassable because drivers ignore the warnings and drive without chains during a blizzard," Margo bristled. "I happen to have a license to drive those trucks."

"How did you know where I was staying?" Leigh straightened her posture indignantly.

"Karen said she saw a key card for the Gaylord Hotel in your wallet. I called and the desk clerk said you were eating lunch in the restaurant. So here I am. Any other questions, Ms. Insley?"

Leigh checked the card as if looking for defects then slipped it in her wallet.

"No. And thank you for returning the card." She planned a call to customer service to check on unexpected charges to her Visa account.

"Why the Gaylord? I thought you had a cabin here in Aspen."

"I had a little problem with the cabin."

"What happened? Power outage? Or too much snow to get up there?"

"Neither. I had a robbery. Someone broke in and trashed the place."

"Wow. A robbery? I'm sorry to hear that. Did they take much?"

"Enough so I couldn't stay in it." Leigh wasn't sure the details were any of Margo's business. She was about to change the subject when she noticed a woman a few feet away. Like Margo, she was bundled against the weather. She was younger than Margo by several years and had delicate features. Margo saw where Leigh's gaze had moved and looked back at the woman, holding up a finger as if telling her she'd be there shortly.

"Thank you again for returning my credit card," Leigh said, diverting her stare from the woman. "I should have paid more attention."

"Karen said Lindsey was being a butt-itch. I forgot they were coming in. I should have been there."

"I think they were looking for Lindsey's mother."

Margo chuckled. "Yeah, I was at the hardware store."

"You're Lindsey's mother?"

"Yes." Margo shifted her weight and scowled down at Leigh. "You don't have much confidence in anything about me, do you?"

"I didn't say that. I just thought…" Leigh closed her mouth. She was not about to say that Margo was anything but the mother nurturing type. They didn't look much alike. Margo had dark hair, dark eyes and chiseled features. Lindsey was blond, blue-eyed and petite. But that would explain Wendy and Lindsey being at the store discussing parental issues.

"Margo?" the woman in the parka called. She nodded toward the door as if to hurry her along.

"Gotta go," Margo said, replacing her hat and gloves. "Sorry about the card. Karen should have made sure you had it back before you left the store."

"I share the responsibility. But thank you."

Margo turned to leave then looked back and said, "Sorry

about your cabin trouble. I hope you get it fixed." She smiled back at Leigh then followed the woman out of the restaurant.

Leigh watched until they were out of sight. So, Margo, the truck driver is a mother, Leigh thought. She'd never guess that. In fact, her first instinct was to assume Margo was gay, like herself.

Chapter 6

It was dinnertime but Leigh wasn't hungry. She was frustrated. The hotel's Internet was down and would be until morning. She'd spent most of the afternoon on her laptop with follow-up phone calls to three clients. She'd been on the phone for an hour talking a woman out of creating a trust fund for her cats. Leigh usually didn't interfere with her clients wishes but leaving two hundred thousand dollars to a pair of aging Siamese seemed excessively eccentric. Now she needed a break. It was better than pacing the confines of her room in frustration. Normally she could find something to do with herself, something in her briefcase or on her laptop to keep her busy. Whether it was meeting Gwen or the repeated confrontations with Margo, something blocked her ability to focus. And that wasn't like her.

Maybe a breath of fresh air and a cup of coffee or a glass

of wine would put her in a better mood. She slipped a proposal in her purse to look at later and headed out the door. A flyer in her hotel lobby for The Sweet Spot, an inviting looking bistro two blocks away, seemed like the perfect place for a change of atmosphere and a little work-related dinner.

The brick-fronted building in mid-block was crowded, filled with patrons clad in everything from business suits to ski wear. The waitresses were dressed in red and white striped shirts and bowties, reminiscent of turn-of-the-century malt shops. Leigh couldn't help but notice the decadent-looking desserts in the glass case along the front of the store. She strolled the case, her mouth watering at the cheesecakes, pies, cakes and pastries lined up like calorie-laden soldiers waiting for a parade. Maybe she was a little hungry after all.

After waiting ten minutes for a table she was escorted to the balcony and a small table against the railing. The walls alongside her were decorated with abstract art and ski posters. She ordered the special—Italian meatball soup, a slice of dark rye bread and a slice of cheesecake for dessert. She hadn't had cheesecake in months and the dozen or so varieties to pick from all looked wonderful. The problem would be settling for just one.

Leigh sat bouncing the tea bag up and down in the little teapot and watching the passing scene while she waited for her order. She had a good view of the steady stream of customers on the floor below. The hearty soups and decadent-looking cheesecake seemed to be the popular menu choices. From the buzz of conversation around her about the fresh powder on Aspen Mountain she wondered if she was the only person in town who couldn't strap on a pair of skis and schuss their way down the mountain.

As she scanned the crowd someone caught her eye. Margo and several women were crowded around a table in the far corner of the café. Leigh couldn't hear what they were saying but they were obviously having a good time, laughing uproariously and pointing at an attractive blonde. Margo was wearing a fleece top and black ski pants with a gray scarf draped around her neck. She was probably the oldest of the group, but her body was just as trim and athletic as the twenty and thirty-year-olds sitting with her. She must exercise a lot to stay in shape, Leigh thought.

The blonde seated next to Margo flipped her long hair and leaned against Margo's shoulder. Leigh recognized her as the woman with Margo at the hotel, the impatient one. She was drop-dead gorgeous. She had on tight-fitting ski pants that looked like spandex and a Nordic ski sweater. Margo leaned into the middle of the table to hear one of the women then threw her head back and laughed, draping her arm around the blonde's shoulders. The blonde buried her face in her hands as if embarrassed by what was said. Margo rubbed her back, reassuring and soothing her, then kissed her forehead. Leigh watched, magnetized by the sight.

As the waitress brought Leigh's dinner to the table, she noticed Margo and the other women getting up to leave. There was a confident swagger to Margo's stride and a radiant smile lighting up her dark eyes. What was it about this woman that had Leigh craning her neck? Her fascination had always been with professional, well-educated and personable women able to carry on a conversation on a wide range of subjects. Not a truck-driving arrogant boob whose idea of a stylish wardrobe was a flannel shirt in every color of the rainbow. Leigh had no idea what the attraction was but whatever it was, she couldn't shake it. And she felt silly for it. Thankfully they all filed out, leaving Leigh to enjoy her dinner in peace.

The soup was delicious. So was the raspberry swirl cheesecake but she could only manage a few small bites of it. She asked for a to-go box, resigned to enjoying the rest of it later in her room. While she waited in line to pay her check she noticed a woman loading a tray of desserts into the case. She had raspberry red hair and wore black granny glasses. Leigh hadn't paid much attention when the menu referred to Tink's Homemade Cheesecakes but she instantly recognized the hair and the glasses on the round-faced woman.

"Miss Winecroft?" Leigh exclaimed.

The woman looked up and squinted then squealed wildly.

"Leigh Insley," she squealed, throwing her arms open as she rushed up to Leigh and wrapped her in a hug. "I can't believe it. It's so good to see you." She continued to hug and sway.

Katinka Winecroft, or Tink as her students lovingly called her, was a home economics teacher extraordinaire. Tink hadn't changed. Her eyes were still bright pools of happiness. Her hair was still a very unnatural shade of red. She still had a wonderfully warm hug. Somewhere in her sixties, her energy and enthusiasm still oozed from every pore.

"It's not Miss Winecroft anymore, honey. It's just plain old Tink." Her laugh was more of a chortle. "And what are you doing in Aspen?" she asked, pushing Leigh back by the shoulders to take a look at her.

"I should ask you the same thing. I heard you retired but this hardly looks like retirement." Leigh tugged at Tink's apron playfully.

"Retirement isn't all it's cracked up to be. It was at first. But after the first month I knew I had to do something with myself or go crazy. I wasn't meant to sit on the sidelines and watch. So I put my recipe box under my arm and went in search of a little place I could call my own. And here I am. What do you think of my little piece of paradise?"

"You own this? Tink, it's wonderful. I love the soup and the cheesecake." She closed her eyes and moaned, "The cheesecake is soooo good. But I couldn't finish it. I'll treat myself to the rest of it later." She held up her to-go box.

"Let me give you a fresh piece, honey." Tink took the box and went to the case.

"Tink, thank you but I don't need another piece. This is fine."

"I'll give you a little piece of key lime so you can compare." She cut a generous piece and slipped it in the box as well. She then took Leigh by the arm and led her into the office. "Come visit with me one minute. I have to hear all about what you've been up to since graduation. How long has it been? Eighteen years? Twenty?"

"Thirty."

"You're kidding. Are you sure?" Tink frowned in disbelief. "Gosh, that makes you forty-eight. You know, I can't remember all my students but I remember you like it was yesterday. You were so smart and always on time. You did your assignments and cleaned up after yourself. You were a pleasure to have in class, Leigh. But if you don't mind me saying so." She pinched Leigh's arm and whispered. "You couldn't cook worth poop."

"I still can't," Leigh confessed and they both laughed.

"You were the organizer and negotiator in class. So what did you do after graduation?"

"I attended CU then Yale Law School."

"Really? You are a lawyer?" Tink sounded more proud than skeptical.

"Yes. You were a great Home Ec. teacher, Tink, but I'm afraid I don't possess even a shred of domesticity."

"Oh, I bet you do. But that's okay." She patted Leigh's hand. "We don't all have to like cooking. Look at me. I can bake up a storm but when it comes to sitting at a desk." She shuddered. "I hate it. I'd rather filet a moose than do bookwork."

"But you were always so organized, so efficient."

"Me? Lord no." She shook her head and smiled reflectively.

Tink had always been the teacher students could turn to. Leigh had. When she was wrestling with the inner turmoil of her sexual orientation, hanging out in Miss Winecroft's room was her safe haven. Even though she had never come out to her, she felt better. It was as if she had mystical powers to solve any problem. The fact that Tink never married only strengthened her sanctity and validity in Leigh's eyes. Miss Winecroft was so dedicated to her students there was nothing left for a husband or family. At least that's the way the students saw it.

Tink ran her fingers through her hair then squashed the curls back into place. She looked tired. Common sense told Leigh she was just another mortal with flaws and defects like everyone else. But she was also Miss Winecroft, teacher and mentor.

Leigh gave Tink a hug and said, "It's so good to see you."

"How long will you be in Aspen?"

"Two weeks. I came up to get my cabin ready to put on the market."

"You have a cabin here? Why haven't I seen you before now?"

"Because I don't get up here very often. I don't have time for it." Leigh knew that sounded like a flimsy excuse.

"Tink, we need change in register two," a woman said, sticking her head in the office door.

"Okay, Sally. Be right there." She groaned as she pulled herself to her feet and straightened her apron.

"I better let you get back to work," Leigh said, tucking her to-go box under her arm as she pulled on her gloves.

"I hate for this to end." Tink locked her arm through Leigh's as they headed for the front. "Promise you'll come back and see me before you go home. Okay? I want to hear all about you and your work and your partner." She walked her to the front door and opened it.

"I'm not married, Tink," Leigh confessed.

"I know, honey. Me either. They won't let us." She winked. "Zip your coat and keep warm, honey."

Tink kissed Leigh on the cheek then went back to work, leaving Leigh struck dumb with astonishment. Had Miss Winecroft just outed herself? That explained a lot. How many more surprises were there going to be this trip?

Leigh stepped out onto the sidewalk, her box of cheesecake under her arm. She had originally planned to eat dinner then return to the hotel for a hot bath and a little work before bed. But seeing Tink after all these years had been a hoot—and a revelation. She was invigorated and decided a little walk would be good. She headed up the sidewalk, blending in with the pedestrians strolling downtown Aspen. The chilly evening was amazingly still under the sparkle of streetlights reflecting in the snow like diamond dust.

Leigh's breath curled around her face as she stood at the corner waiting for the traffic light to change. She could hear faint sounds of laughter from across the street. Several people were running across the park, scrambling from tree to tree to avoid flying snowballs. A row of non-combatant spectators lined the sidewalk, cheering as the missiles found their targets. The teams seemed to be a group of teenage boys using the Victorian gazebo as their fort and an equal number of women hiding behind whatever they could find.

"No ice balls, Lucas," a woman yelled, throwing one back and hitting him square in the chest.

"All's fair, Margo," he replied then scooped up two hands full of snow, formed a ball and let fly. She ducked and it sailed over her head, striking the woman behind her.

"Sorry, Karen." Margo laughed uproariously.

This must be where the women were headed when they left Tink's. Leigh watched as Margo dodged several shots then dove behind a park bench. She rolled to her knees and threw two successive shots, striking two boys as they advanced on her position.

"No fair making them ahead," another boy yelled. "You have to throw them as you make them."

"All's fair," Margo scoffed and threw another, striking him in the knee.

One of the boys threw a snowball that missed everyone and rolled to within a few feet of where Leigh was standing on the sidewalk.

"Hey, hi Leigh," Karen called from behind a nearby bush. "Toss me that one."

Leigh obliged.

"If she helps, she's enemy," Lucas shouted, pointing at Leigh. He then launched several snowballs in her direction. Leigh squealed and ran down the sidewalk to avoid being hit. But his aim was too good. He led her just enough and pelted her in the back of neck.

"I'm just a spectator," she screamed, hunching her shoulders as the snow drifted down inside her jacket.

"Not anymore you aren't." He threw another one. It hit the to-go box and knocked it out of her hand.

"Hey, that's my dessert," she declared, scrambling to retrieve it. Another snowball struck the box again, dumping the cheesecake in the snow. "Who did that?" Leigh scowled. Her nostrils flared as she scooped some snow and threw it. She didn't pack it well enough and it flew through the air like pixie dust.

"Nice throw, lady," Lucas scoffed. He stood up and waved his arms. "Wanna try that again? Come on. I dare you."

"Knock his block off," Karen shouted. "Hit him in his big mouth."

Leigh was mad. Tink had given her that cheesecake. She scooped again and pressed the snow into a tight ball then threw it but he ducked and it floated over his head. She quickly reloaded and held the snowball over her head as she ran toward him, determined to get close enough to hit him.

"Oh, shit," he yelled and took off running, Leigh right behind. She chased him around one tree then another.

"You better run, sonny. I may not be a good shot but I'm fast." Leigh was closing in on him. She hadn't run like this since high school track. She cocked her arm and let fly, striking him in the back of the neck. He yelled and cursed as the snow settled down the inside of his jacket. Leigh was immediately met with a barrage of snowballs from all directions.

"Over here," Margo shouted, waving her over.

Leigh scrambled behind the bench, narrowly missing another shot. Margo brushed the snow from Leigh's hat and collar. "I'm sorry about your to-go box. What was in it?"

"Cheesecake. Chocolate raspberry and key lime."

"Damn. Two pieces? Where from?"

"The Sweet Spot."

"Double damn. Her stuff is good."

"I had plans for my cheesecake."

"I bet." Margo rose up and threw two snowballs then ducked down again.

"Here. Throw this one," Leigh said, handing her the one she had made. Margo heaved it at the two boys sharing a tree. Leigh quickly made another one and handed it to Margo.

Two women who had been huddled behind a snow-covered statue made a run for another park bench but were hit by several snowballs before they could jump to safety.

"Not in the face," one of the women shouted angrily. "You could put an eye out."

That's the blonde. Who'd have thought she'd participate in something like this?

"They're getting murdered. Come on. We're moving over there." Margo pulled at Leigh's sleeve.

"How did I get roped into this?" Leigh followed, covering her head as she ran.

The four women huddled together while snowballs flew overhead.

"Load up, girls," Margo ordered, sounding like the captain of a special ops team. "We're taking back the gazebo."

The four women armed themselves. On Margo's count they sprang from behind the bench and charged the boys' position in the gazebo. Karen and several other women mounted an assault from the other side. The boys were surrounded. They had depleted their snow supply and were left with only the scattered remnants of broken snowballs.

"Get 'em," Margo yelled, throwing bravely and accurately. Leigh wasn't a very good shot but she stood her ground. Karen threw with both hands. The blonde did more ducking than throwing.

"Watch out," Karen yelled. "They're going to make a run for it."

"Get 'em, get 'em, get 'em," Margo shouted as the boys ran across the park and down the street. Several of the girls followed to the edge of the park, firing their last snowballs at them. The women climbed the steps of the gazebo, cheering victoriously and sharing hugs and high fives.

"That was fun," Leigh declared, catching her breath. She removed her hat and shook off the snow and ice pellets. "Who was the enemy? Anybody dangerous?"

"Lucas, the one you were chasing, is Karen's brother," Margo replied, laughing and brushing the snow from Leigh's back. "He and his friends challenged us to a snowball fight. It's kind of a tradition. They call it the battle for the park. It's just a bunch of us locals acting stupid. Two of the gals are cops. One is a teacher at the elementary school. Her son is on the boy's team. The guy in the camouflage coveralls is the mayor's son. The rest are just friends of friends."

"Then I shouldn't have interfered," Leigh said. "I'm sorry."

"Heck, yeah, you should have. We were outnumbered. This is the first time we've ever won. Usually the boys have the women screaming and running down the street before we even get warmed up."

"I bet I looked ridiculous. I can't believe I did that."

"You were good. Or at least you were fast. I'm just sorry you lost your cheesecake. I'll be glad to replace it for you."

"Heavens, no. You didn't make me drop it. Besides, I don't need it."

"Are you sure?" Margo removed her stocking cap and leaned over, ruffling the snow from her hair.

"Quite sure."

"I need something hot to drink. How about an Irish coffee?" Karen asked the group of women.

"Make it double on the Irish part," the blonde added with a shiver.

"Come with us, Leigh," Karen said, stomping her feet to warm them. "We're going to the Silo. They've got great chocolate thunder."

"What's that?"

"Hot cocoa with peppermint schnapps." The blonde grinned wickedly.

"Thanks, but not tonight," Leigh replied. "Maybe another time." She was cold and she could feel snow melting down her pants. A bath and dry clothes sounded better than getting drunk on peppermint schnapps.

"Hot chocolate thunder will warm you better than a hot bath," Karen insisted.

"I'm sure it would but I don't think so."

"Leave her alone, Karen," Margo said. "She isn't interested in your lush-fest at the Silo. And she isn't interested in seeing you flash the bartender to get a free drink."

"I only did that once," Karen argued. "It was my birthday and I was dared."

"Let's go. I'm cold," the blonde said impatiently. "Come on, Margo."

"You go ahead. I've got to pick up Lindsey. Next time."

"'Night, Leigh," Karen called as she headed across the park.

"Good night," Leigh replied, waving then turning the other way toward the hotel.

"I bet you're cold," Margo said, trotting up to the corner as Leigh waited for the light to change. "You're not dressed for a snowball fight."

"If I'd known I was going to participate I would have dressed for it." She shivered.

"Can I buy you a cup of coffee?" Margo asked as they passed a walk-up window to a coffeehouse. In spite of the chilly temperatures it was bustling with business. "They have hot chocolate," she said with an encouraging smile.

"Well." The idea did sound tempting.

"Whipped cream with chocolate sprinkles on top?" Margo asked, digging a money clip from the pocket of her coveralls.

"No sprinkles, please."

Margo stepped to the window and said, "Hi, Megan. Two hot chocolate, one with whipped cream."

"Hi, Margo. Large or small?" the woman asked, peeking through the window to see who was with her.

"Large. No sprinkles."

Margo handed one of the cups to Leigh, saying, "Be careful. It's hot."

"Smells fantastic," she replied, smelling the rich chocolate aroma. "Thank you."

"Ghirardelli chocolate, I think." She blew across the top of her cup then sipped carefully. "So you really don't ski?" Margo nonchalantly stepped to the outside of Leigh as they walked along.

"Nope. Not a smidge. I tried when I was a kid but I was a clutz."

"How old were you?"

"About ten. My sister and I took lessons from the YMCA but the only thing I learned was how to fill in my sitz mark when I fell."

"Maybe you should try again."

"I don't think so," Leigh said, holding her cup close to her face to allow the steam to warm it. "I nearly got frostbite on my fingers. And I stabbed my chin with my pole."

"Damn. I can see why you didn't enjoy yourself."

"Like most sports, it looks easy when the experts do it. Like that poster in your store, it looks so easy to float down the hill. Do you ski?"

"Yeah. I was born here in Aspen. It's written on our birth

certificates. We are required to learn to ski." Margo chuckled then pushed the pedestrian light to cross the street. "This is where I leave you." She nodded toward the Polar Bear Shop across the street in the other direction.

"You're sure working late." She glanced over at the store. It was closed but the display windows were brightly lit.

"I've got to pick up Lindsey at a birthday party. She'll be on a sugar high for sure." She tugged at the neck of her coveralls. "But I need a shower first. I think there was sand in the snowballs."

"You shower at your store?"

"I live up there," she replied, nodding toward the four tall windows on the second floor. "I converted the storeroom to an apartment to save on rent."

"So you live in the storeroom." Leigh tried not to sound judgmental but the idea of living in an upstairs storeroom over a clothing store with a child didn't conjure up images of cozy comfort.

"Yeah. It's not much but at least I'm seldom late for work."

"I like the detailing across the top of the building," Leigh said, trying to find something nice to say.

"It was built in eighteen ninety-nine. It was a boot store until the early nineteen fifties. Rumor has it Teddy Roosevelt ordered a pair of riding boots from the store. He wanted them made out of elk hide."

"Wow. You live in a historic building."

"Most of downtown Aspen has some history to it. Silver mining was a big deal a hundred years ago. Now the only silver mining around Aspen is the outrageous prices the jewelers charge." The light changed but Margo didn't cross. She waited then pushed the button again. "How's the cabin repair coming?"

"Several things will have to be special order, but hopefully I'll be able to move back in within a few days. Replacing the door to the deck and the carpeting are the biggest jobs."

"Anything I can do?" Margo sounded genuinely concerned.

"Thank you but the contractor seems to have things under control. And thank you for the cocoa." Leigh took the last swig then dropped the cup in a trash barrel. The light changed. "Good night, Margo," she said, stepping off the curb.

"Watch out!" Margo yelled, grabbing for Leigh's arm when a car rounded the corner on the red. Leigh gasped and jumped back. "Asshole," Margo shouted at the driver.

"Thank you. I guess I should look before I leap," she said. She looked both ways then crossed.

She could feel Margo's eyes watching her until she stepped up the other side. She turned and clasped her raised hands together victoriously. Margo gave her a thumbs-up then grinned and waved before trotting across the street in the other direction.

Chapter 7

Leigh slept curled up under a comforter while an icy snow pelted the window of her hotel room. The mere sound of the crystal pellets against the glass was enough to send a chill coursing through her body. By morning an iridescent crust clung to the windowsill. She ordered coffee and toast from room service, determined to finish her correspondence before heading out for the day.

"What's this, Maureen?" she muttered, skimming through an email flagged high priority. She scrolled down through the greetings and office updates.

Regarding the Aspen property—Helen estimated about ten acres on a dead-end street. She wasn't sure but thought the street was something like Pinion or Primrose. It's an abandoned three-story brick building. Said you can't miss it. Most of the windows are broken out and there is a chain-link fence around the parking lot on the back of the building. I couldn't find an MLS listing for it. Maybe it's for sale by owner or tied up in probate.

Leigh typed a reply.

It could be under contract waiting for a title search or financing. Let's establish a physical address for the property then take it from there. I'll see what I can find.

Google Earth provided Leigh a possibility but Maureen was right. She could find no reference to commercial property for sale at that location. No permit or license of any kind had been issued. Leigh was tempted to call Gwen and see what she knew about it but she knew better than to tip her hand. If the property was available and could be purchased without a real estate commission, it could mean significant savings to Helen and the owner. Not to mention opening the door to Gwen's clients and driving up the price.

Leigh decided to take a look herself first. If the property had liens or a disputed title, she'd worry about that later. Helen Vick had never been intimidated by complicated property sales before. That's what she paid Leigh to handle. Wading through the mine field of legalities was all in a day's work, although Leigh didn't usually do the preliminary legwork. The law firm had gofers for that. But Leigh decided to check it out herself. After all, it might be fun. She hadn't done that since her early years as a legal aide when she was sent all over Denver, often on wild goose chases.

Leigh pulled up to the chain-link gate. The snow-covered parking lot inside the fence was untouched but for a few squirrel tracks. Just as Maureen had described, many of the windows on the three-story brick building were broken out with no effort made to cover them from the weather. A row of rusty Dumpsters lined the corner of the building. No Trespassing signs, many of them bent and graffitied, were prominently displayed but that didn't deter Leigh's curiosity. This building had obviously been empty and abandoned for some time and she didn't have time to go looking for some out-of-town property owner. Besides, who would know if she took a little look around for business purposes?

The gate latch was secured with a heavy padlock but when

she pushed on it a gap opened, wide enough for a slim person to slip through. Leigh wrapped her coat tightly around her body and eased her way through. The door at the corner of the building was locked. So was the overhead door at the loading dock. She circled the building, peeking in windows. The ground-floor windows, though broken out, were covered with bars. A metal fire escape, partially hidden behind a scraggly tree growing at the end of the building, led to a second-floor landing and a rusted metal door. Next to the door was a broken window, jagged pieces of glass still clinging to the frame.

One look inside. That's all she wanted. One look to see if this property was worth pursuing. Sure, it would probably be torn down but she wanted a look inside anyway. The worse the structure, the better the bargaining chip. She stood on her tiptoes but couldn't reach the fire escape ladder. It wasn't that far out of reach if only she had something to stand on. She combed the parking lot and found a five-gallon plastic paint bucket. Her form wasn't graceful but she was able to reach the ladder and pull it down, the rusty metal guides squealing and creaking loudly. She teetered on the bucket as she climbed onto the ladder and started up. As she suspected, the door on the landing was locked. But the window wasn't blocked. She carefully plucked the last fragments of glass from the window frame and hoisted herself up and over the edge.

"And I needed a law degree for this?" she groaned, pulling herself through the opening. "I look like a criminal."

The second floor of the warehouse was one immense open room with metal support posts every few feet, a freight elevator on one end and a door to a staircase on the other. A few remnants of metal shelving and wire racks littered the floor. A section of heating duct that ran across the rafters was disconnected and hanging loose. The faint smell of varnish lingered in the air along with a musty stench. The wooden planked floor was stained with splotches of paint and grease and creaked when she walked on it.

Leigh crossed her arms over her chest to keep warm as she stood at a broken window and stared out at downtown Aspen. Even if the building was worthless, the land it sat on was definitely a developer's dream. Just then a pigeon flew from the rafters and dove at her head then veered out the window. She screamed and ducked, frantically waving at the air. She didn't like birds, at least not ones free to swoop down and peck at her.

"The owner needs to cover the windows so birds can't get in here," she grumbled.

She didn't expect the elevator to work but she pushed the button anyway. To her surprise the motor engaged, raising the elevator on rusty rails.

"That needs some oil," she muttered, looking down through the metal grate as it slowly ascended the elevator shaft. The closer it got the louder the screech. Suddenly the elevator stopped a few feet short although the motor continued to hum. She pushed the buttons again but it didn't move. "This can't be good." She pounded the heel of her hand against the buttons, trying to dislodge it. She didn't need to be a mechanic to know a motor straining against a stuck object would soon overheat and be a fire hazard. She scanned the wall for a switch, something to cut the power to the motor. She was surprised the electricity was on at all in an abandoned building. She pounded the buttons but the motor continued to hum, the faint smell of burnt rubber coming from somewhere inside the elevator shaft.

Leigh's legal brain could just imagine the police report and the newspaper headlines.

Denver attorney Leigh Insley was arrested and charged with trespassing and criminal mischief in the fire that destroyed a three-story abandoned building on Aspen's north side. According to counsel for the property owners, a lawsuit filed against Ms. Insley is asking for monetary as well as compensatory damages. Criminal prosecution to the full extent of the law is expected.

"Come on, baby. Unstick yourself," she said, pounding her fist on the buttons. She added a kick to the elevator gate. A wisp of smoke drifted up through the gaps in the shaft. Leigh squatted and peered through the grate, trying to see where the smoke was coming from. "Where's the damn fire extinguisher?"

She continued beating the buttons. A bang and a pop like a Fourth of July firecracker startled her and she jumped back. "What was that?" The wisps of white lacy smoke changed to noxious black smoke, billowing from the edges of the elevator shaft. She knew she had waited long enough and pulled her cell phone from her pocket and keyed in nine-one-one. But her phone chimed, indicating low battery then shut off.

"Oh, no. Not again. I just charged you last night. You can't be dead already." She shook the phone and tried again but it was stone-cold dead. She wondered how long it would take her to retrace her steps out the window, down the fire escape and to her car where she could plug in the mobile charger. Too long. By then flames would be shooting up the shaft and spreading to the wooden floors. She smacked the buttons again, pressing her face to the grate to see between the cracks for signs of flames.

"What the hell are you doing in here?" a voice echoed, startling Leigh into a scream. The shadowy figure of a person stood in the open door to the stairwell. "You're trespassing. Can't you read?"

The figure filled the doorway menacingly. Leigh's heart pounded.

"Who's there?" she snapped, her voice quivering.

"It's Margo, Ms. Insley." She started toward her with long strides. "And you are trespassing."

"The elevator is stuck. I think the motor is overheating," Leigh said, frantically pointing at the smoke.

Margo formed a fist as she walked toward her, raising it over her head. She had an ominous look in her eye, one that had Leigh trembling in her dress boots and wishing she hadn't ignored the No Trespassing signs.

"I didn't mean to cause any damage, really I didn't." She had no escape and flinched as Margo's arm descended. "I'm sorry."

Margo's gloved hand sailed past Leigh's head and punched a red button at the side of the elevator gate. The motor immediately fell silent. Within a minute the smoke dissipated, leaving only the smell of burnt rubber.

"Oh, thank God," Leigh said gratefully.

"Can't you read, Ms. Insley? This building is off limits. No trespassing."

"Yes, I know. I just wanted to take a look around. I didn't want to bother the owner. How did you know I was here?"

"I'm psychic." She opened the cover to a wooden box on the wall, flipped a breaker switch then slammed it shut. "Karen saw your car turn north on Madison. The only thing out here is a Goodwill store, a truck repair shop and this building. You don't look like someone who shops at thrift stores and you don't drive a truck. How did you get in?" Margo asked, looking around.

"Through there," she said, nodding toward the window.

"The window off the fire escape?" She scowled at it then back at Leigh.

"The door was locked."

"That's what you do when you don't want anyone inside. You lock the doors."

"Yes, I know," she replied sheepishly.

"Why?"

"Let's just say I'm investigating real estate potential for a client."

"I prefer to call it what it is, trespassing."

"Yes, but it was purely business curiosity. I had no criminal intent." Leigh didn't know why she was explaining this to Margo. After all, it wasn't any of her business. Yes, she was grateful she happened along and knew how to avert a disaster but that's where the obligation stopped. "Say, how did you get in?"

"I used these," Margo said, holding up a ring of keys. "I'm the owner, Ms. Insley. This is my building and you are trespassing."

"*Your* building?" That took Leigh so completely by surprise, she didn't know what else to say.

"Yes. Mine. I own it, pay taxes on it, insure it and don't want anyone in, on, or around it. That's why I posted No Trespassing signs." She had a smug look on her face. "As you can see, it isn't safe. I don't want to be paying hospital bills when someone falls and hurts themselves. So I need you to leave and not come back. Okay?"

"*You* are the proprietary owner of this building?"

"Yes." She cocked an eyebrow at Leigh. "Surprised?"

"Forgive me, but yes. A little."

"Let me guess. You want to buy the building, tear it down and build upscale condos. Right?"

"I don't want to buy it, no."

"Oh, come on, Ms. Insley. Don't give me that. You wouldn't be climbing up my fire escape in three-hundred-dollar leather dress boots just to sightsee. I get calls and proposals all the time. I'll tell you the same thing I tell all of them. I own it. All by myself and I'm keeping it. I don't want to sell it, lease it, rent it or subdivide it. I don't want to enter in a consortium or partnership either."

"Wow, you have had offers, haven't you?" That didn't surprise Leigh. With housing at a premium in Aspen and vacant property prime for development, it was no wonder Margo had other interested parties. Leigh would be more surprised if she hadn't. "How long has it sat empty like this?"

"A while. Why? What did you plan on doing with it?" she asked with a cocky smile.

"I personally don't plan to do anything with it. I'm a corporate lawyer, Ms. Tosch. I represent clients who would like to invest in property development."

"I've had my share of those barking up my tree."

"I am not a vampire out to suck your blood. I don't want to take advantage of you."

"You represent one who does though."

"No, I do not." The hair on the back of Leigh's neck bristled at the suggestion she did anything unethical or illegal. "I assure you that is not the kind of investor I represent."

"I can hear it now. Offer the mountain girl a couple thousand for the place. She's too stupid to know what it's worth. We'll bulldoze the building and slap up condos before the ink is dry on the check. She'll never know the difference. Tell her we'll throw in a new pickup truck. That'll seal the deal." Margo smirked at her.

"If that's the kind of offers you've received I don't blame you for the cynical attitude. But I assure you the clients I represent would never do anything like that. I wouldn't represent them if they did. We negotiate in good faith, using the appraised fair market value. I wouldn't be in business very long if I didn't. We encourage all parties to have legal representation. We're not out to scalp anyone."

"Very eloquent, Ms. Insley. Very legal sounding. But you can save your breath. It's not for sale." She held open the door to the stairwell for Leigh.

"Do you mind if I ask what plans you have for it?"

Margo looked back at the empty room. Her eyes narrowed as if she were deep in thought. She seemed to see something Leigh hadn't as a slow satisfied smile settled across her face.

"It must be something very special," Leigh added, watching her expression.

Margo gave a last look then locked the door and started down the stairs. "Time to go, Ms. Insley. I've got things to do."

"What? Driving a snowplow again tonight?" Leigh hadn't meant for that to sound condescending. It just came out that way.

"No." Margo unlocked the door to the first floor and held it for Leigh.

"I didn't mean to sound sarcastic about driving a snowplow."

"Oh, that was sarcasm? I thought you were just being a bitch." Margo gave a chuckle.

Leigh gasped, ready to make a smart retort. But Margo was probably right. She was being a bitch.

"Margo, I need to apologize. For trespassing, for overheating your elevator motor, for suggesting driving a snowplow was anything less than an honorable profession and for any other comment I might have made to upset you. I'm truly sorry."

"Okay." Margo crossed to the back door of the warehouse, the footsteps of her hiking boots echoing through the rafters.

"So you accept my apology?" Leigh asked, the heels of her boots clicking a faster pace as she hurried to keep up with Margo's long strides.

"Sure. I don't hold grudges. That's a waste of time. You apologize. I accept. Done deal." She unlocked the back door that led out into the parking lot. As soon as she opened the door a blast of wind struck Leigh in the face, taking her breath away. Margo seemed to accept the bitter cold as easily as she had accepted Leigh's apology. "I imagine you lawyers are used to arguing. Isn't that what you do for a living?"

"No. And I'm not a litigator. My work is more proposals, agreements and contracts. I agree with you though. When people have to resort to screaming and raising their voice, their people skills are seriously lacking."

"How are the repairs coming on your cabin? Have you moved back in yet?"

"Not yet. The carpet is going in tomorrow."

"Wow. It really must have been bad if you need new carpet."

Leigh curled her lip and said, "It was disgusting." She swallowed back the queasiness the memory of it provided.

"Any suspects yet?"

"I haven't heard. The crime lab lifted quite a few fingerprints so a conviction should be doable if they can catch the little creeps."

"Assholes." Margo's empathy was another surprise. "Living in a hotel must be getting old. I don't care how swank it is, it can't compare to sitting by your own fireplace."

For sure. Even a four-star hotel like the Gaylord was still just a room.

"I have to go, Ms. Insley. Please stay out of my building, okay?" Margo's eyebrows arched.

"Call me Leigh. I think we can be on a first-name basis. Don't you?"

"I guess so. After all, my daughter saw you naked." Margo checked the padlock on the gate, rattling it to make sure it was secure.

"Thank you for showing me around," Leigh said, hiding a mischievous grin.

Margo gave her a cutting stare then climbed in her truck, started the engine and pulled away. As she roared down the street, Leigh could see Margo watching her through her rearview mirror. It wasn't a critical stare but more of a one-last-look stare.

Leigh started the engine and sat waiting for the defroster to clear the windshield. She was cold, as cold as she had been standing on the side of the highway in the blizzard. The floors of the building had been freezing, numbing her feet. The wind had stung her ears and face. Why the hell did I do that, she thought, looking up at the broken window she had climbed through. *And how many times is Margo's path going to cross mine?*

"Sorry, Helen. I seem to have come up empty on this one," Leigh muttered, giving one last look before backing away from the gate.

Chapter 8

It didn't take much snooping to find Margo was right. She did own the property free and clear. She'd inherited it from her father, Melvin Tosch. He had employed twenty-six people and manufactured much of the metal fittings for the ski lifts in the inter-mountain area. It was a small operation but one that adapted its tool and die machines for custom work, something larger manufacturers were less likely to do. It's bottom line showed a profit for six consecutive years in a competitive market controlled by overseas production and foreign-owned companies. They seemed to have found a formula for success. So why had Margo turned to selling ski parkas and driving snowplows? Why not continue her father's business? Was she responsible for the systematic degradation of a thriving business? Did a lack of business savvy mean the demise of a business her father had struggled to build?

Leigh stood at the window of her hotel room, sipping a stale cup of coffee. She knew all she wanted to know about Margo Tosch and the property at the end of Pinion Street. She had more important things to do than wonder why this woman refused to sell an empty building she obviously didn't have the resources to renovate. Maybe it gave her a feeling of power, status in the community to be a property owner. That had to be it. That or she was just stubborn.

After a call to the contractor to see how the repairs were coming, she read over the room service menu, wondering if she really wanted hotel food again. The special was herb-crusted Tilapia with asparagus tips and Mediterranean rice pilaf. That sounds a little pretentious, she thought. Just as Margo had said, hotel living was getting old. She couldn't wait to sit in front of her own crackling fire and eat a bowl of soup from her own dishes.

"I bet Margo isn't eating herb-crusted anything," she muttered. "She probably eats meat. M-E-A-T," she added in a deep gravelly voice then chuckled to herself. She tossed the menu on the desk and went to take a shower. Maybe she'd walk down to Tink's for a sandwich. A change of scenery sounded good.

Twenty minutes later as she made her way down the sidewalk, avoiding patches of ice, she glanced over at the Polar Bear. The shop was dark, all but the lights in the window display. The lights were on in the upstairs row of tall windows. Leigh stood staring up at the windows from across the street, arguing with herself.

Don't do it. Don't even think about it. She doesn't want to discuss it with you. She doesn't want to sell it. Don't do it. You can't reason with someone who has no business sense.

But Leigh *was* thinking about it. Call it a business meeting. Call it professional networking. Call it curiosity on several levels. While she waited at the corner for the light to change Leigh wondered if she'd even be invited in. After all, the scowl on Margo's face this morning had been anything but cordial.

She climbed the stairs and as she knocked on the door to Margo's apartment she could hear music coming from inside. She knocked again, pounding to be heard over the heavy techno beat.

"Hi, Leigh," Karen said with a broad smile. She had her cell phone to her ear but Leigh didn't know how she could possibly hear anything over the blaring music. It reverberated against her ears, making her wince with every beat.

"Hi, Karen," she stammered, assuming she was interrupting something.

"Come on in." She waved her inside. "We sent text back and forth until after midnight," she said to the caller, practically having to shout. "I gotta go. Call me later."

"I'm sorry. I'd didn't mean to interrupt."

"You're not. You're right on time." She took Leigh by the hand and pulled her into the living room where eight or so women were visiting and laughing. A few were dancing, seemingly oblivious to the ear-pounding noise. Karen pulled off Leigh's coat and added it to the pile draped over a chair. "Come on into the kitchen."

When Margo had said she lived in the storeroom over the store, Leigh expected it to be drafty windows and rooms crudely partitioned by stacks of boxes. The main room was an open, well-lit space. A small fire crackled in a corner fireplace where two women sat on the semicircular brick hearth, sipping glasses of wine. A cinnamon colored leather sofa and matching chair faced the fireplace. The brick walls were decorated with a pair of antique skis, a section of an ornate iron gate, a framed picture of a skier at sunset and another of Margo and Lindsey, dressed in matching snowsuits. The space had polished wood floors and exposed beam rafters giving it a homey feel. The kitchen area at the end of the room had granite countertops and stainless steel appliances. It was a small area but looked efficient and clean. Two women leaning against the end of the counter smiled and nodded at Leigh. She smiled back.

"What do you want?" Karen shouted over the music. "Beer or wine cooler?"

"Nothing, thank you. I just thought I'd visit with Margo for a minute." She scanned the room, looking for Margo. "Is she here?"

"Who?" Karen shouted, bobbing her head to the music.

"Margo," Leigh said, enunciating clearly.

Karen shook her head and pointed to her watch then with her fingers indicated ten minutes.

"One sec," she shouted, answering her cell phone. Leigh wondered how she could possibly hear it ring over the din.

Leigh meandered across the living room to the tall windows that looked out onto the street below. The condensation on the glass transformed downtown Aspen into a Christmas village of twinkle lights and artificial snow. The music changed to a song with more melody and less thump-thump. A tall, attractive woman who smelled like beer and pretzels asked Leigh to dance. She declined with a smile, feeling guilty for crashing Margo's party. Although the smiling acceptance from the women in the room made her wish she had been invited. There was nothing pretentious about them. Leigh had started back for the pile of coats when Margo and the blonde from the snowball fight came through the door carrying a stack of pizza boxes. They were greeted with cheers and hoots.

"Come and get it while they're still lukewarm," Margo shouted. "And turn the damn music down. I can hear it on the sidewalk." She set the boxes on the kitchen counter and flipped the lids open.

"What kind did you get?" one of the women asked, leaving her dance partner and heading to the kitchen.

"Cheese, supreme, Hawaiian, vegetarian. You name it, we got it," the blonde said, aligning the boxes to fit on the counter.

"Save me a piece of veggie, you animals," one of the women said. "I have to go pee."

"First come, first serve," the blonde shouted as she snagged a piece, trailing a string of cheese back to her mouth.

Like vultures on a carcass, a crowd swarmed around the food. Margo stuck a slice of pizza in her mouth then wrestled her jacket off her shoulders as she worked her way through the crowd. She was wearing jeans and a white button-down shirt. She pulled off her stocking cap and gave her head a shake as if that was enough attention to her tousled hair. It took a minute before she noticed Leigh.

"Well, well. If it isn't the trespasser," she said, chewing the bite of pizza.

"I'm really sorry for barging in on your party like this."

"Want some pizza?"

"No, thank you. I just wanted to have a few words with you."

"About trespassing?"

"Do we have to call it trespassing?"

"Okay, what do you want me to call it?" Margo folded the pizza slice in half and took another bite.

"Could we call it professional curiosity?"

"Criminal curiosity." Margo gave a chuckle then looked Leigh up and down. "Nice sweater. Cashmere?"

"I don't remember. Just wool, I think."

"Are you sure you don't want some pizza? It's not bad."

"Thank you, no. I don't need any pizza. Margo, could I have a minute of your time?"

"Are you one of those shy wallflower types? The kind that stand around and watch until you end up with the last stale piece of pizza with all the toppings picked off."

"I'm not a wallflower."

"How about something to drink? Beer?" Margo retrieved an opened bottle of beer from the top of the refrigerator and took a drink.

"No, I don't drink beer."

Crap. That sounds like I expect champagne.

"By the way, I know why you're here," Margo said.

"You do?" Leigh asked skeptically.

"Sure." Her eyes drifted down Leigh's body, stopping at her bust line. "It's written all over your face."

As if Margo had blown across her nipples, Leigh felt a chill race up her body, making her shiver.

"Are you cold?"

"I'm fine."

"You need to layer. Silk or microfiber long sleeve tee under a sweater will keep you warmer."

Something in the way she said it made it sound invasive, as if she slipped her hand under Leigh's sweater to check for herself.

Oh geez, my headlights are on and she is staring at them.

Leigh crossed her arms and said, "I didn't know you were having a party or I wouldn't have come."

"I bet you wanted to see what a storeroom apartment looked

like." She took a long draw on her beer. "You thought I'd have a dirt floor and snow shovels on the wall, right?"

"No, not at all." *Okay, so the thought crossed my mind.* "Your apartment is very nice. Very cozy."

Margo looked around as if scrutinizing her handiwork.

"It's adequate for a bachelor pad, I guess."

"Bachelorette pad?" Leigh offered.

"Whatever."

"What about Lindsey? I think technically you're not a bachelorette. You're a single mother."

"I'm not into the politically correct euphemisms. I'm just me."

Leigh scanned the room, wondering where Lindsey was.

"Where is she anyway? Watching TV?"

"Probably playing video games."

Margo placed her fingers at the corner of her mouth and gave a loud shrill whistle then gave a thumbs-down to the woman at the stereo.

Leigh felt her cell phone vibrate in her pocket. Normally she wouldn't answer it because of the background noise but it was Bev. She still hadn't gotten past the urge to answer her calls.

"Excuse me. I need to take this," she said, stepping away. "Hello."

"Hi. What are you doing? What's all the noise?"

"I'm at a party. The music is a little loud." Leigh stepped around the corner into the hall and cupped her hand around the phone. "Is that better?"

"Yes. Whose party?"

"Just a bunch of people here in Aspen I hardly know. I heard you had some trouble getting to the airport."

"Cripes, yes. Transit strike. Hell to pay finding a rental car just to get to Heathrow."

Leigh wanted to ask about Lisa but decided she'd rather not know.

"Anything new on the business end? Any proposals I need to look at?" Bev asked.

"I don't think so. Maureen would know if there is anything pending that needs attention."

"Maybe we need a quick meeting to touch base on some things."

"I won't be back in the office this week."

"Yeah, I heard that. What are you doing in Aspen? You don't ski."

"I'm getting the cabin ready to go on the market."

"When will you be back?"

"By the fifteenth at least. Did you have a good trip?" Leigh couldn't help asking although she wished Bev would just say it was fine and drop it. Or better yet, say she had a terrible time and would never do that again.

"Whitehaven was gorgeous. I'm telling you, Leigh, you have to see the Lake District at least once. It's incredible. Cobblestone streets, quaint little shops and pubs. We could have stayed a month. The B&B was adorable."

"We?" *Why did I say that? I don't care.*

"Yeah. Did you know the Brits eat fried tomatoes and baked beans for breakfast?" Bev said nonchalantly.

Leigh didn't want to hear the details of their stay at a bed-and-breakfast. It would only resurrect memories of the last time she and Bev had stayed at one near Lake Tahoe. It had been one of those incredibly romantic and peaceful moonlight moments. At least it was for Leigh. She had no inkling the airplane ride home would shatter that memory.

"I have to go, Leigh. Call me when you get back to town. We need to revisit the Jamison contract. I think we can save that one."

"Yes, I will," she said as the phone went dead without a goodbye. She slipped it back in her pocket, wondering what suddenly had pulled Bev away. If it was Lisa, she didn't want to know. "Why the heck do I care what she does?" she muttered to herself.

"There you are," Karen said, coming up behind her. She had her cell phone in her hand with a text message on the screen. "Margo said you were a lawyer. Is that right?"

"Yes." Leigh had heard that before. Someone wanted free legal advice often without sufficient details for her to offer an informed opinion. Not that she minded but, like a doctor asked for a snap diagnosis without test results, it was hard to give legal advice without a clear picture of both sides of the situation.

"Can I ask your opinion on something? You're older, right?"

"Yes, I'm definitely older," Leigh said with a tentative smile.

"If someone sent you a text and asked what your favorite flavor of ice cream is, would you think that's suggestive?" She studied Leigh for an answer.

"Suggestive? No, not suggestive. Curious maybe."

"You don't think they are asking if you like oral sex?" Karen looked dead serious.

"I think they are asking if you like chocolate mocha fudge or maybe vanilla bean. Not if you like oral sex." It was all Leigh could do not to laugh out loud at Karen's big-eyed naïveté. For a knowledgeable sales clerk, she sounded emotionally immature.

"Are you sure?"

"What were you texting before the ice cream question came through?"

"We weren't. I was just standing over there talking to Margo when I received it."

"What did Margo tell you?"

"She thinks I'm nuts. She said you can't judge someone just on texts and emails."

"She's right. You can't. It takes face-to-face communication to really know someone."

"But you can learn a lot about someone from the way they write. You can tell if they're smart or not, whether they have a sense of humor, stuff like that."

It wasn't Leigh's place to argue with Karen or burst her bubble. If ever there was a place someone could hide their true personality it was through the written word. And with all the acronyms used in texts it was hard enough to tell what people really meant anyway. Leigh wondered what her clients would think if she used single letters for words and no capitalization or punctuation.

"Is this someone you've met online?"

Karen nodded and said, "She lives in Manitou Springs." She looked to see if anyone else was listening. "And she is hot."

"So you've met her in person?"

"No, not yet. We want to get to know each other a little more first."

"Then how do you know she's hot?"

"That's what Margo said." Karen pulled a folded piece of paper from her pocket and handed it to Leigh.

"What's this? I don't want to read anything personal."

"Open it. I printed it from her website."

Leigh unfolded the crumpled paper. It was pixelated and faded in spots but it was a small picture of a woman in running shorts, tank top and sun visor. She looked exhausted and sweaty.

"That's Jenny," Karen said, beaming at the picture. "That was taken during the Pikes Peak Run. She finished sixth in her division. God, she's so hot."

Sweating like that, yes, she probably is hot.

"Very impressive." Leigh refolded the paper and handed it back to Karen.

"So what should I say?"

"Tell her what flavor ice cream you like."

"But I don't like ice cream. It makes my teeth hurt and gives me a headache. If I tell her that, she'll think I don't like to...you know." Karen blushed.

"Ahhh, you are referring to the licking reference."

"Yes."

"What if she actually likes ice cream and just wants to know if you do?"

"Believe me, it can't be that simple. You don't know Jenny like I do. She is way cerebral. I'm sure there is a secret meaning to her question. She's very scientific. She teaches kinesiology at a college in Colorado Springs."

"My advice, answer the question on its face value. Tell her your opinion on ice cream and only ice cream. Remember, it's just a text. If she is as smart as you think she is, she won't read more into it than that."

"Okay, thanks," Karen said, a worried look on her face. A hand came between them with a glass of wine in it.

"Here," Margo said, handing the glass to Leigh. "What are you doing hiding back here?"

"Thank you," she said, taking a sip. "We were just visiting."

"About ice cream?" Margo looked at Karen suspiciously.

"Nooooo." Karen smirked and walked away.

"She's got a new online girlfriend. They text a hundred times a day. Drives her crazy when she can't get a cell."

Margo followed Leigh back into the living room where three couples were dancing to a slower song. Leigh was about to break the ice and ask Margo what she planned to do with the building when the blonde came up behind Margo and wrapped her arms around her waist.

"Dance with me, Margo." She began to sway, pulling Margo back and forth. "You promised."

"Go ahead," Leigh said. She knew if she was going to get any information from her, she would have to be patient.

"Come on, Adriana." Margo steered the blonde out into the middle of the living room to join the other couples dancing.

Leigh perched on one of the stools at the counter and sipped her wine while she watched Margo and the blonde move to a Madonna song. Leigh knew the song but wasn't familiar with the latest dances. Virtually anything after she joined the law firm was a complete mystery. It wasn't that she didn't like to dance. In her carefree days she used to know all the latest steps and loved to spend an evening with friends, dancing the night away. But as a corporate lawyer she didn't have time. That didn't stop her from swaying in time to the music.

Margo molded herself against the blonde's slender body, holding her around the waist as they dipped and moved to the music.

"Isn't she good?" Karen said, popping the top on a beer and taking a drink.

"Yes, they all are."

Call it dancing if you like but it sure looks like that woman is humping Margo's thigh.

"You wanna?" Karen nodded toward the dancers.

"Me? No, no." Leigh didn't mean to suggest Karen's invitation was ridiculous but she wasn't sure she knew her well enough to rub bodies like that.

Karen took another swig then set her beer on the counter. As if she hadn't heard Leigh's refusal, she pulled her into the middle of the floor.

"I don't know how to do this," Leigh said, shaking her head and trying to pull away.

"Sure you do. Anybody can do this. Just bend your knees and shake your ass."

"No, really. I'm not a good dancer."

"Can't hear you." Karen grinned and continued to dance, rubbing and bumping against Leigh playfully.

"I feel like a stripper pole," she muttered as she raised her arms over her head to keep from being squashed between the dancers. She flexed her knees and bobbed a little to look like she was participating.

Margo pulled the blonde closer, her pelvic bone massaging the woman's butt. She lowered her eyes and rolled her shoulders into the woman, sliding her crotch down the blonde's hips, then back up again.

Karen occasionally bumped against Leigh but seemed lost in her own moment. Leigh couldn't take her eyes off Margo. It was as if she were peeking through the curtains of her bedroom, ashamed at herself for watching their lovemaking but mesmerized at what she saw. She wanted to blame the crackling fireplace and the wine for the moisture she felt between her legs. It couldn't be the erotic dancing this mountain woman was performing. At least she didn't think it was. Leigh wasn't that easily turned on. She wasn't a prude either. The first time she saw Bev she was wearing an Armani suit with just enough cleavage showing to make Leigh wish she were two inches taller so she could see down between those gorgeous breasts.

The difference between Margo and Bev was startling. They were as opposite as two women could get. Bev's cheeks would flush and she'd feel a giddy buzz on a single glass of wine. Margo looked like she was well on her way to finishing a six-pack, something that meant talking business was out of the question tonight. Leigh knew better than to initiate corporate dialogue with a soon-to-be intoxicated prospect. Nothing substantial would come of it. And Margo looked well on her way to a hangover. At least she didn't have to drive home. When the party was over and the guests all left, she wondered if it would be Lindsey's job to put Mom to bed.

Leigh inched her way through the crowd of gyrating bodies, moving ever closer to the door. Karen was preoccupied with her dancing and didn't seem to notice until Leigh waved goodbye and reached for the doorknob. Leigh couldn't tell if Margo noticed her leave or not. Slipping out unannounced the same way she arrived was the best choice. She didn't want to see what probably came next between Margo and the all-too-eager blonde. Why did she care? And why did she wonder what it would be like to be object of Margo's dance moves.

Chapter 9

Leigh left her cell phone in the car while the construction foreman gave her a tour of the cabin repairs. She watched as the workmen lifted the new piece of granite into place for the kitchen countertop.

"They must have really worked hard to break the corner off your counter," the foreman said, lending a hand as they eased the heavy slab up snug against the wall.

"Yeah. I'm sure it was no accident."

Leigh remembered falling in love with the gold, green and tan granite the first time she saw it eight years ago. Now she had to settle for something else since Venetian Glory was no longer available. She ran her hand over the newly placed stone, the surface still cold from the ride up the mountain in the back of a truck. Maybe it was better Venetian Glory wasn't available. Something new might help erase the memories she associated with the old one and the evening Bev lifted her onto the countertop. The earth had moved that evening, at least it had for Leigh. Bev was probably already making plans to end their relationship.

A ray of sunlight streamed in the kitchen window, illuminating the turquoise fleck in the granite Leigh hadn't noticed before.

"I wasn't sure I was going to like this color, but I do," she said, sweeping away the dust. "Yes, I like this a lot."

"It should last you a lifetime, ma'am."

"Or someone," she muttered, the haunting reality that she planned to sell the cabin returning.

By the time she was satisfied with the progress and received the good news she could move back in possibly the day after tomorrow she had three missed calls on her phone. She pressed the Bluetooth button on the steering wheel as she headed back to town.

"Call Gwen Foley," she said clearly.

"Leigh, hi." Gwen sounded cheerful. "I was about to call you. Good news, honey. I'll have a preliminary draft of your contract in my hands this afternoon. I have an idea. Let's meet for dinner and we can go over it." Gwen's words bubbled with enthusiasm. "There's a great place downtown within walking distance of your hotel. I've got a showing this afternoon but it shouldn't take long. These people have no business looking at a three-hundred-thousand-dollar loft." She gave a patronizing chuckle. "What do you say? Scrumptious dinner on me. A little shop talk. Sevenish?"

Leigh was an old hand at combining work and dinner. There were many times it was the only way she could be guaranteed a meal. "Sounds good. What's the name of the place?"

"Freddo's. You can't miss it. Oops, my other line is ringing. See you at seven."

"Seven," Leigh said and pressed the button on the steering wheel to end the call.

Leigh headed back to the hotel, optimistic she'd be back in her cabin within two days with a real estate contract ready to sign. Maybe the Aspen trip was coming together after all.

Except for Margo's unwavering refusal to discuss selling her property.

She spent the afternoon working, that is between thinking about Margo, the party last night and why she had such a curious fascination with the woman. She finally gave up on the emails and changed for dinner.

The sidewalk had a thin dusting of snow on it as she made her way toward Freddo's. Gwen's idea of walking distance from the hotel—twelve blocks in frigid temperatures—and hers weren't exactly the same. The crisp wind stung her earlobes like a thousand tiny needles and by the time she opened the door and stepped inside, her body was shaking from the cold. Believing Gwen, she hadn't dressed for a winter outing.

According to the online reviews, Freddo's was an upscale eatery with enough ambiance for even the most discerning clientele. The perfect place for a sophisticated first date or a business lunch, according to the Aspen Chamber of Commerce. Leigh took that to mean she wouldn't see jeans and sweatshirts. She hugged herself, wiggling inside her coat to warm up while she waited for the hostess to return from seating a party of four.

"Good evening, ma'am," the hostess said, returning to the podium. She was dressed in a simple, though elegant, black dress with a single strand of pearls at her throat. Freddo's was indeed intended for the upscale crowd. The foyer had marble floors fanning out into several dimly lit dining areas. Racks of expensive looking wine bottles lined two walls. "Welcome to Freddo's."

"You happen to have a reservation for Gwen Foley for seven."

The woman scanned the open book on the podium and said, "Foley? No, I'm sorry."

Gwen came through the door holding her cell phone to her ear with an angry scowl on her face.

"I don't care, Roberta," she snapped. "Have the fucking carpet cleaners finished and out of there by one. The open house is at four. And make sure they do a good job of sucking up the water. I don't want people wading through a damn swamp." Gwen smiled

at Leigh and held up a finger. "I'll call you later, Roberta." She
closed the phone without waiting for a reply. "Leigh, I'm so glad
you could make it." She hugged her warmly, her temperament
turned jovial. "Did you have any trouble finding the place?"

"No. It was right where you said it was. It looks charming but
I think we have a bit of a problem. No reservation."

Gwen frowned at the woman at the podium and said, "Gwen
Foley, party of two."

"I'm sorry, ma'am. I don't have a reservation in that name,"
the hostess said politely but firmly, folding her hands over the
stack of menus.

"Sure you do. I called this morning and spoke to J.J." Gwen
scanned the memory on her cell phone. She held it up so the
woman could see. "Call time, four minutes. It certainly wouldn't
have taken four minutes if I hadn't made a reservation. That is
your number, isn't it?" The woman seemed intimidated by Gwen's
evidence and the matter-of-factness in her tone. "Where's J.J.?"
Gwen demanded, squinting into the darkened restaurant. She
turned to Leigh and said, "J.J.'s the owner's wife. Last year's
Chamber of Commerce President. Excellent businesswoman."

"I'm sorry but she isn't here right now. Let me see what I've
got, Ms. Foley," the hostess said, going in search of an empty
table.

"Yes, you do that, honey." Gwen peeled off her leather
gloves, a tiny smirk of frustration on her face. "So, how was your
afternoon?" she said in Leigh's direction, smiling warmly.

"Busy. How did your showing go?" Leigh didn't feel like
enumerating the endless details of her day.

"Dreadful. Terrible. Awful. Does that pretty much explain
it?" She laughed.

"What happened?"

The hostess returned and escorted them to a cozy table in
the corner near the window with a view of both the fireplace and
the snowscape street. Gwen took the seat in the corner, draping
her coat over the back of the chair.

"They brought the guy's mother with them," she answered
Leigh and rolled her eyes. "Everything I showed them, she had
to have an opinion. I showed them the granite countertops. She

said the grout seam was too wide. I showed them the walk-in closet in the master. She said *only one?* I showed them the new appliances. She said, *what? No stainless steel?* I tell you, by the time we were finished I was ready to strangle her."

"I thought you said they couldn't afford the place anyway," Leigh said, hitching in her chair and slipping out of her coat.

"Oh, they can't. She made that very clear. Come to find out, she's financing it. Or rather, she's buying it as a trustee to her dead husband's estate. They have some sort of private trust thing. I didn't ask."

"Discretionary trust." Leigh opened the menu and began scanning the choices.

"Whatever," Gwen said, shuddering indifferently. "All I know is if Momma doesn't like it, they don't like it."

"So she didn't like the condo?"

"I have no idea. They drove away without saying no, yes or maybe. What looks good?" Gwen flipped the pages, giving little attention to the items. She finally closed the menu and slammed it down on the table. "You know what pisses me off? She didn't even ask her daughter-in-law if she liked it. Nothing. It was as if her opinion didn't matter. This poor girl was going to have to cook, clean, decorate, propagate and sleep in it. Yet she never opened her mouth. Not one word. She never said I like the fireplace or I like the spacious kitchen or even I like the fucking carpeting. She just followed along like a puppy." She picked up the menu and began reading again. "Gave me the creeps to see a woman act like that." She leaned over to Leigh and whispered, "I wonder if mommy-in-law tells her when she can have an orgasm."

Gwen ordered a filet mignon and a baked potato, giving the waiter careful instructions on how she wanted it cooked. She also ordered a Long Island iced tea with two cherries. The cherries seemed to be important somehow. Leigh ordered spinach and mushroom ravioli. She would rather have a cup of hot tea but decided the occasion warranted a mixed drink and ordered a glass of cranberry juice with a shot of vodka in it.

They chatted about more inconsequential topics until the food arrived.

"And guess what?" Gwen said, cutting into her steak and

examining the inside. "I have an offer on the cabin already." She gave a little wink.

"Already?" Leigh assumed this meant Gwen had clients on a waiting list for certain types of property, not an unusual practice for agents handling high-end clientele.

"It's very preliminary and I really haven't had a chance to flesh out the details so I hesitate to mention it."

"Sounds suspiciously like there's a caveat attached. What's the offer, Gwen?" Leigh asked then tasted her ravioli.

Gwen looked around at the nearby tables. Someone must have looked like they were eavesdropping because she took a piece of paper from her purse and scribbled a figure on it then slid it in front of Leigh. Leigh studied the amount, trying hard not to laugh out loud.

"I know. It's not your listing price. But, honey, it's a cash offer." Gwen raised her eyebrows as if that fact alone made all the difference.

"How a buyer pays for the property isn't my concern. That's between the buyer and his mortgage lender or bank account. My price is the same whether they pay with dollars, Euros or Krugerrand." Leigh slid the offer back across the table. "Tell your client thank you but no. I'm not interested."

"Give me a few days to work on him. I can get it up, I'm sure."

"Unless he's willing to double that figure, I don't need to hear back from him." Leigh gave her a friendly but firm look.

"Okay, okay. I hear you. But I had to ask. It's my job. So, I owe you one." She took another bite of steak before nodding for the waiter. She held up her drink, signaling for a refill. "You want another one, honey?"

"No, this is fine." Leigh took a sip then sat her drink aside. "I do have a little question for you. I've got a client looking for either undeveloped or available property, preferably commercially zoned."

"What do they want to do with it? Retail stores?"

"Probably residential. Condos, apartments."

"How large are we talking? Multi-home development? Two hundred lots?" Gwen's eyes glistened with the possibilities.

"No, no. Nothing that dramatic. Couple dozen acres. A vacant lot. Abandoned building. Imminent foreclosure. Good location."

"So this client of yours is shopping for residential in-fill."

"Or urban. In fact, she prefers inner city potential."

"But location, location, location, right?" Gwen grinned knowingly.

Leigh smiled in return and said, "But at the right price."

"Of course." Gwen thought a minute. "I don't have anything in town right now, at least nothing you'd want to demolish. Everything I've got with that kind of potential is already developed. I've got a sixteen-unit brick apartment complex within walking distance of one of the elite shopping districts. Over eighty percent occupied. Real nice."

"And probably real pricey."

"Very. But this is prime location, Leigh. And I mean super prime for Aspen."

"I'm sure it is but I need undeveloped."

"One place you don't want to bother with is the abandoned building on Pinion Street. I do have five acres in Wingo if you don't mind being out of the Aspen district. It's wide open to zoning. It's a blank slate. Great potential."

"Let me guess. Rock-bottom price and motivated seller." Leigh gave Gwen a quirky smile. "What is it, Gwen? Disputed title? Forty percent grade?"

"Okay, so it has a few rocks."

"So we're talking five vertical acres?"

"Not entirely." Gwen looked up. She saw Leigh's suspicious stare and burst out laughing. "It would make a great outdoor climbing wall."

"Or a cabin on two-hundred-foot stilts?"

"Something like that. The owner should just give it to the park reserve as an animal habitat. I've been trying to sell it for a year and no one even wants to look at it."

"Is that the problem with the place on Pinion Street? No one wants to look at it?"

Leigh hadn't planned on asking Gwen about Margo's property but she'd brought it up.

"Just the opposite. Everyone wants to look at that place. The building's best days are behind it but the location is prime. Paved dead-end road, good services, the total package."

"Then what's the problem? Liens on the property?"

"The owner." Gwen rolled her lips back like a vicious dog then cut a bite with a sharp thrust as if taking her anger out on her steak. "The bitch," she muttered between chews.

"Sounds like a seller with a hidden agenda. What's the problem? Asking twice the value?"

"She won't give me an asking price."

"Maybe she hasn't made up her mind." She didn't want to tip her hand that she knew all about Margo Tosch and her abandoned warehouse but rather goad Gwen into divulging what she knew.

"The day I talked to her she had on a greasy flannel shirt with rips at the elbow and enough grease under her nails to lube my SUV." She leaned into Leigh and whispered. "It was disgusting. I didn't shake her hand. I was afraid of what I'd catch."

"What does that have to do with selling her piece of property?"

"If there is one thing I've learned to do it's read people. The woman doesn't have the slightest idea how to conduct business. She's completely clueless."

"That seems kind of harsh. What is this woman doing? Trying to sell it herself?"

Gwen rolled her eyes and chuckled. "She probably doesn't know a lien from a loan. I wouldn't be surprised if there's hazardous materials issue. The idiot wouldn't even discuss it."

"You seem to have very low regard for the owner."

"I could have made her a very wealthy lesbian, at least wealthy in her eyes. She could have bought that stupid snowplow she drives and all the skis in Aspen."

"What does her property appraise for?"

"The warehouse? Not much, even to rent. The acreage?" Gwen's eyes flashed as she drew a knowing smile.

"So the property is a keeper but the owner isn't."

"Absolutely." Gwen looked around then whispered to Leigh, "Although if I was into that kind of woman, she does have a cute ass. I wouldn't mind having a body like that on top of me."

Leigh had to agree. Under the flannel and denim, Margo probably had a chiseled body that could melt butter in the Arctic. Leigh would put Margo's athletic hot body up against Karen's new girlfriend's any day.

"Are you okay, honey?" Gwen said, giving Leigh a worrisome stare.

"Yes, why?" she replied, returning to reality.

"You had this funny look on your face like you were a million miles away."

"Did I?" She took a long drink, reliving one last moment of the image.

Gwen seemed disappointed in her steak and pushed the plate aside, leaving over half of the forty-dollar entree untouched.

"So, how's Bev?" she asked, the question coming out of the blue.

Leigh didn't expect the topic and momentarily choked on a bite before saying, "She's fine, I guess." She assumed Gwen hadn't heard they were no longer together.

"Really?" Gwen inquired skeptically.

"She's been busy with a merger but as far as I know, she is fine."

"Is it true, Leigh?"

"Is what true?" *She knows. Now she wants to know the details. Why can't people just let it die?*

"You know what. You and Bev. Did you two really break up?"

Leigh refolded her napkin across her lap as she decided how much information to offer.

"Bev and I are no longer seeing each other, if that's what you mean." *Please, let it go, Gwen. Please. Don't ask me to rake up all the ugly details.*

Gwen stared at her for a long moment, her expression slowly changing from patronizing concern to relieved contentment. If Leigh didn't know her better she might have thought Gwen was happy she and Bev had ended their relationship. Could Gwen be secretly interested in Bev? Was she waiting for confirmation that Bev was once again single so she could pounce? Gwen's expression made Leigh think so.

Thankfully, the conversation moved to other subjects.

"Thank you for dinner but I wish you'd have let us go Dutch treat," Leigh said, following her out the door. She zipped her coat and hunched her shoulders to the cold wind that blew off Aspen Mountain and right up her pant legs.

"I'll walk you to your hotel," Gwen said, slipping her arm through Leigh's as they hurried down the sidewalk.

"You don't have to," Leigh said then added, "but thank you." She wasn't helpless but Gwen was welcome to walk along with her. They passed the park where Leigh had participated in the snowball fight, bringing a grin to her face. Gwen didn't seem to notice. It was just as well. Leigh didn't want to explain it. Nor did she want to hear Gwen's opinion. Running through the park, giggling and throwing snowballs, was probably the last thing she'd be caught doing.

"It's a real shame you're going to sell your cabin." Gwen snuggled closer as they walked along. "I know I said it before but I'll say it again. I think you'd really like Aspen if you'd just give it a chance. I'm thrilled to be your agent but I think you're going to miss it, Leigh."

"I haven't sold it yet," Leigh said, ducking her chin inside her collar.

"Remember that client of yours who wanted me to sell his mother's condo in Denver to settle her estate? He insisted I list it at four hundred thousand. Not a penny less. I had half a dozen offers the first week but he wouldn't consider them even when I showed him the comps. I had three-fifty cold, in his hand, but he refused it. The damn place sat empty for months. Then he got desperate. You know what he finally settled for?"

"Two-seventy, wasn't it?"

"Yes. Two hundred seventy thousand instead of three-fifty. He didn't jump on the decent offers when I had them and ended up with the bottom of the barrel."

"I'm not desperate. And I've checked the comps."

"Don't worry. I'll take good care of you, honey. I'll get it sold."

"Good evening, ladies," the hotel doorman said, opening the door for them and tipping his hat. Leigh pressed the elevator button for the third floor. When she swiped her room card she expected Gwen to say good night but she followed her inside.

"This is nice, Leigh," she said, dropping her big purse on the bed. "Flat-screen TV, minibar, leather sofa. Not bad." She checked the contents of the minibar while Leigh hung up her coat.

"Help yourself if you'd like something." Leigh hadn't planned on entertaining anyone this evening but Gwen was an old friend. There was no reason to be rude.

"Share a little bottle of wine with me?"

"Sure."

"White or red?"

"Doesn't matter."

"White," she declared, as if the occasion called for white wine. She shed her coat and went to work pouring two glasses. She handed one to Leigh then held her glass up for a toast. "Here's to old friends and new business."

"Hear, hear," Leigh agreed and took a sip. She stood at the window with her back to the heater vent, facing Gwen. She had dressed for a business meeting, not a hike in the snow, and was still cold.

"Hmmm, this feels good all the way down." Gwen took a slow sip then closed her eyes and sighed. "Not as good as Chardonnay but nice." She poured a little more in her glass before moving to the window. "I'll tell you who has a great wine list. The Sundeck. Too bad they're only open for dinner once a month. I'd love to take you up there for dinner. They do have a nice variety for lunch though."

"The Sundeck?"

"Yes. You know. The restaurant on top of the mountain." Gwen studied Leigh a moment then asked, "You've been up there, haven't you?"

"On top of the mountain?"

"At the top of the gondola ride. The restaurant snack bar place. Oh, my God. You've never ridden the gondola up the mountain." She made it sound like a crime.

"I don't ski, Gwen."

"So? You don't have to ski to ride the gondola up there and

have lunch. When you're done you just ride it back down. Sure, it's a little pricey if you're buying the lift ticket just to eat at the restaurant but it's so worth it. The view alone is worth the cost of the ticket."

"That good?" Leigh had trouble imagining any view more spectacular than the one from the deck of her cabin.

"Put it on your to-do list, honey. I mean it. You'll love it. Just be sure to dress for it. Warm boots are a must." She gave a deliberate shiver. "I about froze my tits off the last time I went up there." She drank down the last of her wine and set the glass on the table. "I better get going. Do you want me to leave the contract for you to look over?" She pulled it out of her purse and handed it to Leigh.

Leigh flipped through the pages, checking the details.

"No, this looks good." She took a pen from the desk and signed it. "Just no more low-ball offers."

"I promise," Gwen said with a chuckle.

But Leigh knew the rules real estate agents lived by. An offer was an offer and a commission was a commission. Even the most ridiculous offer would somehow work its way into a phone conversation, just in case her willpower softened.

Leigh opened the door for Gwen. She expected a hug or perhaps a little kiss on the cheek. But to her surprise, Gwen kissed her gently on the lips and winked before saying good night and heading down the hall to the elevator.

Chapter 10

Leigh stood on the sidewalk, rubbing her gloved hands together to warm them. The morning sun shone bright on downtown Aspen, the smell of burning fireplaces filling the crisp stillness. And Leigh had no idea why she hadn't just walked right in the Polar Bear Shop. Why was she standing outside, staring mindlessly at the window display? There were probably a dozen shoe stores in downtown Aspen specializing in winter boots. Why here? She scanned the boots in the window, wondering which ones were the warmest, the ones with fur trim or the ones with quilted liners.

"Hey there," Karen said, opening the door and smiling at her. She was dressed in black ski pants and a yellow fleece top. "Are you just window shopping or are you coming in?"

"Coming in," she said, stepping inside.

"What's your need? Sweater? Pants?"

"Boots. Snow boots. Really warm ones. Something with better traction." Leigh discreetly scanned the store for Margo but unless she was in the storeroom, Karen was alone.

"We don't have a very big selection. We're more clothes than footwear but we do have a couple to pick from." She headed to the rack near the counter. "We've got suede ones with sheared lining. Also fur-trimmed leather ones, or these. They're quilted with Thinsulate lining. They're waterproof and very lightweight." She handed one to Leigh to examine.

Karen's cell phone jingled. She didn't answer it but Leigh could tell she wanted to. "Do you need to get that? It might be important."

"Thanks." Karen's face brightened. She giggled as she read the text and typed a reply.

"Good news?"

"Yes. Well, at least it could be." As soon as she sent the text another was waiting to be answered. Karen read it and blushed. "I already told you that," she muttered as she clicked out a reply.

Leigh strolled the store, looking at boots and winter apparel hoping Margo might come in, while Karen received and sent two more texts. From her expression and giggling, Leigh guessed they were probably from Jenny.

"I'm sorry, Leigh," she said, slipping the phone back in the holster. "Would you like to try on some boots? The suede ones run a little small so you'll need at least a half size larger."

"How about the ones with Thinsulate lining? They look warm. Seven and a half."

"Margo has a pair of these. If she wears them they have to be good. She doesn't give a crap about style or what they look like. Functionality." She used a deep voice to mimic Margo, pointing a discriminating finger at Leigh. "It's all about functionality, little lady. Fashionable won't keep you warm in a blizzard." She laughed.

"You do her very well. Especially the raised eyebrow thing."

Karen's cell phone jingled again.

"Go ahead and answer that while I try these on."

Karen read the text but frowned then replaced the phone without replying. "How do they fit?"

"A little snug."

"Let me find an eight." She turned her back to Leigh while she searched. It didn't take a private detective to see that the text had upset her.

"Karen, is everything okay? Was that bad news?" Leigh asked, sensing something was suddenly very wrong.

"No," she said quietly, handing Leigh another pair.

"Gosh, you could have fooled me. These are sixes, hon. Not eights."

"Sorry." Karen turned back to the stack, her shoulders slumping noticeably. "Can I ask you something?"

"Sure."

"If someone says they want to be your friend, that means they don't really like you very much, right?" Karen looked back at Leigh, her eyes moist.

"What? No, it doesn't. If they want to be your friend, they obviously like you. Why else would they say it?"

"But if you thought this person was going to be something way more than just a friend, and then they say let's be friends, that means they don't like you as much as you like them, right?"

Not the most succinct explanation in the world, Leigh thought. But she got the general idea. It sounded like Karen just got dumped, a feeling with which Leigh could well identify.

"I think it depends on a lot of things," Leigh said, brushing a lock of hair out of Karen's face. "How long have you known Jenny?"

"Not very long."

"So she's a new friend?"

Karen nodded.

"Six months?" Leigh asked carefully. "Three months?"

Karen lowered her eyes and said, "Three weeks."

"Oh, so very new." Leigh took a deep breath, deciding what advice to offer.

"She said she wants us to be friends."

Normally that statement would be good news but the pain in Karen's voice made it sound tragic. This was the second time

Karen had asked for her opinion. Didn't she have someone else to confide in, like Margo? Karen struck her as smart—at least she knew her merchandise. But when it came to relationships, she seemed to be floundering in insecurity.

"Maybe you need to sit down and talk to her and find out exactly what she means."

"That's the trouble. I'm not sure if I'm ready to meet face-to-face." Karen swallowed hard. "Not if she wants to tell me she just wants to be my friend."

"You mean you still haven't met her in person?"

Karen shook her head.

"Maybe there is something she hasn't told you. Something in her life that keeps her from offering more than friendship right now. Is she in a relationship already? Maybe she's not out."

"She says she's single and totally out. One minute she says I've been on her mind lately. The next minute she says let's be friends. I know what that means."

"Maybe. Maybe not. Karen, I have to ask why you want my opinion? Don't you have someone else you could talk to about this? I barely know you."

"Margo? Yeah, right. Like Margo is going to give me advice. She has enough trouble of her own. Besides, I respect your opinion. You're really smart and practical. I'm not practical at all and I don't want to mess this up."

"I don't know that I'm all that practical. But, honey, I think Jenny is right. You have to build a relationship on a foundation of friendship. Be friends first. My best advice, go slow. Learn about each other. Open a line of communication and not just texting on this thing," she said, patting Karen's cell phone. "Find out what you have in common, what your interests are. Maybe you'll be great friends who one day discover you want more." Leigh wrapped an arm around Karen's shoulders. "She wants to be your friend. Isn't that what you want too?"

"So it's not an entirely bad thing that she wants to be my friend?"

"Not at all." Leigh smiled encouragement. "Now, how about those size eights?"

"Sure," Karen said, brightening.

The bell over the door jingled and a voice called, "I'm back." It was Margo carrying two large boxes with shipping labels on them. She was wearing cargo pants and a bulky sweater. No gloves, no coat and no hat. Her cheeks and ears were pink from the cold. "I think we got the rest of the vests."

She hadn't noticed Leigh sitting on a chair trying on the boots. When she did she stopped in her tracks and smiled down at her. "Hey, hi. You buying boots?" The telephone on the counter rang and Karen went to answer it.

"Maybe, if they fit and will keep my feet warm." Leigh stood up and stomped then walked up and down the aisle to test the fit.

"Those are good ones. Be sure and get them big enough. Boots that pinch your feet can't keep them warm. You have to have room for the insulation to work." Margo stood holding the boxes as Leigh tried them out. "Wiggle your toes."

"I've got two pair of socks on and they still seem to be plenty roomy."

"Take your time. Wear them around the store awhile. Be right back. I need to put these down." She headed to the storeroom.

She returned a few minutes later, having combed her hair. "So, what's the verdict, counselor? Do they fit?" She stuffed her hands in her back pockets and rocked back on her heels, studying the way Leigh walked in them.

"I think so." Leigh wiggled her feet inside the boots just to be sure. "Will these keep me warm up there?" she asked, nodding toward Aspen Mountain.

"You mean in the snow?"

"No. I mean riding the gondola up to the top."

"They should. What else are you wearing?"

"The new coat I bought last week and wool slacks."

"Wool dress slacks? That's all?"

"Yes. And a sweater. Why?"

"It's none of my business but you're going to freeze your ass off. The wind chill on top of Ajax is ten to fifteen degrees colder than down here in town. You'll need thermals and a wind layer. You've got to dress like a skier, even if you don't ski."

"But I just want to ride up there and have lunch at the Sundeck Restaurant. I heard it has a great view."

Margo chuckled. "You sound like a tourist. You've got a cabin. Don't you have any winter clothes?"

"I had some winter clothes but I told you, everything was ruined in the break-in. Now I'm just trying to get by until I go back to Denver."

"You do know the gondola cars aren't heated."

"Oh." Leigh hadn't thought of that.

"And the ride to the top takes about twenty minutes," Margo added as if reading Leigh's mind. "Twenty minutes back down again, too."

Leigh stared down at the boots. Margo was probably right. She needed appropriate clothing if she planned on riding to the top of the mountain, any mountain with snow on it.

"Okay, show me. What do I need?"

Margo nodded toward a rack of quilted snow pants. Some had zippered legs, Leigh assumed for fitting over ski boots. Margo picked a pair that looked like bib coveralls.

"These will keep the wind out and keep you warm. They're lightweight but rated for twenty below. They're waterproof with sealed seam construction. I sell a lot of these to skiers. But they'll do for what you need." She turned the tag so Leigh could read it. "And they aren't real expensive. Mid-range."

"Do I wear them over my slacks?"

"Actually, no. You wear them over your base layer. Thermals. Long underwear."

"Like the waffle weave ones you were wearing?"

"What waffle weave ones?" Margo scowled then laughed. "Oh, you mean when I was driving the snowplow. Yeah, I wear those old things because it's easier to wash out the diesel smell. But I wear the silk or nylon thermals when I'm on the mountain."

Margo took a pair of the white silk thermals from the shelf and held them up. "These are what you need. They fit like a sausage casing but they'll do the job." She headed toward the dressing room with the coveralls and thermals. "Try on the snow pants and let's see how they fit. I've got a couple different styles."

"Margo," Karen called from the counter, cupping her hand over the telephone receiver. "Adriana for you. She wants to know what time."

"Tell her I'll call her later," Margo replied in curt dismissal.

"I really hadn't planned on trying anything on," Leigh said, slipping off the boots.

"I recommend you do. Every style is different. Some styles ride up in the crotch."

"Really?" Leigh felt herself blush. "We can't have that," she muttered under her breath.

"By the way, how are the cabin repairs going? Finished yet?"

"I should be able to move back in tomorrow afternoon. The refrigerator is being delivered in the morning."

"I bet you'll be glad to be in your own place." She hung the coveralls on the hook in the dressing room and held the door for Leigh. "Let me know if you need a different size."

"Thank you." Leigh stepped in and reached for the handle to close the door but Margo held it open.

"I've got other colors too. I just thought silver would look good with your new parka." She looked Leigh up and down, her eyes hesitating at the chest bulge in Leigh's coat.

"Thank you," she repeated, tugging at the door.

"You can try on the thermals too, if you want." Margo still hadn't released the door.

"Yes, I will."

"How about a fleece pullover as your mid-layer?" she added softly with a gentle smile.

"We'll see." Leigh pushed Margo's arm off the top of the louvered door and closed it, flipping the lock.

"By the way, the lock doesn't work on this dressing room."

Leigh opened the door and peered out at her, then closed it again and relocked it anyway. She could hear Margo chuckling as she walked away.

"Try on the coveralls over the silks," Margo called.

"I am." Leigh pulled on the skintight long underwear then stepped into the coveralls. She barely finished zipping them when she realized they would indeed keep her warm. She already felt perspiration forming.

"Warm, aren't they?"

"Yes, very." She opened the door and stepped out, adjusting the straps.

"They look good on you. Turn around." Margo leaned against the side of the full-length mirror with her arms crossed, grinning. Leigh turned, checking her look in the mirror. "How do they fit in the crotch? Too tight?"

"No, I don't think so."

How are snow pants supposed to fit in the crotch? They don't ride up or invade anything. They must be okay.

"And the silks, are they long enough? You need them to at least cover the ankle bone and the wrist and not gap at the waist. I usually recommend tall sizes to most of my customers, unless they're really short."

"What do you wear?" Leigh asked, still checking the look in the mirror.

"I wear extra talls." She took Leigh's hand and examined the sleeve length. "They look okay."

"You were right about them fitting like a sausage casing," Leigh said, running her finger around the neck. "Instead of fleece could I wear a sweater?"

"Sure. Wool is best but anything with a close weave will help insulate." She continued to hold Leigh's hand, smoothing the sleeve but her gaze was on the tight fit only partially blocked by the bib of the coveralls. "When do you plan on riding the gondola? The last run is at four." Her eyes met Leigh's and held them.

"I thought maybe today." Leigh felt a bead of sweat form on her upper lip she assumed was from the long underwear and snow pants. Before she could wipe it away, Margo gently ran her thumb across it and smiled.

"Warm, huh?" she said softly.

"Yes, very." Leigh found something mesmerizing in Margo's gaze, something soft and mellow and inviting. What was it about this woman that caused Gwen to have such a passionate dislike for her? And why would Karen not want to seek her advice? There was a purity and innocence to her. Uncluttered and simplistic. She was without pretense.

"I'll take these. All of them," Leigh said, swimming in Margo's bright smile. "They're perfect," she heard herself say breathlessly.

Margo said something about washing instructions and care but Leigh wasn't paying much attention. Much to her surprise, she was busy imagining what Margo looked like in her sausage casing.

Leigh collected her purchases and hurried back to the hotel. She dashed through some emails then changed into her new clothes and headed to the Silver Queen Gondola terminal. She couldn't wait to ride to the top of the mountain and see what was so special about the Sundeck Restaurant and Aspen Mountain, or Ajax, as the locals seemed to call it. She had slipped a few pages of a contract she needed to look over into the inside pocket of her parka, justifying the afternoon outing as work-related.

She bought a day-pass and waited in line. She noticed she was the only person riding to the top of the mountain without skis or a snowboard. Thanks to Margo's guidance she was not only dressed for the occasion but was toasty warm in her silk thermals and high-tech Thinsulate snow pants. And for the first time since she arrived in Aspen, her toes were warm and snug in her lined boots. She hadn't gotten used to the tassels hanging from the ear flaps of her new stocking cap but Karen assured her this was the latest must-have, even if she did feel like a complete geek.

"One more," the gondola attendant announced. She waved Leigh to enter the waiting car where three young men with snowboards, bagging pants and wicked grins eyed her up and down.

Those three are going to grow up to be pinchers, if they aren't already, she decided.

"You go ahead," she said to the middle-aged man in line behind her. He stepped in, carrying his skis and poles.

"Thanks," he said, nodding politely as the door closed.

"Hi, Leigh," a voice called from back in line. It was the blonde, Margo's blonde. Adriana. She was dressed in a teal blue ski outfit and carrying black and teal skis. Leigh's first thought was that she looked like a giant bruise.

"Hi." She waved back.

"You going skiing?" she shouted, as if the six people in line between them were invisible. Leigh shook her head. "Going to the Sundeck?" Leigh nodded. "You'll love it. The wok menu is incredible."

"Going up, ma'am," the attendant called to Leigh, ready to load the next car.

Leigh rode to the top with three skiers who spent the twenty-minute ride discussing the ramp angle of bindings. She considered herself a literate person but she had no idea what they were talking about. Instead she concentrated on the breathtaking winter scenery passing below.

It didn't take long for the gondola to rise above the city congestion and into the mountain calm. It slipped along above snow-covered trees, the ratcheting chug of the overhead pulley slicing through the pristine beauty of the frozen mountain. Patches of fog had settled in the crags and crevasses below. Leigh could see why Gwen recommended a trip up the mountain. It was gorgeous. She stood at the front window, staring out at the thick blanket of white speckled with patches of pine trees as far as she could see. So this was Margo's world. How could she not love it?

At the top she stepped off the gondola and followed the signs to the Sundeck Restaurant. It was an imposing looking building with a vaulted roof line and stone façade. Massive windows looked out in all directions at the majestic Rocky Mountains. The area outside the restaurant was crowded with racks of skis and snowboards, waiting for the customers to finish their respite and return to the slopes. Inside was just as crowded. The cafeteria-style restaurant was bustling with hungry customers, their ski boots clomping across the floor. Leigh selected a hearty bowl of soup and a cup of herbal tea before threading her way to a vacant table by the window. It didn't seem to matter where you sat, the scenery was awe-inspiring from any seat. She spent over an hour leisurely enjoying her lunch and watching the people come and go. She took the contract from her pocket, intending to read it but she never got beyond the first paragraph, not with the view of a ski run right outside the window.

She was standing outside the restaurant, pulling on her gloves and ready for the ride back down the mountain, when from the corner of her eye she caught sight of something teal. It was Adriana. She was adjusting her ski boot in the binding while another skier in white ski pants and a white parka stood next to her, watching and apparently offering advice. Leigh shaded her eyes from the bright sunshine, squinting at the skier in white. Even behind the mirrored sunglasses and snow-blown hair, there was no mistaking her. It was Margo. The perfect date for a crisp Aspen afternoon, Leigh thought. Just as Adriana finished adjusting her skis, another skier, a child, eased up to them, snow-plowing to a stop. It was Lindsey. She looked like a giant pink marshmallow. Her snowsuit, helmet and gloves were all various shades of pink. She had a serious expression on her face.

"I'm ready," Lindsey said, still holding her position. "Can we go now?"

"I want to see a couple more turns first," Margo said, pointing to a flattened area. "Let see what you've got."

Lindsey groaned. "I know how to turn."

"Show me or we ride back down in the gondola." Margo leaned on her poles. "What's it going to be?"

In grumpy obedience she pushed off, slowly picking up speed as she started across the snow. Margo watched as she made several diagonal passes, each pass a little steeper and a little faster.

"Pole the turn, babe," Margo shouted.

"I did," Lindsey yelled back, concentrating intently.

"Bend your knees and lean more." Lindsey continued to ski back and forth, her arms and hands leading her around the turns. "Good, that's good."

"Can we go now?" Lindsey asked, sliding back to Margo's side.

"Are you ready?" Margo asked, tightening the strap on Lindsey's helmet.

"Yes," she said eagerly.

"Okay. Go ahead and start but take it easy."

Lindsey made a wide turn and headed down the hill, slowly gaining speed. Adriana followed, giving her a clear path. Margo waited until they were well out in front then pushed off, cutting a straight line to where Lindsey was zigzagging her course.

Leigh hurried to the edge of the staging area but they were rapidly disappearing down the mountain, Adriana athletically carving her path through the deep powder, Lindsey cutting short zigzags back and forth, her arms out and balancing her flight, Margo gracefully descending the slope, making it look effortless.

Leigh squinted for one last look, then tugged down the ear flaps of her cap and set off toward the gondola terminal. A strange sense of serenity settled over her. It was as if she shared in Margo, Adriana and Lindsey's moment of togetherness. Or was she jealous of it. It didn't matter. Whatever it was put a contented smile on her face.

Chapter 11

Leigh waited in line at Bed, Bath and Beyond to pay for new sheets, comforter, pillows and towels, the last things she needed before moving back into the cabin. The thought of using filthy linens left on the floor by the burglars, even after repeated washings, was too gross to consider. She didn't have to argue much with her insurance agent when she offered to reuse them only if the agent washed and slept on them first.

She conducted a conference call from the hotel and finalized a deal before loading her suitcase in the car and heading for the cabin. She was as giddy as a kid at Christmas as she roared up the mountain road, the cabin keys burning a hole in her pocket. It had been a week since she came to town, hitching the memorable ride in Margo's snowplow. She was finally able to spend her first night in her cabin, sitting by a roaring fire and reveling in the mountain splendor. She couldn't wait to unpack, slip off her shoes and sip a cup of tea in her own place. She had work to do but even that was something to look forward to in her own living room.

It was early evening when Leigh leaned back in the chair and rotated her neck. She didn't know how long she had been hunched over the desk but it felt like years. She stood and stretched, her back popping back into place. Time to reheat her coffee—for the third time. She noticed the sun was taking aim on the rim of Aspen Mountain. She opened the refrigerator, hoping to find something she could call dinner. She didn't feel like cooking nor did she feel like going back into town to eat.

"Don't I even have a can of soup?" she said, checking the cupboard. There was a knock at the door. "Please let it be a lost pizza delivery man."

"Can we sled your hill?" Lindsey asked, her face beaming.

"Can you what?" She smiled down at her bubbling enthusiasm.

"We want to sled your hill. Can we? My mom said you've got the best sledding hill in all Aspen."

"I do?" Leigh chuckled and looked past her to where Margo was climbing out of her truck.

"I told her this might not be a good time for you but you know how kids are when they set their minds to something." Margo pulled off her gloves and stuffed them in the pockets of her snowsuit.

"No, no. It's not a bad time. But I wasn't aware I had a good hill for sledding."

"The best hill," Lindsey insisted, clapping her mittened hands together as if she didn't know what to do with them.

"Calm down, young 'un. Leigh might be busy."

"You're not busy, are you?" Lindsey pleaded.

Leigh had been rewriting a merger proposal so technical even she had to rethink the phrasing but how could she say no to a six-year-old in a purple snowsuit, pink boots and lime green hat with a big pom-pom on the top?

"Yes, I'm very busy," Leigh said, tweaking Lindsey's nose. "I'm busy watching you sled down my hill."

"Oh boy," she squealed. "She's going to let us." Lindsey

grabbed the surprised Leigh around the waist, hugging her tightly.

"Are you sure you don't mind?" Margo asked, leaning against the tailgate of the truck. "We can do this another time."

"She said it was okay, Mommy." Lindsey frowned back at Margo.

"Where exactly is this best hill I'm supposed to have?" Leigh asked.

"It might not all be yours but the top of it probably is. It's on the other side of the trees." Margo nodded toward the back of the cabin then released the tailgate. She pulled out three large black inner tubes, each with a rope tail.

"You're sledding on those?"

"Inner tubes are fun," Lindsey said, with a gleam in her eye. "They go really fast."

"Why three?" Leigh asked. "Now wait. You don't expect me to go sledding too?"

"Sure." Margo tossed the last one on the snow and slammed the tailgate.

"Don't you like to sled?" Lindsey asked.

"I used to, I think. But that was years ago." Leigh couldn't remember the last time she'd slid down a hill.

"It's not hard. All you do is run and jump on," Lindsey said. "The hard part is pulling it back up the hill. Sometimes Mommy pulls mine." She turned to Margo and asked, "Will you pull Leigh's too?"

"I don't need help pulling an inner tube up the hill," Leigh chuckled.

"So, you'll join us?" Margo asked, grinning approval.

Leigh looked down at Lindsey's smiling face and said, "I guess I could do one run. After all, it is my hill. Would you two like to come in while I find appropriate sledding attire?"

"Okay," Lindsey said and marched inside.

Leigh waited for Margo and asked, "Isn't it a little late in the day for sledding?"

"Best time of day for two reasons. Less wind in the late afternoon and less daylight means fewer runs." She winked as if divulging a secret.

"Ahhhhh."

"She'd go all day if I let her." She leaned into Leigh and whispered, "My ass can't take more than a few runs down the hill."

Oh, geez. I have the urge to touch her ass and offer sympathy. Why would I do that?

"What should I wear?" Leigh quickly asked, hoping to ward off a blush at the thought of Margo's nicely rounded ass.

"Warm and waterproof."

"My new snow pants then."

"Wait." Margo trotted out to the truck and returned with an ugly army-green colored snowsuit rolled up like a sleeping bag. "You can wear this." She gave it a shake.

"Couldn't I wear my new ones?"

"I wouldn't. You might snag them on a rock or branch and rip them. These aren't the best color in the world and will be a little big on you but you can't hurt them." She held them up to Leigh for size. "Yep, they'll work. Sorry about the wrinkles."

Leigh wondered how long they had been stuffed behind the seat of the truck. But obediently took the snowsuit upstairs to the bedroom and changed. When she reappeared, Margo was waiting at the bottom of the stairs like Rhett Butler in *Gone with the Wind*. Leigh half expected her to say you look mighty fine this afternoon, Miss Scarlett.

"How does it fit?" she asked, watching Leigh descend the stairs. "Oh, wow. Big, huh?"

"A little," Leigh said, turning the sleeves back six inches just to find her hands. The crotch hung halfway down her thighs and the hem of the legs had to be cuffed up several turns so she didn't walk on them. "Do I look as awkward as I feel?"

"Actually it looks good. Very blue-collar," Margo said, snickering as she looked her up and down. "You should wear that to town sometime."

"Uh, I don't think so."

"Come on, snickerdoodle," she called to Lindsey. "Let's get at this before it gets too dark."

Leigh followed Margo and Lindsey around the cabin, each of them dragging an inner tube by the rope. They made their way through the grove of trees and stood facing the snow-covered valley stretched out like a landing strip. It had a gentle unobstructed slope perfect for sledding. Leigh had never considered it a good spot for sledding but then she didn't take time for such things. It was a nice vista, nothing more.

"Wow," Lindsey gasped. "Can I go first?"

"Be my guest," Leigh said, adjusting Lindsey's stocking cap to cover her ears.

"Can I go down on my tummy?" Lindsey asked Margo hopefully.

"No. Set your bottom in here and hold on to the rope." Margo steadied it while Lindsey backed up and lowered her rear into the hole. She held the rope between her legs and gave a few body jerks but couldn't get herself going. "Push me."

"Ready?"

"Ready!" She hunched her shoulders and held the rope as if it were the reins of a horse. Margo gave the inner tube a nudge, sending it on its way. Lindsey immediately started to squeal and kept it up all the way down. Leigh and Margo watched, laughing as she spun and slid her way across the valley.

"Good run, kiddo. Keep going," Margo shouted, her voice echoing.

"She's good at this, isn't she?" Leigh declared.

"I told you. She'd stay out here all day if I didn't stop her. She'd have frostbite and still wouldn't quit." Margo watched proudly, cocking her head and smiling at the child's antics.

"Should we join her?"

"You bet." Margo steadied Leigh's inner tube while Leigh eased herself onto it. "Keep the rope in your hand in case you fall off. That way you won't have to chase it down the hill."

"Good idea," Leigh said, winding the rope once around her hand. "I'm ready, I think." She pulled her hat down snug.

"Okay, here we go." Margo gave her a shove.

It took a moment to gather speed but soon she was spinning in circles and sliding down the hill. Leigh couldn't help but giggle. This was fun, more fun than she had had in years. The more she spun, the more she laughed.

"Wheeeeee," she squealed.

"Watch out below," Margo shouted as she caught up with

her, spinning and hopping over little bumps in her path. She too was laughing at the fun. "Left turn," she said, leaning to avoid crashing into Leigh. She stuck her hand out and gave Leigh's tube a spin, making her laugh all the more.

Lindsey was still sliding, her smaller body carrying her at a slower rate. Margo kept an eye on her, as if making sure they weren't on a collision path. Lindsey finally came to a stop but kept rocking, trying to get going again. Leigh and Margo slid a few yards past her before coming to a stop, both of them still laughing as their tubes bumped together.

"That was fun," Leigh said, trying to catch her breath.

Lindsey hadn't yet climbed out of her inner tube when she said eagerly, "I want to go again."

"Start back up." Margo rolled off and climbed to her feet, offering Leigh a hand up.

"Will you bring my tube?" Lindsey said, handing her the end of the rope.

"How did I know you'd ask that?" Margo tossed a handful of snow at her and chuckled. Lindsey started back up the hill, her determined little legs marching through the snow.

"I bet it takes a lot longer going up than it did coming down," Leigh joked and started back up, dragging her tube behind.

"Give me your rope," Margo said, holding out her hand.

"I've got it."

"I'll take it for you." She looked at Leigh, a confident smile on her face. Margo's offer didn't sound like a chore, but a gift, a gift Leigh couldn't find it in her heart to refuse.

"Thank you. I have a feeling this is going to take some getting used to."

"You mean accepting my assistance?"

"No, I mean walking up the hill in this snowsuit."

"Hurry up," Lindsey called, looking back at them.

"We're coming, Lu-Lu," Margo replied, wrapping the three ropes into one as she started up the hill.

"My name isn't Lu-Lu," she shouted, listening to the echo. "That's cool. HELLO!" The sound of her high-pitched little voice bounced from one hillside to the other. "Shout something, Mommy."

"LU-LUUU," she shouted then laughed as if knowing it would raise a response from Lindsey.

"Not that!"

"All right. How about LINDSEY LOUISE?" Margo bellowed. Lindsey giggled and continued tramping up the hill. "What's your middle name, Leigh?"

"Nothing near as lyrical as Lindsey Louise."

Margo raised an eyebrow at her.

Leigh finally said, "Okay, it's Leigh Eden."

"Eden?"

"Yes. My dad's idea of a biblical name."

"I kind of like it. Leigh Eden Insley. Yep. I do."

"It certainly has its fair share of vowels, doesn't it? What's your middle name? Margo what?"

Margo shook her head.

"Oh, come on. I told you mine. Now you tell me yours. It can't be any worse than Leigh Eden."

"I'd tell you but I don't have a middle name."

"You mean it's just Margo Tosch?"

Margo nodded then looked up, her eyes scanning the rim of the hill. She finally said, "Mom and Dad couldn't agree on one so they left the place blank on the birth certificate."

"You can add one, you know. It's not a difficult thing to do."

"I know." She kept her eyes on the hill, but they narrowed as if something had just come over her, some memory she'd rather not relive. "Are your folks still living?"

"Yes. They live in Castle Rock, south of Denver."

"Retired?"

"Years ago. Dad was a lawyer."

"And your mom?"

"Mother was a housewife. She kept Dad and me fed and comforted. Lovely woman. Non-confrontational. Just duty bound. Yours?"

"Mom has been gone for several years but worked in my dad's business. She was a bookkeeper, shipping clerk, warehouse manager, you name it."

"What kind of business?"

Margo took a few deep breaths. Leigh couldn't decide if she was catching her breath from the walk up the slope or formulating an answer.

"Dad had several businesses over the years. Commercial laundry, cleaning service, appliance repair, heating and air conditioning, ski equipment manufacture."

"Wow. Sounds like a very handy guy to have around the house."

"Sometimes. How you doing? Going to make it to the top?"

"I'll make it. I'm no sissy, Margo."

Margo smiled over at her and said, "I didn't say you were."

"Hurry up," Lindsey called from the top of the hill. "I want to go again."

"We're coming," Margo said.

"Can I go on my tummy this time? Please?" she pleaded dramatically.

"If I let you will you promise to keep your face up off the snow this time?" Margo said gruffly.

"YES!"

"No fooling around?"

"I promise."

"Okay, but I'll be watching you." Margo squatted and held the inner tube as Lindsey climbed onboard. "Scoot back a little," she said, tugging at her leg.

"That looks scary," Leigh said.

"It's fun. You can go really fast." Lindsey exclaimed and braced herself for launch.

"With your face just inches off the snow you'd think so," Leigh muttered under her breath.

Margo wound the rope around Lindsey's hand and adjusted her hat. "All set?"

"Yes," she squealed and kicked her feet. "Push me."

"You keep your face up, you hear me?" Margo gave her a playful pinch on the rear then sent her on her way. "And remember you're pulling your own tube up the hill this time."

"I know," she said between giggles.

"I'm not doing that tummy thing, that's for sure," Leigh said as she watched Lindsey float down the hill, her nose practically dragging the snow. When her tube bounced over a rough spot, Leigh turned her back. "I can't watch. Is she all right? Did she scrape her face off?"

"She's fine. She's a toughie."

"Tell that to my stomach that's about to come up." When Leigh turned around Margo had tied the two inner tubes together side by side. "What's that for? Are you going down face first?"

"No. We won't run over each other this way. Hop on."

"Oh, good idea. I wouldn't have thought of it."

"Lindsey doesn't like it when I tie them together. She thinks I slow her down." Margo looked up at Leigh with a sparkling smile and bright eyes, extending her hand. "We old folks can go slow. Take our time."

Leigh felt a twinge of excitement. She heard exactly what Margo said and knew what she meant. But something inside had taken the idea of going slow and taking their time in a surprisingly different context. It had nothing to do with sliding down a hill on conjoined inner tubes. And it gave her a flutter.

"I gotcha," Margo said, steadying the tube while Leigh settled onto it. "Ready?"

"We're going to spin like crazy, aren't we?"

Margo just grinned then climbed on and gave a push.

"Oh, nooooo. Margooooo," Leigh squealed as they went careening down the hill, the tubes bouncing and spinning wildly. They sailed past Lindsey, hopping over one mogul after another. Leigh grabbed for Margo's arm, giggling so hard she couldn't talk.

"Lean to the right," Margo shouted as they bore down on a clump of aspen in their path. Leigh leaned but it didn't seem to make much difference as they kept spinning toward the trees. "Abort. Abort," Margo said, rolling her body toward Leigh and causing the inner tubes to flip, dumping them in the snow. Leigh was still giggling as she rolled to a stop face down. Margo ended up next to her, also face down. "Houston, we have a problem," she said, laughing.

"You are a lousy driver, Ms. Tosch," Leigh teased, flipping a handful of snow at her.

"At least I didn't run over you." She pulled herself to her knees and caught her breath. "You okay?"

"I can see why your derriere can only take so many of these of runs." Leigh sat up, brushing the snow from her chest.

"Is your ass sore?"

"A little."

Margo climbed to her feet then looked down at Leigh with a crooked smile and said, "You don't have much meat on your rear to absorb the shock."

"If that's a compliment, thank you." Leigh held up a hand. Margo took it and helped her to her feet then brushed the snow off Leigh's backside.

"Are you up for one more run?" Margo started up with the tubes.

"I'm not sure. I'll decide when and if I make it to the top."

"One more is all, Lindsey," Margo called to her, already halfway up the hill. "It's getting too dark."

The sunset left a glow over the valley as if coloring the snow with iridescent orange pixie dust. The air was still and the only sound was their breathing and the crunch of their steps. When Leigh started to fall behind, Margo took her arm and helped her up the slope. Lindsey was already at the top.

"You going to make it?" Margo asked, her strong arm boosting Leigh along.

"Yes, but I might need to get a better fitting snowsuit before we do this again. I appreciate you letting me borrow this one but I feel like a penguin."

"It is a little big on you, isn't it?" She grabbed the back waist and hiked it up. "Is that better?"

"Actually, yes, thank you." They climbed the last few steps that way, Margo holding the back of Leigh's snowsuit up while she climbed the hill.

"Make it a quick one, Lu-Lu."

Lindsey flopped down on her tube and used her feet to get going. She was halfway down the hill before Leigh caught her breath from the last climb.

"Are you game for one more?" Margo asked, readying the tubes.

"I don't think so. You go ahead. I think I need to work up to three runs." Leigh leaned over and propped her hands on her knees to rest, gasping for air.

"You don't have your mountain wind yet. High altitude takes some getting used to."

"I've lived in Denver most of my life. I can handle high altitude." Leigh took a few deep breaths but it wasn't helping.

Margo removed one of her gloves and took Leigh's wrist, feeling for her pulse.

"Yep, your heart is racing trying to pump more oxygen. Do you feel light-headed?"

"A little but not bad." Leigh gulped for air.

"You need to sit down."

"I need to go inside and warm up. You stay here and sled some more with Lindsey. Come up to the cabin when you're finished and we'll make hot chocolate." She headed back through the trees, her head swimming strangely.

"Do you need some help getting back up there?" Margo called.

Leigh shook her head.

"Are you sure?"

Leigh nodded and kept walking. Once in the cabin, she changed out of the snowsuit and into a fleece jogging suit. She heated a cup of tea and sat down on the hearth to warm herself by the fire. She was tired. The two sled runs had zapped the strength right out of her. She had never been a great athlete but she wasn't a wimp either. She never expected that walking up that hill twice would drain her energy. I bet Margo could walk it all day and not complain, she thought.

Leigh moved to the sofa, covering herself with an afghan to keep warm while she waited for them to return. When she opened her eyes, it was dark outside. It was after nine o'clock and she wondered where Margo and Lindsey were. She opened the front door but Margo's truck was gone. So was the snowsuit hung over the post at the bottom of the stairs.

"Why didn't you wake me?" she said, staring into the darkness, and wondering why she cared.

Chapter 12

Leigh touched the screen on her cell phone to dial her office and waited for Maureen to answer while she reread the email flagged high priority.

"Maureen, what is this? RMST versus Diane Nelson? When did this happen?"

"We just got the paperwork yesterday." Maureen sounded as upset as Leigh. "Rocky Mountain Securities Technologies has filed against Diane and her parent company, Nelson Thomas Industries. They are asking for two hundred sixteen thousand for goods and services plus legal fees. I'm sorry to bother you with this while you're out of town but Bev insisted I let you know."

"Is Bev there?" Leigh squinted at the screen, rereading a paragraph.

"Let me see if she's still in her office."

"Leigh?" Bev sounded exasperated. She didn't extend the normal telephone pleasantries but Leigh didn't mind. She didn't call to have a chit-chat with her ex. "RMST is suing Diane and she hasn't even moved to her new offices yet. We're looking at a couple hundred grand here. You need to get back here and have a talk with this asshole at RMST. I don't have time and Diane trusts you."

"Slow down, Bev." Quiet practicality was never Bev's long suit. "First, the lawsuit has something to do with the security system installed last month, right?"

"Damn right it does. Those idiots can't read their own work orders. They installed their crap all over the building, even the basement parking garage, BY MISTAKE. They even admit it was a mistake. They were supposed to be across the street in the Kline Building. I've gone around and around with these people. I spent two hours on the phone with the supervisor. They're going forward with this thing. I told the guy they can't win and they're going to end up paying Diane's legal fees as well. We'll countersue."

"No, we won't, Bev," Leigh said, leaning back in her chair.

"What do you mean we won't sue? What's wrong with you, Leigh? Has that thin mountain air made you loopy? They installed that stuff in the wrong building. They admit it. They'll have to eat it."

"Bev, I read the email. Diane's brother-in-law let them in the building. They told him what they were there to do. He knew Diane hadn't signed a contract for security yet. She wasn't sure which company she wanted to use. It was in the memo. RMST was on the premises for four days and no one said a word to them. No one asked for verification. Doug was even overheard telling Diane not to worry about a security system. Because the brother-in-law failed to stop the installation, with the intention of benefiting from the mistake, the court will create a quasi-contract. Knowing that it was a mistake and failing to stop the installation will be interpreted as an implicit agreement to pay. The court will treat it as if there was an actual contract. Bev, this is law 101. If a painter paints a house by mistake while the owner watches, he can sue for payment."

"Leigh, this is Diane Nelson we're talking about. Not Clem Kadiddlehopper. We know her. She's a friend."

"She's a business associate. And that has nothing to do with it. She can't benefit from a mistake they could have stopped. She is liable."

"What's wrong, Leigh? Have you given up on friends? Is hiding in that cabin of yours making you cynical? You didn't used to be like this."

"Be like what, Bev? Have common sense?"

"Wooo," Bev chuckled sinisterly. "Are you saying I don't?"

"I didn't say that. I'm just saying in this case the omission of responsibility doesn't exist. RMST has a case and they will win. I'd suggest Diane agree to a settlement. Pay the money and avoid a huge legal fee. We can't win this case. And that's what I'm going to tell her."

"I'll take care of it," Bev snapped. "I've got a meeting with Diane tomorrow."

"I'll be back in town sometime next week. I talk to her then."

"No, no. I'll do it," Bev argued defensively. "You stay up there. Maybe you do need some time to re-acclimate."

"Re-acclimate to what, Bev?" *Don't do it. Don't go down this road. There is nothing to gain.* But Leigh couldn't stop herself. "When did discussing a client's legal options become open season on my personal life? I don't need to re-acclimate to anything. Just because I don't agree with you doesn't mean I'm incompetent."

Bev hissed like a cat backed into a corner then laughed and said, "Wow, I must have touched your hot button."

"I'm sorry." Leigh closed her eyes and massaged her forehead. She was getting a headache. Maybe that's why she snapped at Bev like that. "I'll call Diane first of the week."

"I have to go. Staff meeting in ten minutes." Bev ended the call.

Bev had made her mad. Was it her inability to place basic legal expertise above friendship or her accusations Leigh needed a break from? It didn't matter. She closed the email, shut down her computer and carried her coffee cup to the kitchen to reheat it, muttering to herself.

"Re-acclimate, my ass. Try re-acclimating to practicality, Bev. Remember you're a lawyer. Not a playground buddy twirling a jump rope." Leigh crossed her arms and leaned against the counter, frowning fiercely. The longer it took her coffee to heat in the microwave, the more she fumed and stewed over Bev's insinuations. "I don't need to stay in Aspen to re-acclimate to anything." She left the coffee cup in the microwave and went to find her coat. Maybe coffee at Tink's Sweet Spot in town would help defuse her anger. She slammed the front door to the cabin, still muttering to herself as she zipped her coat, climbed into her car and headed for town. She circled the block and pulled into a parking spot in front of the Sweet Spot, Bev's call still rolling over in her mind.

"Hi, Leigh," Tink said, waving from behind the cheesecake counter as Leigh stepped through the door. Tink was busy loading desserts into the glass case, all of them looking scrumptiously delicious.

"Hi, Tink. Those look wonderful."

"Which one would you like? The almond amaretto is deadly good." The wattle under her chin jiggled as she laughed.

"I'm sure it is but I just need a cup of coffee."

"What's wrong, sweetie," she said, narrowing her eyes sympathetically. "Is everything all right?"

"Everything is fine. I only have a few minutes so I thought I'd grab a cup of coffee and say hi." Just the sound of Tink's concern was reassuring.

Tink filled and carried a cup to a nearby table and sat with Leigh, discussing the latest town news.

"Have you sold your cabin yet?" Tink dabbed a corner of her white apron across her brow. She looked tired.

"No. And I don't expect a quick turnaround. It could take weeks in this market."

"Why not keep it and wait for better times? Maybe you'll find the time to come to Aspen more often." Tink grinned encouragement. "And you never know, you might find a reason to stay." She leaned in and whispered, "I have."

"I agree. The Sweet Spot is fabulous. You should have done this years ago. You are a natural, Tink."

"No, I mean a real reason." She winked.

"You mean a person reason?" It was surprise enough that

Tink had outed herself to Leigh. Was she now admitting she had a girlfriend?

Tink nodded. "Her name is Kate and she is so wonderful I can't believe it. Where has she been all my life?" Tink clutched her hands to her chest and sighed deeply. "I can't wait for you to meet her."

"I'd love to."

"I better go check the oven and see what I'm burning," she said, hugging Leigh and kissing her cheek. She pointed a menacing finger at Leigh. "Tomorrow, cheesecake, you hear me?" She grinned and returned to the kitchen.

Leigh finished her coffee, refreshed and happy she had stopped by Tink's.

On her way down the sidewalk to her car she noticed the window display in the Polar Bear was empty but for a naked female mannequin. Her first thought was that Margo had closed the store, perhaps for financial problems. Her second thought was how could she help? She crossed against the light, scurrying between oncoming cars to get a closer look.

The store was open. All the lights were on but there was nothing in the window, not even items waiting to be dressed on the mannequin. She stepped inside, the bell over the door announcing her arrival.

"Be right with you," Karen called cheerfully from somewhere in the storeroom. "Have a look around."

"It's just me, Karen," Leigh replied, glancing around for signs of impending doom.

"Hi, Leigh. I'm steaming a sweater. Be right there."

"Take your time. Is Margo here?"

"She ran upstairs for a minute."

"Did you know the window display is empty?"

Karen laughed and said, "You're the fourth person to say that. Everybody thinks we're closing."

"Are you?" Leigh came to the storeroom door, braced for the bad news.

"No. But we had to empty the window so the guy can reinforce the flooring." She made an ugly face. "Termites."

"Oh, wow. That's not good news."

"Yeah, Margo isn't very happy about it. Fortunately it's only in that one spot under the window." Karen turned off the steamer and hung the sweater on a hanger. "She about blew a gasket over the cost of the repair. Aspen's a small town. Those guys know they've got you."

"Did she shop around and get estimates?"

"Yes, she did," Margo said, coming up behind her. "I got three estimates, each one higher than the first. And before you ask, no, I didn't have a contract for services with an exterminator. I have no recourse other than to pay it and forget it."

"I didn't say anything," Leigh replied. The telephone on the counter by the cash register rang. Karen moved to answer it but Margo waved her off, picking it up instead.

"Polar Bear. Can I help you?" she said in a pleasant business voice. "Yes, we are open regular hours, Stephanie. Sure." She hung up, shaking her head. "We need to get something in the window before people start reading the newspaper for my obituary. Put that new apple-green parka on Tillie."

"With the forest green snow pants?" Karen suggested.

"How about the white ones with gray trim?" Leigh said nonchalantly.

Margo looked over at her, considering the idea. "I like that," she said, brightening. "Yeah. The white ones. Very good, counselor."

"You're welcome." Leigh curtsied playfully. "How about no hat, just sunglasses?"

Margo's brow wrinkled curiously.

"Yes, I saw you the other day," Leigh said. "You and Lindsey and Adriana up by the Sundeck Restaurant."

"I thought that was you," she said with a chuckle. "How did the snow pants work out for you?"

"I was toasty. Thank you. And I see Lindsey is learning to ski."

"Did you let Lindsey ski Ajax?" Karen demanded, overhearing their conversation.

"She was ready," Margo replied. "She did great."

"What's wrong with Lindsey skiing Ajax?" Leigh asked.

"Ajax is for intermediate and advanced skiers. Not beginners," Karen exclaimed.

"Is that true?" Leigh couldn't imagine Margo would allow Lindsey to do something dangerous. "It's not safe for kids?"

"Now wait one minute." Margo bristled, holding up her hands as if to stop the barrage of questions and accusations. "Lindsey has been skiing Buttermilk for three years. She's not a beginner. And I was with her. It's not as if I threw her down the mountain. I promised she could try Ajax this season. She wants to enter the Ski Bunny Race and she needs the experience. If she can't ski Copper Bowl or Little Nell, she can't enter her division."

"If she walks in here on crutches I'm turning you in to DFS," Karen scolded playfully.

But Margo didn't seem to take it that way. "Don't even joke about that," she shot back angrily, the veins at her temples popping out.

The telephone rang again but Margo didn't move to answer it. She still had Karen locked in an angry stare. The phone continued to ring but neither one answered it, Margo fuming over Karen's remark and Karen too intimidated to move.

"Should I get that?" Leigh asked, instinctively trying to break the ice between the two.

"I've got it," Margo said, tossing one last harsh look at Karen.

"Oops," Karen whispered in Leigh's direction then gasping in relief. "My bad."

"What was that all about?" Leigh whispered back.

Karen waved her off, as if it was a forbidden subject better left alone.

"Sorry but Lindsey's school is out for teacher meetings tomorrow," Margo argued to whoever had called. "My babysitter is out of town. I can't do it, Frank. I can't help it. You'll have to get someone else." She rolled her eyes. "You can offer double time but I still can't do it." Margo frowned disgustedly. "The cleanup will have to wait. Have them work the push-back on the highway first."

"This happens a lot," Karen said to Leigh. "The county gets shorthanded and they call Margo. They know she'll do it. Hell, if I knew how to drive one of those big snowplows I'd do it. You can make some serious money."

"Why not learn how then?" Leigh thought that was the logical resolution to that situation.

"You can't have a ticket in the past five years to apply," she said with a sheepish smile.

"Ah-ha. And you don't qualify?"

Karen shook her head and held up two fingers.

"Frank, let me explain this again," Margo said flatly. "Wendy is in Glenwood Springs. School will be out. I can't drive tomorrow. Period."

Before Leigh could stop herself she said, "I'm not doing anything tomorrow."

Margo overheard her and rolled her eyes to Leigh. "You'd watch her?"

"I guess so. Sure." Leigh shrugged. "How hard could it be?"

"Hang on, Frank." She covered the receiver with her hand and stared at Leigh. "You're sure you'd be willing to watch Lindsey for me?"

"How early?"

"About eight."

"That's not very early. Can you bring her up to the cabin?" Leigh was usually up and already two hours into her workday by eight.

"You bet. Wow, that'll be great. Thanks. She won't be any trouble." She smiled and went back to her call. "Frank, I'll be there. And I'm holding you to that double time."

The Polar Bear became noisy with several customers shopping for ski apparel. Leigh wanted to talk with Margo about her warehouse, a topic she had wanted to discuss since she was caught trespassing, but like other times, the opportunity melted away before she could broach the subject. Perhaps tomorrow evening after babysitting.

The next morning Margo dropped Lindsey off a few minutes early but it didn't matter. Leigh had been on the computer since six thirty and she needed a break.

"I really appreciate this," Margo said, setting a package of juice boxes in Leigh's refrigerator. "Behave yourself, Lu-Lu," she said, unzipping Lindsey's parka. "You do what Ms. Insley tells you, okay?"

"When will you be back?" Lindsey asked, looking up at Margo hopefully.

"I don't know but it won't be too long." She swept the hair from Lindsey's forehead. "You've got lots of stuff to do in your backpack. You won't even miss me." Lindsey pursed her lips as if expecting a kiss. Margo gave her a cocky grin and asked, "What am I supposed to do with that?" Lindsey whined and continued to pucker. Margo finally relented. She gathered Lindsey in her arms and lifted her off the floor, giving her a little peck and a big hug. "See you later, baby." She set her down and hurried out the door without a backward look.

"I'll take good care of her," Leigh said, standing in the doorway. She wrapped her arms around herself against the cold. "Don't worry."

"I won't," Margo called as she climbed in the cab of her pickup, the engine still running. She shifted into gear and roared away, Lindsey watching from the window.

Leigh wasn't sure what to do first. Offer support that her mother wasn't abandoning her forever? Or find a distraction to take her mind off her uncertainty at being left with someone she barely knew?

"Can I have a juice box?" Lindsey asked as soon as Margo's truck was out of sight.

"Absolutely," Leigh said, assuming that was what they were for.

Leigh went back to her computer and soon became consumed with work. Lindsey sat at the counter kneeling on a barstool, digging through her backpack and sipping a juice box while Leigh put the finishing touches on an involved email. What was so hard about babysitting, she thought. Nothing to it. Lindsey was a quiet child. She colored two pages in a coloring book, spent a few minutes combing the mane and tail of a plastic horse before taking out a handheld video game.

She slurped the last drops from a juice box then said, "Can I have another one?"

"Yes, I suppose so. Do you need me to get it for you?" Leigh asked, looking over her shoulder.

"I can get it." She hopped down and went to the refrigerator.

The door was open a long time, longer than Leigh thought it should take to select another box of juice.

"Did you find it?" she called.

"Why do you keep cookies in the refrigerator?"

"So they don't get stale. Would you like one?" Leigh couldn't imagine Margo wouldn't allow just one.

"What kind are they?"

"Amaretto shortbread." Leigh came into the kitchen to hurry things along. "They're good. Very light and buttery."

Lindsey scrunched her face and said, "I like chocolate chip."

"I'm sorry but I don't have any chocolate chip." *Sounds good though.*

Lindsey had lined up the juice boxes in a neat row across the front of the shelf.

"Which one do you want?" Leigh asked, finding the child's compulsion for order cute.

"Grape. Do you want one?"

"No, thanks." Leigh's cell phone rang. "Maybe we should close the refrigerator door soon," she said, going to the desk to answer it.

"Hi. It's Margo." The sound of rushing wind in the background made it hard to hear.

"Hello. And yes, she's fine. Having juice." Leigh assumed she was calling to check up on her daughter.

"Good. Say, are you doing anything this afternoon?"

"Just babysitting Lindsey." Margo didn't need to hear a list of contracts she needed to look over.

"Yes, I know. But I got a call from Dr. McGuire's office. She's Lindsey's pediatrician. They had to change Lindsey's appointment for her flu shot. The doctor will be out of town for a couple weeks. Some kind of family emergency. I really hate to ask you but is there any chance you could take her? I can cancel it but they don't know when they'll be able to reschedule."

"I heard flu shots were available at the pharmacy downtown on a walk-in basis for thirty dollars."

"Yeah, I know but she had a reaction to one a couple years ago so I want the doctor's office to do it."

"What kind of reaction did she have?" Anaphylactic shock came to mind.

"Nothing major. I mean she wasn't foaming at the mouth or anything. But that's okay. I'll take care of it later."

"No, wait, Margo." Leigh looked over at Lindsey who was mopping a juice dribble off the counter with her sleeve. *How hard can it be? Drive her to the office. Wait. Drive her home.* Leigh took a deep breath and said, "I can take her. But you'll have to call and give parental consent for treatment." The legal implications immediately popped into Leigh's mind.

"I already did that. I really appreciate this, Leigh. Thank you. I want her to get the shot before the kids at school start sharing the flu."

"When is the appointment?"

"As soon as you can get there. I'll call and let them know you're on the way."

Leigh got the details from Margo and headed into town with Lindsey.

"Why do I have to sit in the backseat?" Lindsey complained from behind her.

"Because it's safer." Leigh checked her in the rear view mirror. "Is your seat belt good and tight?"

"It pinches."

"It needs to be snug. If we're in an accident I don't want you flying through the windshield."

"Mommy sings the seat belt song. Do you know it?"

"I didn't know there was a seat belt song."

"Sure," Lindsey said cheerfully then began to sing. "Buckle up for safety, buckle up. Pull your seat belt snug, give an extra tug. Everybody BUCKLE UP!" She finished with a broad gesture and shrill notes.

"Very good. No, I haven't heard that one." Leigh smiled at the child's performance and at Margo's wisdom for teaching her a lifesaving habit.

A few minutes later Leigh pulled into the clinic parking lot. Lindsey took her hand as they crossed the parking lot to Dr. McGuire's office door.

"Hello, Miss Lindsey," a nurse in teddy bear scrubs said from behind the counter. "I like the pigtails."

"I got beads in them. See?" Lindsey flipped her hair.

"Yes, I see. I like them." She pulled a folder from the stack and opened it. "I see you are here to get a toy from the treasure chest and a sucker from the tree." She grinned at her. "Right?"

"Yes. I want a ring this time. A pink one."

"We'll see if we can find you one." She turned to Leigh and said, "And you're Ms. Insley?"

"Yes." Leigh produced her ID, assuming they would ask to see it. But the receptionists didn't even look.

"You two can come right on back." The nurse stood at the open door to the hall.

"You need me to come too?" Leigh somehow thought Lindsey would be escorted to the exam room by the nurse and returned to her when it was all over.

"Yes. We always have parents accompany the child."

Lindsey headed down the hall as if she knew where to go. Leigh followed nervously. She was in virgin territory. She had never accompanied a child to the doctor's office before.

"You'll do fine," the nurse said, patting Leigh on the back.

Lindsey turned the corner and stopped at an alcove with two chairs, one with a frog painted on it and the other with a penguin on it. She sat down on the penguin chair and began swinging her legs.

"Have a seat, Ms. Insley. I'll be right back."

Leigh perched on the edge of the frog chair, wondering if she should reassure Lindsey everything would be okay. But she didn't want to scare the child unnecessarily. Lindsey seemed happy enough at the moment and perhaps oblivious to what was coming. Just the thought of having a shot made Leigh's palms sweaty. She had been that way since childhood and a particularly unpleasant experience with a myopic school nurse.

"Here we go," the nurse said cheerfully, hiding a syringe in one hand while producing a large gold key in the other. Lindsey's eyes lit up as if curtains had just parted on Santa's workshop.

"Can I hold the key?" Lindsey asked gleefully.

"Let's get your pants down a little first then you can." The nurse looked over at Leigh and said, "We find using the thigh muscle is a little meatier on some of these petite kids. Less soreness. She may experience a little redness and a slight temp but that's normal." She pulled Lindsey's pants down enough to expose her pale little thigh. "Okay, Lindsey. Find the ladybug."

Lindsey scanned the vine painted across the ceiling. Leigh had only vaguely noticed it and the colorful bugs, flowers and animals hidden among the leaves. While Lindsey searched, the nurse swabbed her thigh with alcohol and pinched up a chunk of muscle.

"There it is," Lindsey said just as the needle jabbed her skin. "Ouch," she gasped, stiffening.

"All done," the nurse said, wiping the swab across a tiny bead of blood.

But Lindsey was still sucking wind, her eyes welling up with tears. Leigh knew it was just a matter of time before the terror on her face changed to shrieking sobs.

"Here's a Barbie Doll Band-Aid for you, sweetie," the nurse said, applying it gently.

Lindsey looked down at it, her chin quivering. Two large tears dropped onto her bare skin. Her mouth was poised to scream but she didn't make a sound. Leigh bit down on her lip to stop her own tears of sympathy and braced herself, ready to swallow Lindsey in a hug to soothe her crying.

"Let's get your pants pulled up so you can use that key." The nurse was all business, ignoring the tragic look on Lindsey's face.

Lindsey stood up, clutching the key to her chest as the nurse hoisted her pants into place. As soon as she was finished, Lindsey ran across the hall, sliding the last three feet on her knees, to a wooden box painted to look like a pirate's treasure chest. She slipped the key into the lock and lifted the lid. She still hadn't uttered a peep. She wiped away the tears with the back of her hand as she peered into the box of trinkets and small toys. Her face had changed from one of shock and pain to absolute ecstasy.

"Dig down there and get you a good one." The nurse looked back at Leigh and asked, "Are you okay? You look a little pale." Leigh nodded. "See? That wasn't so bad, was it?" She chuckled and headed up the hall.

"Look, Leigh. A diamond necklace." Lindsey held up a piece of plastic bling. The tracks of her tears were still visible.

"Wow, that's gorgeous. But I thought you wanted a ring."

"Oh, yeah." She went back to sorting through the treasure chest. "I got Mommy a bracelet last time. It had red diamonds and kitty-cats on it."

"That sounds adorable." She wondered if Margo knew how brave her daughter was. "Look, there's a ring." Leigh knelt next to Lindsey and plucked a pink plastic ring from a far corner of the box.

"Can I have it?" She held out her palm eagerly.

"It's may I have it and absolutely, you may," Leigh said, slipping it on her ring finger.

"Not that one. This one." She quickly changed it to her index finger.

"But this one is called the ring finger." Leigh showed her the amethyst ring she wore on her ring finger.

"Mommy said it's bad luck to wear a ring on that finger." The child said it as if it were gospel.

"I didn't know that." Leigh wasn't going to argue. She wondered what terrible thing happened to Margo to taint such a time-honored tradition. "Do you like cheesecake, Lindsey?" she asked, wanting to reward Lindsey's remarkable bravery through the ordeal.

"Uh-huh," she replied, admiring her new jewelry.

"Come on. Let's splurge a little."

They left the car in the clinic parking lot and walked the five blocks to Tink's Sweet Spot. It was after two and the lunch crowd had dissipated. The customers were predominantly a coffee and dessert group. Tink wasn't there, something about going home sick. Leigh made a mental note to call and check on her.

"What would you like?" Leigh stood behind Lindsey with her hands on her shoulders while they scanned the choices. Lindsey stared with wide eyes, much like the look she gave the contents of the treasure chest.

"Is that chocolate cake?" Lindsey pressed her newly-ringed finger against the glass.

"Raspberry Decadent Double Fudge," the lady behind the counter said, waiting to take their order.

Lindsey frowned up at Leigh.

"That means it's chocolate cake with raspberry filling between the layers," Leigh explained.

"Oh." Lindsey went back to studying the choices. "What kind is that?"

"Walnut carrot cake with cream cheese frosting," the lady replied. "My favorite."

Leigh wondered if that was true or only her way of speeding up the selection process.

"What are you going to have?" Lindsey asked Leigh.

"Cherry cheesecake."

Lindsey gave it some thought then said, "I'll have that too."

"No chocolate cake?"

Lindsey scrunched her face as if she couldn't decide.

"Could we have one of each, please?" Leigh ordered then gave Lindsey a playful squeeze. "We'll share. Okay?"

"Okay."

"We'd also like a glass of milk and a cup of coffee, black. You do drink milk, don't you, Lindsey?"

"Can I have a Coke?" The uncertainty in her voice told Leigh she didn't expect her to agree.

"No. Milk."

They climbed the stairs and sat at the railing on the balcony, eating decadent double fudge cake and cheery cherry cheesecake. Lindsey ate like she was starving, gobbling down big bites and mashing the crumbs with her fork. She drank her milk without objection, leaving a milk moustache on her upper lip.

"Was that good?" Leigh enjoyed watching the child. Her enthusiasm for the desserts made the trip through the snow well worthwhile.

"Yeah. My mom doesn't let me have cake for lunch."

It suddenly dawned on Leigh she hadn't fed Lindsey lunch. As a busy lawyer, she seldom had a predictable lunch hour. It hadn't occurred to her Lindsey might be hungry. Sugary juice boxes and chocolate cake weren't exactly healthy choices for a six-year-old.

"Would you like a sandwich? How about a veggie wrap?" Leigh asked, reading the placard on the table for suggestions.

"No." Lindsey pulled her portable video game from her coat pocket and turned it on.

"How about a bowl of soup? They have incredible chicken gumbo."

"No," she mumbled distractedly then looked up. "Do you want to play my DS?" Lindsey offered as if it was a privilege reserved for close friends. "You use the stylus like this." She demonstrated.

Leigh wondered how many kids would have known the term stylus twenty years ago.

"Thank you but you go ahead and play it. Are you sure you wouldn't like something else to eat. Fruit maybe?"

Lindsey sat swinging her legs as she studied the tiny screen, tapping it with the stylus. Occasionally she rubbed her thigh but never complained.

"Shall we go?" Leigh asked after replying to a cell phone text from an associate.

Lindsey followed her down the stairs and out onto the sidewalk, still concentrating on her game. Leigh was tempted to close it, exercising the parental prerogative to limit her screen time. But Lindsey had been so brave at the doctor's office she decided she deserved it.

They had only been back at the cabin a short time when Margo knocked on the door. "How did it go?" She looked past her to where Lindsey was sprawled on the floor in front of the TV watching a cartoon.

"Everything went well. She was very brave at the doctor's office."

"Yeah, I called and they told me. Thanks for taking her. Hey, Lindsey, time to go," she called. "Get your stuff." Margo dug in her pocket and handed Leigh two twenty-dollar bills and several ones. "Is this enough?"

Leigh pushed it back at her and said, "I don't want that."

"Sure you do."

"Margo, I don't want your money. It was my pleasure."

"We had chocolate cake for lunch," Lindsey said cheerfully as she grabbed onto Margo's arm.

"Wow. Chocolate cake?" Margo flexed her arm, supporting Lindsey while she swung on it.

"It wasn't so much lunch as it was a treat," Leigh quickly inserted, knowing it sounded irresponsible to have fed her cake.

"We had cheesecake too. How come you won't let me have cake for lunch?"

"Because I think fruit and vegetables are better for you." Margo cast a curious look at Leigh.

"Okay, I admit it. I'm a terrible babysitter. I forgot lunch."

"How can you forget lunch? It comes around every day at the same time. Noon."

"Not for me. Some days my lunch is a granola bar between meetings. I'm sorry. I just forgot. At least she had milk with the cake." Leigh hated sounding incompetent and for some reason it was even worse in front of Margo. "I didn't do it intentionally. Lindsey isn't diabetic, is she?"

"No, she's just a growing six-year-old who will now be bouncing off the walls because you fed her sweets for lunch."

Lindsey wrapped her legs around Margo's leg and shinnied up like a monkey climbing a tree. "See what I mean? Lindsey, go find your coat and your backpack. We've got to go."

"I'm really sorry, Margo." Leigh helped Lindsey into her coat and hung her backpack over her shoulders. "The cake was a reward for how well she behaved at the doctor's office." She couldn't tell how upset Margo actually was with her. Enough not to trust her again with Lindsey?

"It's okay. Next time I'll leave a set of instructions and an alarm clock." She chuckled. "Let's go, short stuff."

"Can we have cake for dinner, too?" Lindsey said, beaming up at Margo.

"No. You're having an apple."

"I don't want an apple." Lindsey crossed her arms and scowled.

"Too bad. And don't give me that pit bull face. It won't work."

Leigh watched the two duel, amused at the variety of faces each displayed. Lindsey arched her eyebrows to almost vertical then dropped them to a dramatic pout. Margo's mood could be read in her eyes, dark and piercing when she was mad. Bright and twinkling with sparks of light when she was happy. No wonder Lindsey studied Margo's eyes before making her next reply.

"Can I have ice cream then?"

Margo burst out laughing. "We'll see. Run out there and get in the truck. Watch the ice," she said, holding the front door. "Thanks, Leigh. I really appreciate this."

"No problem. Glad I could help. I'm really sorry about lunch."

"She'll live. Are you sure you won't take the money?"

"I'm sure. Spend it on her." Leigh watched as Lindsey walked out to the truck, testing the ice for traction.

"I wanted to thank you for letting us sled on your hill the other day."

"It was fun. I had a good time. Why did you leave without waking me?"

"You looked peaceful. I didn't want to bother you. And you probably needed your sleep. Are you still feeling light-headed?"

"No, I'm fine. And I wasn't light-headed. I was cold. Weren't you?"

Margo gave her a quirky grin and said, "City girl."

"Hey, I can handle myself in the mountains."

"Like installing tire chains?"

"Yes, like installing tire chains," Leigh replied defiantly but finally gave in and joined Margo in a good laugh. "Maybe I should buy some new chains and have you teach me how to put them on."

"Excellent idea. Look for the ones with steel cables along the sidewalls. Galvanized is the best. When it comes to tire chains, you get what you pay for."

"Galvanized steel cable sidewalls, right?" Leigh was making a mental note of what to ask for.

"Tell you what," Margo said, pulling on her gloves. "You buy them tomorrow and we'll stop by about four." She nodded toward Lindsey, tromping a circle in the snow. "I'll let her sled the hill while I show you how to install them. How's that?"

"Good idea. I can make up for my babysitting faux pas by making dinner." *And give me an opportunity to talk with you about your warehouse. A little dinner, a little congenial conversation and maybe we can come to an agreement.*

"You don't have to do that."

"Hey, Lindsey," Leigh shouted out the door. "Would you like spaghetti or hamburgers for dinner tomorrow night?"

"Basgetti," she replied, continuing to stomp the circle.

Leigh looked back at Margo and said, "We're having basgetti." She smiled smugly.

"Then we'll be here." Margo went out to the truck, tossing a look back at Leigh. "Thanks."

"You're welcome," she said, leaning against the doorjamb. She would swear she saw Margo wink at her. A cold wind sent a shiver through Leigh, making her sneeze but she stood her ground, watching until Margo's truck disappeared down the driveway. I wonder what she likes with her spaghetti, she thought.

Chapter 13

Leigh overslept. She attributed it to the thin air and was determined not to let it happen again. But climbing out of bed was a struggle. She sat on the edge, rubbing her neck and waiting for her head to stop spinning. She felt like she had a hangover but she hadn't had anything to drink since her dinner at Freddo's with Gwen.

"I need to get up," she groaned then flopped back on the bed. "In twenty minutes."

She opened her eyes and squinted at the clock. That can't be right, she thought. Two hours had passed. She stumbled into the bathroom, hoping a shower would wake her up. She turned on the water then sat down on the side of the tub to wait for it to come to temperature.

What day is this? Tuesday? No, Friday? What was I going to do today? I can't remember.

This couldn't be the result of sledding down the hill on an inner tube. That was three days ago. But every muscle in her body ached. She propped her elbows on her knees and rested her forehead on her hands. Steam from the hot water filled the bathroom but she was too stiff and sore to shower. She turned off the water and went to dress. She'd shower later.

She pulled on a pair of Spandex jogging pants and a fluffy sweater. They didn't match but she didn't care. She was cold and hoped the sweater would warm her until the furnace kicked on. It wasn't until she had rummaged in the kitchen for a cup of herbal tea and a bowl of instant oatmeal that she remembered Margo and Lindsey were coming over for dinner.

She sat at the counter, slurping her tea, wondering why she didn't have any energy. She hadn't turned on her computer and had no interest in doing so. She instinctively reached for the phone to let Maureen know she was sick but she was too weak and tired to place the call. She'd tell her tomorrow. Maureen would have to hold down the fort, something Leigh had every confidence she could do.

"I wonder if the grocery store delivers," she mumbled, finally pulling herself to her feet and going to change her clothes. Maybe a trip into town to buy tire chains and groceries would wake her up. The trouble was, right now, she couldn't care less about tire chains. But she might as well get them while she was there.

It took an hour to pull herself together and head into town. What was it Margo said? Sidewall something. She strolled the aisle at the auto parts store, reading the boxes and hoping something jogged her memory. All she could remember was Margo saying you get what you pay for in tire chains. Leigh gave up and bought the most expensive set, calling it good. She didn't feel like stressing over the choices.

The trip to the grocery store was no better. She bought a box of pasta, a jar of spaghetti sauce, garlic bread and a bag of salad, not what she normally bought for company but she didn't feel like spending hours in the kitchen crushing garlic and snipping fresh basil leaves. She bought a bottle of red wine and a package of juice boxes for Lindsey. She tossed a package of chocolate chip cookies in the basket for good measure. Maybe Margo wouldn't notice she shortcut the menu.

"That's it. I'm done," she said, heading to the register, squinting at the headache trying to form behind her eyes. "Time to go home."

At the cabin Leigh made a half-hearted attempt at straightening the place but her headache made running the vacuum impossible. She had just dumped the sauce in a pan to simmer when she heard a knock at the door.

"Hi," Lindsey said, smiling brightly as she came bubbling through the door.

"Hello." Leigh couldn't stop a cough and sneeze as soon as the cold air brushed her face. "Sorry," she said, ducking her head behind the open door as she coughed again.

Lindsey's hair looked freshly combed and decorated with several pastel-colored barrettes. Her pink parka was zipped to the neck but she had it opened and off before she crossed the foyer. Margo looked clean and combed as well. The collar of a navy blue turtleneck extended out the top of a solid gray flannel shirt. Both were tucked neatly into the waistband of her jeans with a black and silver Navajo-style belt, a handsome accent to her dark hair. She wore a narrow silver bracelet with native-American markings on it, visible when she pulled the door out of Leigh's hand and closed it.

"Are you okay?" Margo frowned deeply.

"Sure. I just felt a chill. I like the barrettes, Lindsey." She led the way into the living room. "If it's okay with you I thought we could visit a little before we do the tire chain thing."

"Did you get a new set?"

"Yes. They're in the trunk of my car."

"Galvanized chains with steel cable sidewalls?"

That's what it was. I wonder if that's what I got.

"Are you sure you're okay?" Margo scowled at her as if she were looking at a freak.

"Yes, I'm fine. Why?" Leigh ran her fingers through her hair, wondering if she had forgotten to comb it recently.

"You look a little flushed. Actually, you look a lot flushed."

"I'm just a little tired. I didn't sleep very well last night. But I'll be fine as soon as we have some dinner." Leigh smiled over at Lindsey. "And I've got some chocolate chip cookies for dessert."

"Really! Can I have one now?" Lindsey grinned up at her.

"No, you can't," Margo said as she escorted Lindsey over to the TV and flipped it on. "You sit here a few minutes and behave, okay?"

"After dinner, Lindsey," Leigh offered. A chill shot up her back and made her shiver.

"I think you should sit down," Margo said, guiding Leigh onto a nearby barstool. Her hand lingered on Leigh's. "Damn, you've got a fever."

Leigh placed her hand on her forehead and said, "No, I don't."

"Come on, counselor. You know as well as I do you can't take your own temperature like that. Your hand is just as warm as your head. Do you have a thermometer?"

"I'm telling you I don't have a temperature." She stood up but the room began to spin and she sat back down. "I had a little headache this morning is all. Nothing dramatic. I'm fine." Leigh took a deep breath then coughed a raspy bark.

"Oh, yeah, that sounds like you're fine."

"How about we have dinner?" Leigh said, using the counter for support as she moved to the stove to check on the spaghetti sauce.

"How about you sit down and let me do that?" Margo said, coming to help.

"I'm sorry it won't be very fancy. Just pasta and sauce." Leigh opened the refrigerator, the cool temperature inside feeling good on her face. But she couldn't remember why she opened it in the first place. She looked back at Margo with a blank expression. "What was I going to get?" Her head and chest felt heavy but her legs felt like rubber and about to give out on her. "Do you mind if I sit down for just a minute?" she said, stumbling back to the barstool.

Margo wrapped an arm around Leigh's waist and eased her down. Then went to the stove and snapped off the burners.

"I haven't cooked the pasta yet," Leigh said softly, the headache pounding just below the surface.

"Lindsey and I aren't staying for dinner. You're in no shape to have company. You're sick and need to go to bed. You've got the flu, Leigh." She put the box of pasta in the cupboard and the contents of the saucepan into the refrigerator. "We'll do this another time. Do you need help getting upstairs?"

"No," Leigh said after coughing into her hands. "I can do it. I'm really sorry, Margo. I don't know what happened. I must have picked up a little head cold somewhere." She sneezed.

"Go to bed. Drink liquids but go to bed and sleep it off." She handed Leigh a paper towel to wipe her nose.

"I will." All Leigh could think of was a long warm, comfy nap. And an ibuprofen tablet the size of a ski boot. "I'll make a cup of tea and go right to bed."

"I'll make it," Margo said, searching the cabinets. "Where's the tea?"

"In the tea caddy," she said, closing her eyes and resting her head against her arm.

"Do you have any booze?" Margo asked, opening and closing every cabinet in her search. "Aha," Leigh heard her say but didn't open her eyes to see what she had found. "I'll fix you right up, counselor. You're going to sleep like a baby."

"Uh-huh." Leigh's mind was wafting through a dizzying sea of yellow and feathers. Nothing made sense. She felt herself drifting off.

"Here we go," Margo said, lifting Leigh's chin and holding the cup up to her lips. "Little sips." She helped Leigh take several sips of lukewarm tea as she cradled her in her arms. "Little bit more, counselor."

Leigh obeyed but her eyes refused to stay open. She could feel the soft comfort of a blanket around her shoulders and her bed beneath her. How had she gotten here? She didn't remember climbing the stairs. She didn't remember changing into her flannel pajamas either but they felt good. She cuddled against Margo's warm shirt as the tea slowly slid down her throat.

"One more," Margo coaxed, rubbing her cheek gently. Leigh opened her mouth and sipped. She swallowed then coughed, turning her face into Margo's chest to catch it. "Now sleep," Margo whispered as she lay her back on the pillow.

Leigh opened her eyes a slit and tried to focus but all she could see was the dark shadow of a woman's face staring down at her.

"Good night," Leigh tried to say but it came out slurred. She closed her eyes.

The last thing she felt was a hand stroking her forehead and a pair of lips on her cheek. She wanted to reach out and take Margo's hand but she didn't have the strength. She wanted to feel her strong protective hand against her as she slept. Instead she heard the bedroom close and her world was silent but for the pounding in her head.

Chapter 14

"Lindsey, come to dinner," Wendy called as she set a bowl of mashed potatoes on the kitchen table.

Margo came through the back door, stomping the snow from her boots and leaning a snow shovel in the corner.

"All done," she said, peeling off her hat and coat. "Something smells good." She ruffled her hair then went to the sink to wash her hands. "I really appreciate this, Wendy."

"No problem. I've got plenty of leftovers. Lindsey, wash your hands," she shouted toward the living room. "I thought you were going up to that lawyer lady's cabin for dinner tonight."

"We did but she's sick. I think she has the flu."

"It's going around, all right. Lindsey Louise!"

"Hey, Lindsey. Dinner," Margo said with a booming voice as she stood at the sink, washing her hands with dish soap.

"Turn off the DS before I take the batteries out of that thing."

"Why the heck you gave her that video game for her birthday is beyond me. Why not a nice Barbie Doll?"

"Come on Lu-Lu."

"Don't call me that," Lindsey said, still playing the game as she came into the kitchen but Margo held out her hand. Lindsey quickly keyed in two more moves then reluctantly placed the DS in Margo's hand.

"Did you save it?"

"I can't," she whined.

"That's okay. You can play it later." Margo wrapped an arm around Lindsey's head and drew her close, kissing her hair. "Dinner's ready. I want you to eat your vegetables without complaining, okay?" she whispered.

"What is it?"

"It doesn't matter."

Lindsey took her place at the table, groaning at the bowl of peas and carrots. Margo took her place at the far end. She scanned the table then tilted her chair back, opened the refrigerator and took out catsup and barbecue sauce.

"Looks wonderful, Wendy. Thanks for making us dinner." Margo nudged Lindsey under the table.

Lindsey seemed to realize what was expected and said, "Thank you for dinner, Wendy."

"You're welcome. Now eat before it gets cold." Wendy took her place, closed her eyes and mumbled something before passing the plate of meatloaf. Margo and Lindsey waited, respecting her wishes that they allow her that moment of thanks.

"How was the trip to the doctor?" Wendy asked as she spooned mashed potatoes onto Lindsey's plate.

"Leigh took me and I got a shot," Lindsey said with sad eyes, milking it for sympathy.

"Yes, I know, honey."

"Then we had chocolate cake for lunch." She brightened.

"Don't remind me," Margo grumbled, taking a slice of meatloaf for Lindsey and one for herself.

"Sounds to me like that lawyer lady doesn't know anything about kids."

"It was just an oversight." Margo explained. "She apologized. Catsup or Sweet Baby Ray's on your meatloaf?" Margo asked Lindsey.

"Sweet Baby Ray's." She grinned and reached for the bottle.

"What do you say?"

"Please."

Margo winked and handed her the bottle then gave her half a spoon of peas and carrots along with a stern look.

"Can I put Sweet Baby Ray's on my peas?" Lindsey asked, carefully portioning out the barbecue sauce.

"Don't put that glop on your vegetables," Wendy scolded.

"Try a little on one bite," Margo said. "Remember, you have to eat them all, sauce or no sauce."

"Melody Smith got to have a no-green week," Lindsey said, pushing the vegetables away from her mashed potatoes. "They don't have to eat green vegetables for a whole week." Lindsey looked up at Margo expectantly. "Her mom said so."

"Good for her. But you are eating yours." Margo took a small portion as well. She planned on eating them last. "By the way, Wendy," she said after eating half her meatloaf. "Are you busy tomorrow after school?"

"I don't have to be. What do you need?" She reached over and pushed peas and carrots back on Lindsey's plate that were hanging on the edge. "Are you driving tomorrow?"

"If you don't mind, could she get off the bus here?"

"Sure. Where will you be? Out of town? Private ski lesson?"

"No. I may not need her to stay. I won't know until tomorrow."

"She's going back up there to Leigh's house," Lindsey announced.

"Eat your dinner, Lindsey," Margo said, diverting her eyes from Wendy's cutting stare.

"I am," Lindsey said with a mouth full of mashed potatoes.

"I thought you said she had the flu." Wendy glared over at her.

"If Leigh has the flu, why didn't she get a flu shot?" Lindsey asked.

"Once you're sick, it won't do you any good to get a shot. It's too late," Wendy said. "Aren't you a little worried she might have exposed Lindsey to the flu?"

"I'm sure she didn't do it on purpose and there is nothing I can do about it now."

"Lindsey, look at me, child." Wendy grabbed her chin and looked deep into her eyes as if looking for disease. "Do you ache anywhere?"

"No, but maybe I shouldn't eat my peas," she said, her mouth pinched between Wendy's chubby fingers.

"Oh, yes, you should," Margo said and reached for the bowl. "Maybe you should have some more."

"NO!" Lindsey squealed and blocked her plate with her hands. "I have enough."

"Then eat them."

"You shouldn't go back up there, Margo."

"She got a flu shot," Lindsey said, decorating the top of her meatloaf with a forkful of barbecue sauce.

"When? You never get flu shots," Wendy demanded.

"On the way over here," Lindsey answered innocently. "We stopped at Walgreen's and she got one."

"Lindsey," Margo whispered.

"Well you did. You said you needed one so Leigh wouldn't make you sick."

"Margo, that flu shot won't protect you from the flu that fast. You shouldn't go up there. You can't afford to be sick. If she does have the flu, you'll catch it. You always catch it."

"I do not," Margo argued then calmed herself. "I was just thinking about checking on her. See if she needs anything. It's no big deal."

"I'm not taking care of you when you're sick, you hear me?" Wendy said with a defiant glare.

"Didn't ask you to."

They ate in silence but Margo could tell something was on Wendy's mind by the way she pushed her food around her plate.

"I'll be okay," she said, hoping to reassure her. "I won't let her sneeze on me."

"I had a visitor today," Wendy said softly. She kept her eyes down as if ashamed to admit it.

"Who?" Margo asked but Wendy just looked at her with a vague expression. "Who?" Margo repeated, hunching her shoulders.

Wendy heaved a resolute sigh then shielded her mouth with her hand so Lindsey couldn't see and mouthed the name *Elizabeth*. Margo hesitated a moment then continued chewing.

"What did she want?" she asked indifferently.

Wendy rolled her eyes toward Lindsey then back to Margo.

"What did she want, Wendy?" Margo didn't want to play cat and mouse with her. If there was one subject she had no patience for it was this one. Wendy should know that.

"I thought she was in Pueblo."

"Cheyenne. What did she want?"

"She asked for your cell phone number."

"You didn't give it to her, did you?"

"Heavens no." Wendy smiled at Lindsey fondly, rearranging a lock of hair behind her ear. "She wants to see her," she said regretfully.

Margo dropped her fork on her plate, her appetite gone. She took her dishes to the sink and washed them off without saying a word.

"She looks good, Margo," Wendy said as if that would make everything all right.

"Irresponsibility will do that for you."

"You can't stop her, can you?"

Margo stared out the kitchen window, the slow-motion memory playing in her mind of Elizabeth's long blond hair billowing behind her as she skied across virgin snow at sunset. Her sinewy body, glistening as she stepped out of the shower. The sound of her laughter sprinkled around them as they cuddled naked in front of the fireplace.

"If she comes by again, what do you want me to tell her?" Wendy asked.

"Nothing. I'll take care of it." Margo wiped her wet hands on her jeans and went to put on her coat. "Finish your dinner, Lindsey," she said then grabbed the snow shovel and went outside, hoping the cold winter wind would stop the anger that threatened to overtake her.

In spite of Wendy's warning, after dropping Lindsey off at school and checking in with Karen at the store, Margo headed up White River Road. As far as she knew, Leigh had no one in town to turn to, no one to run to the store for her if she needed a prescription filled or a few groceries brought in while she recuperated. Escaping to the cabin also meant Margo didn't have to deal with Elizabeth, at least not today.

It was almost noon when she knocked on the front door of the cabin. It took several minutes but the lock finally turned and the door opened a few inches.

Leigh looked ghostly white. Her eyes were glassy. She was still in her flannel pajamas and her hair looked like it hadn't been combed since yesterday. She leaned her head against the door, seemingly unable to hold it up.

"Hello," Leigh mumbled then gave one deep raspy bark.

"Hello yourself." Margo pushed her back and closed the door. She carried a grocery sack into the kitchen, leaving Leigh to follow, shuffling along in fuzzy slippers.

"How much booze did you give me last night?" She flopped down on a barstool, propping her elbows on the counter.

"Just a little in the tea. Made you sleep, didn't it?"

"No, it gave me a headache."

"The flu gave you a headache. Not the booze." The telephone on the wall in the kitchen rang but Margo knew Leigh was in no shape to answer it so she did. "Hello. Insley residence."

"Hello. This is Jewel Pesti with Aspen Security Systems. We have an alarm warning on your system. Could you give me your alarm code please?"

"One second," she said then turned to Leigh. "What's your security code?"

"Who wants to know?"

"Jewel Pesti with Aspen Security Systems. You must not have deactivated the code before you opened the door."

"Oh." Leigh's eyes crossed, a confused look on her face as she thought. "Um, nine one nine two. No, wait. Nine one two nine? Dammit." She squinted at Margo. "Ask her what my secret question is."

"What's her secret question?" she said to the caller.

There was a short silence then Jewel said, "Who was your first?"

"Who was your first?" Margo said, passing it on to Leigh. "Your first what?"

"Oh, yeah. One nine eight one," Leigh said then rested her head against her arm.

"One nine eight one," Margo reported.

"Thank you, ma'am. Have a nice day."

"Where's the keypad?" Margo asked Leigh.

"In the closet by the front door." Leigh didn't seem to mind confessing her security code or how to disarm the system and that surprised Margo as she went to reset it.

"What have you had to eat today?" Margo asked, returning to the kitchen.

"Nothing yet. I just got up. I'm not very hungry though. I know I said I wanted you to show me how to install my tire chains but if it's okay with you, could we do that some other time."

Margo laughed and said, "Is that why you think I'm here?"

"Isn't it?" Leigh coughed into the elbow of her pajamas.

"Not hardly. I'm going to make you some soup. You need liquids."

"I do? I thought I just needed to be shot."

"Feel like crap, huh?"

"I'd have to improve to feel that good." Leigh stumbled to the sofa and collapsed onto it, pulling the blanket over herself. "Sorry I'm not being a very good hostess."

"I don't need one." Margo dug in the sack and pulled out a digital thermometer and went to take Leigh's temperature. "Open your mouth and hold this under your tongue."

"I don't have a fever. Just a cough." Leigh coughed then burrowed her face under the blanket up to her nose.

"And a headache and chills and chest congestion and glassy eyes and weakness. Open your mouth, counselor."

"Are you this tyrannical around your daughter?"

"No, because she listens to me." She pulled the blanket back and shoved the thermometer in Leigh's mouth. "You need nutrients. Chicken noodle soup."

"Canned chicken noodle soup is loaded with salt and preservatives."

"Tough. You'll eat at least half a bowl anyway. Stop talking and let that thermometer work." Margo put the soup on the stove then went to check Leigh's temperature. "Told you," she said, frowning at the reading. "One-oh-one point five."

"That isn't much." Leigh sneezed twice then groaned. "I'll be fine."

"Yeah, in about three days you'll be fine. I did a Google search for the flu. You need to keep hydrated. And you need a fever reducer. You also need lots of rest." Margo handed Leigh two tablets and a glass of orange juice.

"I didn't know I had O.J."

"You didn't. I brought it. Drink up."

A few minutes later she sat down on the edge of the sofa and handed Leigh a mug of steaming soup. "Can you sit up long enough to eat this?"

"I think so." Leigh pulled herself up against the end of the sofa, tucking the blanket in around her waist. "Would it be insubordinate if I ask for tea, also?"

"No problem. But you have to eat the soup first. You need nutrients. Not just tea you're going to pee out."

"Thank you for that glimpse into the digestive process." Leigh sniffled then sipped the soup.

Margo went to make the tea but by the time she returned with it, Leigh had fallen asleep, the mug of soup balanced precariously on her lap.

"Shall I save the rest for later?" Margo asked softly. She lifted the mug from her grasp and tiptoed back to the kitchen.

Leigh slept soundly for three hours, something Margo knew she needed. She was standing out on the deck, admiring the view when she heard Leigh call from the stairs.

"Margo?" she said, leaning heavily on the banister.

"Right here," she exclaimed, rushing to her side. "What are you doing up? Are you okay?"

"I'm just a little weak." Leigh used both hands on the railing to pull herself up the stairs, one step at a time. "I just wanted to know what time it is."

"It's about four. But what does it matter? You aren't going anywhere." She hooked an arm around Leigh for support.

"I'm going upstairs to take a shower. I haven't had one in two days. Or maybe it's three. I'm beginning to disgust myself."

"You don't need a shower, not when you've got a fever."

"There's a seat at the end of the shower I can sit on. I'll be all right. Have you been here all afternoon?" Leigh looked over at Margo with a concerned stare.

"Yes."

"Why, for heaven's sake?" Leigh stopped halfway up the stairs to catch her breath.

"In case you needed something."

"I was passed out on the couch. What could I possibly have needed?" She started up again.

"Help to the bathroom. Something to drink. Whatever."

"Thank you for your concern but you can go home. Lindsey will be home alone."

"She's at Wendy's. They're making brownies. And I'm not going anywhere, not if you're planning on taking a shower."

"Whoa, there, mountain girl," Leigh scolded then coughed. "No one, including you, is going to watch me take a shower."

"I didn't say I was. I'm no pervert. But when the hot water makes your blood pressure go down and you pass out in the bathroom, someone should be here, don't you think?" Margo strengthened her grip on Leigh as they climbed the last few stairs.

"I'm not going to pass out."

"Good. I hope not."

"I can take it from here," Leigh said, pushing back on Margo's chest as they reached the top step.

"Promise me one thing. You won't lock the bathroom door."

"I most certainly will."

"It's your cabin but just so you know, if I hear you fall, I'm coming through the door, lock or no lock."

Margo stood at the bedroom door, watching as Leigh gathered clean clothes and headed into the bathroom. Leigh tossed a look at Margo then closed the door. Margo heard the lock click but after a moment, the doorknob turned, releasing it. Margo had no sooner sat down on the edge of the bed to wait than she heard a knock at the door downstairs.

"Are you okay?" she asked, listening at the bathroom door.

"Yes, I'm fine. I'm taking my time."

"Call me if you need something." Whoever was at the front door continued to knock.

Margo hesitated, worried Leigh would need her but finally decided she could do more good discouraging whoever was pounding at the door. She trotted down the stairs to answer it. She opened the door, ready to offer a polite hello to whoever it was but the word caught in her throat.

"Oh my God," Gwen gasped. "What the hell are you doing here?" She was dressed in a fake-fur leopard chubby and form-fitting slacks. She struck a pretentious posture, the same one Margo detested the first time she had met her. Even her gaudy earrings and pointy-toed boots smacked of snobbery.

"What do you want, Gwen?" Margo held the door, blocking her attempt to come inside.

"Where is Leigh?" she demanded. "She's expecting me."

"Leigh is sick. She isn't seeing anyone."

"I spoke with her yesterday. I have a client who is very interested in the cabin." She nodded toward the gray-haired man climbing out of the passenger seat. He looked thin and weathered, the kind that lived out their retirement years in serene solitude, reading classic literature and taking photographs of nature. "She is definitely expecting me." She clutched a leather folder to her chest and leered at Margo.

"Leigh is upstairs and she has the flu. This isn't a good day to look at the cabin."

"Look, Ms. Tosch, I made an appointment. I'm here to show

this property and I have the owner's permission. I don't need yours. So I suggest you move."

Margo shook her head and said, "It's not happening."

"You know, some people actually *want* their property sold once they no longer have a use for it."

"I don't care. You are not coming in here. Leigh is sick, so sick I had to help her up the stairs."

"I'm not only her real estate agent, I'm a very close friend. If she's that sick I want to see her."

"No." Margo stood her ground, staring down Gwen's insistence.

Gwen dug in her pocket and pulled out her cell phone, quickly stabbing in a number. Leigh's cell phone on the kitchen counter began to ring. Margo looked back at it then smiled devilishly and said, "I don't think I need to answer that, do I?"

Gwen narrowed her eyes as she curled her lip and said, "I don't know what you think you're doing, but believe me, you are NOT Leigh's type."

"I'm not doing anything but helping a friend."

Gwen heaved a disgruntled gasp then returned to her car and roared away, slinging ice and gravel in her wake. Margo hurried back upstairs to check on Leigh.

"How are you doing?" she asked, standing at the bathroom door. There was no answer. "Leigh, everything okay?" she called loudly, hoping to be heard over the sound of running water.

"Margo?" Leigh sounded desperate.

Margo burst through the door without asking what she needed. Leigh was sitting on the floor, her head against the wall in the corner. She was naked and clutching a towel.

"Shit! I knew I shouldn't have let you do this," Margo said angrily, rushing to her side. "Did you fall?"

"No. I just got very light-headed." Leigh looked up at her, her face white as a sheet. Her words were thin and weak. "I sat down so I wouldn't fall down."

Margo reached up and turned off the shower. It was hard not to stare at Leigh's trembling body, her skin wet and glistening. Last night's brief glimpse of Leigh in her underwear as she helped her into bed paled in comparison to seeing her naked.

Her breasts were full and round, her nipples pale and dainty. The patch of curly hair nestled in her lap was small but thick and dark.

"Are you sure you're not hurt?" she asked, forcing her mind away from Leigh's crotch and to the job of helping her. Leigh nodded then closed her eyes, breathing deeply, seemingly unaware she was exposed and vulnerable. Margo pulled the towel from her grasp and began blotting her dry, stroking her legs and arms, but reserving the modesty she knew Leigh would want.

"I feel so stupid," Leigh said softly. "I didn't listen to you." She placed her hand on Margo's arm, looking soulfully into her eyes. "I'm so very sorry, Margo."

"Don't be. No one will know but us."

Margo's brain had locked on a thought she was powerless to ignore. *Do you know how much I want to kiss you, woman? Do you know how much I want to feel your wetness?*

"Are you terribly mad at me?" Leigh asked, squeezing her arm.

"No. I'm just worried about you." She gently pressed her lips to Leigh's forehead and held them there a long moment. "You've still got a temperature."

"But I was feeling better. I really was."

"You just wanted to feel better so you could remain in control, counselor. You don't like to give up your independence to anyone, especially me. Now let's get you up before you catch pneumonia sitting on this cold tile floor." She pulled the robe from the hook on the back of the door and wrapped it around Leigh's shoulders as she helped her out the door.

"I think I'll sit here a minute," Leigh said, holding the robe closed as she sat down on the edge of the bed. Margo sat beside her, her arm still offering support. "It's late, Margo. You need to go home to Lindsey."

"She's being taken care of. I'm not worried," she said softly, folding the collar of Leigh's robe closed. "You need me more than she does right now." It was hard for Margo not to allow her eyes to drift down Leigh's cleavage. She knew what was down there and she wanted it so bad she could feel herself throbbing.

"This is new to me."

"What is? Having the flu and not being able to will it away?"

"Having someone take care of me." Leigh lowered her eyes then admitted, "It's usually me taking care of them. I'm not used to it."

"Are you uncomfortable with me sitting here?" Margo kept her arm around Leigh's shoulders. It felt right and she wasn't going to move it unless Leigh said so.

"I'm a little embarrassed. But you don't make me uncomfortable. Your sitting here makes me feel safe. Do you mind?"

"No," Margo said softly, combing her fingers through Leigh's hair. "I don't mind at all."

The protective side that wanted to care for Leigh gave way to a much deeper need. She couldn't help herself. She slipped her hand behind Leigh's head and pulled her close. She knew she shouldn't do it and it was too late. She kissed Leigh, invading her mouth, her tongue lapping and probing like a love-starved teenager. When she finally released her, Margo expected Leigh to draw away but instead she tilted her head and reached for more, hungrily pressing her lips to Margo's. Margo folded her arms around Leigh and leaned into her, their mouths devouring each other. Margo could feel Leigh's hands stroking her back, her nails digging at the hem of her shirt. Leigh broke away, erupting in deep husky coughing.

"Sorry," Leigh stammered but continued to cough and wheeze.

"I don't mind." She brushed the hair away that had fallen over Leigh's face. "I just wish I could do something to help you feel better. You have to be exhausted from all the coughing." Margo held Leigh in her arms, massaging her back as she rested her head on Margo's shoulder. It was several minutes before her breathing returned to normal and the wheezing subsided. Margo hadn't meant to kiss her. She told herself it was a natural reaction to Leigh's vulnerability and her incredibly sensuous body. But now she felt guilty over causing the coughing jag.

As she continued to hold and comfort Leigh, Margo's mind was off on a lusty fantasy. What would it be like to kiss Leigh without her coughing to interrupt it? What would it be like if she wasn't consumed with fever? Margo allowed the image to flourish, her imagination more eloquent than she knew how to be.

In her mind, Margo leans Leigh back on the bed, covering Leigh's mouth and neck with passionate kisses. Leigh pulls Margo down on top of her, moaning with each lick of Margo's tongue. Margo presses her knee up between Leigh's legs. Leigh moans even louder, pushing against it and arching as if searching for more. The prudish lawyer now a woman with feelings and desires and needs. Needs Margo wants to fulfill. Needs she wants to fulfill for herself as well.

Margo imagined her hand inside the robe, stroking Leigh's breast. Her nipple instantly hardening. Leigh opens the robe as if welcoming Margo inside. Margo's eyes drift down Leigh's milky white breasts and abdomen. She takes one of Leigh's swollen nipples in her mouth, sucking at it until Leigh's quiet moans change to guttural gasps. Leigh shifts on the bed with each hard flick of Margo's tongue. Margo feels for Leigh's wetness, cupping her hand over her mound, her pubic hair moist with desire.

Margo slides her fingers inside, plunging deep into Leigh's incredible softness. She begins a slow rhythmic pulse, moving in and out, leaving her velvet softness then returning. Leigh's body begins to move with it, riding each stroke with a small gasp. Margo could feel Leigh tightening, her groans becoming desperate. Leigh folds both hands over Margo's, holding her fingers deep inside and pressing up against them as she screams with ecstasy.

Leigh coughed quietly then snuggled back into Margo's chest. Margo took a deep breath, frustrated at herself for thinking such carnal thoughts. Leigh wasn't that kind of woman. And even if she was, it wouldn't be with a middle-aged ex-ski-bum.

"I think you need some sleep," Margo said, feeling Leigh sag in her arms. "I'm going to bring you ibuprofen for your fever and some tea with honey and lemon. I know you think you are better but give it one more day, okay?"

Leigh relented, nodding approval. Margo helped her into bed then turned to go make the tea but Leigh grabbed hold of her hand and said, "Thank you for taking care of me."

"You're welcome." Margo wanted to say something else. She wanted to tell Leigh she found her very special. She wanted to admit she had feelings for her but she knew Leigh might not feel the same way. The flu had weakened her defenses. The fever and the light-headedness allowed the kiss. Nothing more. She was a gorgeous successful professional who was probably going to regret that kiss come morning. Who was she kidding? Gwen was right. She wasn't Leigh's type. She wasn't even in her league.

Margo made Leigh's tea and got her tucked in before heading to Wendy's to pick up Lindsey.

It was after midnight when she finally completed a few house chores and crawled into bed, her body exhausted but her mind full of the memory of Leigh Insley. She wasn't sure that would ever go away.

Chapter 15

Leigh peeked out from under the comforter. The first rays of sunshine were filtering through the blinds, suggesting it was morning. For a brief moment she braced herself, wondering if the headache, body aches and chest congestion were going to rear their ugly heads again today. So far, so good. It had been two days since Margo had been there and she had slept almost nonstop. Margo's magical tea recipe must have included a little hooch along with the honey and lemon. Whatever the reason, she was cautiously optimistic the worst of the flu was behind her. Her muscles were still exhausted from the coughing but she felt good enough to try a shower, even wash her hair and shave her legs.

"Oh, good grief," she said, staring at herself in the bathroom mirror and the rat's nest on top of her head. "Did I look like this when Margo was here? She must have thought I was a cave woman." Did she care what Margo thought? She wouldn't have thought so but she had to admit she did care. Why, for heaven's sake, she asked herself. Why did she feel guilty Margo might have noticed she hadn't shaved her legs in three days? So what if Margo saw her naked? She couldn't help it. She was sick.

"You probably embarrassed her, you big dummy," Leigh said angrily and went to shower.

Leigh was just coming down the stairs when her cell phone rang. She didn't remember doing it but it was plugged into the charger on the kitchen counter.

"Leigh, honey. It's Gwen. How are you?" Gwen's voice was dripping with concern and sympathy.

"Hi, Gwen. I'm much better, thanks." Leigh suddenly remembered the appointment Gwen had made to show the cabin. "Oh geez, I forgot all about the showing. I had the flu. I've done nothing but sleep for three days. I'm so sorry."

"I came by. Didn't she tell you?"

"You did? When?"

"Four o'clock, day before yesterday. That's what we discussed, remember?"

Margo hadn't said anything and if she had, Leigh wasn't sure she would have remembered. That was about the time she was collapsing on the bathroom floor.

"Honey, *what* is that woman doing in your house? Especially if you were sleeping."

"Margo brought me some soup and ibuprofen for my fever." Leigh stopped short of apologizing further. She didn't owe Gwen an explanation. Her experience as a lawyer told her she didn't have to divulge everything she knew. "When do you want to reschedule? How about today?"

"Howard left last night for L.A. He couldn't wait. And I'm telling you, honey, he was very interested. He especially liked the view and the wraparound deck."

"When will he be back in town? We can reschedule at his convenience."

"Might not be for a couple months. Margo blew it for you, hon. I think he was ready to talk turkey."

"Margo didn't blow it. She wasn't the one with the flu."

"All I know is she refused to let us in. I told her I had an appointment and your permission to show the cabin but she stood there blocking the door like a great baboon. She was downright rude, Leigh. Even Howard thought so. He went away totally disgusted. He may not want to reschedule."

"All I can say is I'm sorry, Gwen. I'll be glad to make the cabin available anytime he would like to revisit Aspen. I'm sure it was just a misunderstanding with Margo. Don't worry. I'll talk with her about it. It won't happen again."

"You don't plan on having her out there again, do you? I told you about her. She is stubborn, conceited, arrogant and downright pigheaded."

"I'll take care of it, Gwen," she insisted, tired of listening to her Margo-bashing.

Leigh couldn't concentrate on work after the call from Gwen. She had to know what happened. If Gwen did bring a client by to see the cabin why hadn't Margo let her in? Margo knew the cabin was on the market. Leigh shut down the computer and headed to town.

"Hello," she called, stepping inside the Polar Bear, the bell above the door jingling brightly. Although no one was at the counter Leigh could hear someone talking in the back room that sounded like a telephone conversation. "Hello," she said again, not wanting to look like an eavesdropper, but Margo's voice was unmistakable.

"Yes, I know what it says. I wrote the contract. But why now? You didn't care last year."

Leigh flipped through a coat rack, trying not to listen but she couldn't help it. Margo sounded angry and defensive. Two women came through the door, talking and laughing loudly. They went right to the sweater rack and began sifting through the stacks.

"Look, Elizabeth," Leigh heard Margo say. "You'll get your visit. But I say when and where. I have to go. I've got customers."

Leigh heard her slam the receiver down.

"Hello," Margo said, appearing around the corner. She

smiled at Leigh then noticed the women picking through the sweaters. "Hello, ladies. Can I help you find something?"

"We're just looking," one of them said.

"Take your time. If you have any questions, let me know." Margo turned to Leigh, a dazzling smile her only greeting.

"Hi," Leigh said, admiring how stunning Margo looked in black ski pants and a gray fleece top.

"Hi and what are you doing in town? You should be home resting."

"I slept like a baby. I have no idea what you put in my tea but it worked. I slept right through yesterday too. I barely got out of bed to do anything but potty and drink water. Are you the one who put the bottles of water on my bedside table?"

"Yeah, I stopped in a couple times to check on you. You didn't need to be going up and down those stairs."

"Well, I feel much better this morning. I wanted to thank you."

"You're welcome."

"By the way, I forgot to tell you my realtor was bringing someone out to see the cabin the other day. I understand you answered the door."

"Yes, it was when you went in to take a shower. I told her you were sick and it wasn't a good time."

"So you told Gwen she couldn't come in?"

"Absolutely." Margo nodded proudly. She didn't try to hide it nor was she ashamed to admit it. "And it's a good thing too. By the time I got back upstairs you were on the floor, white as a ghost."

"Yes, but..." Leigh had to admit she probably wouldn't have let them in either. "Gwen was a little upset is all. Her client flew in from L.A. I guess."

"I don't care. You were in no shape to have strangers roaming around your house. She'll get over it." Margo waved as the women drifted out of the store, flashing one of her dimpled smiles at them.

"I understand you know her from some past real estate dealings, right?" Leigh knew that sounded like a leading question.

Margo chuckled and moved to the counter, occupying herself with busy work.

"I'm sorry, Margo. That was none of my business."

"I'm sure you can guess what kind of real estate dealings we had."

"The warehouse?"

"I told her the same thing I told you. I'm not interested in selling it. She had a little trouble accepting that."

"She's very dedicated to her work. But yes, she can be a little pushy."

"Look, I'm sorry. I might have been out of line but I didn't want anyone bothering you while you were sick."

"I could have just stayed out of the way."

"Sitting in a chair while they looked in every closet and cupboard in your house?" Margo raised a suspicious eyebrow. "That's why I didn't let them in. You needed to be in bed, resting. Not acting congenial." The telephone in the back room rang, snapping Margo's head around.

"Is everything okay, Margo?"

"Sure, everything's fine," she said but with a distracted look on her face.

"Everything is okay with Lindsey, isn't it? The nurse said she might have a little fever from the flu vaccine."

"She's a tough kid. She's fine." She looked away then like a chameleon, her face changed, pensive frown became a timid smile. "Do you have plans this evening? I mean, is Gwen going to show the cabin or something?"

"Tonight? No, she isn't showing it this evening."

Before she could ask why, a customer came in and, asking for her help, went directly to the thermal sock display. Leigh occupied herself with the glove display while Margo gave advice on the best socks for skiing and then finally rang up the sale.

"Say, how about I repay your kindness by taking you to dinner?" Leigh said, once the customer had left.

"I can't. We're open until nine and Karen's off today so I'm minding the store. But thanks."

"I assume you know she idolizes you. You're her hero."

"Me?" Margo chuckled as if to hide her embarrassment.

"Yes, you. You and that woman on the ski poster," Leigh said, pointing to the poster on the wall behind the counter.

Margo gave another little chuckle.

"It's true. She wants to grow up to ski just like that person."

"Didn't she tell you?" Margo gave the poster only a cursory glance.

"Tell me what? Who is it?" Leigh studied the skier's athleticism and grace although the racing helmet and goggles obscured all facial features.

"It's me."

"You?" Leigh exclaimed, going behind the counter to get a closer look.

"Publicity shot for ski equipment. I cut off the ad at the bottom."

"Wow. How old were you?" She stared up at it in amazement.

"Twenty-two." Margo continued to fold and arrange things as if the poster were no big deal.

"I bet you were a very intense twenty-two-year-old."

"I was like every other twenty-two-year-old. Naïve and confident." Margo heaved a reflective sigh then changed the subject. "So, you're feeling better?"

It was an awkward transition but Leigh didn't question it. She would leave that for another day, like Margo's reason for keeping the warehouse.

"Yes, I am."

Margo began to say something else when a young couple came through the door.

Leigh waited for an opportunity then said, "Thanks again, Ms. Tosch. I better get back to work."

"You're welcome," she replied, her eyes falling softly on Leigh's. "I'll talk with you later."

Leigh reached for the door but looked back, sorry she hadn't been able to say everything she wanted to say. If she had embarrassed Margo, she wanted to fix it. "I should probably apologize. Some of what happened the other day should be taken with a grain of salt. Because of the flu, I wasn't really with it."

"No problem," was all Margo said, keeping her attention on her customers.

Leigh wasn't sure what she expected but Margo's indifference was disappointing. They did share a kiss, albeit short and dispassionate. It had to be the fever that had Leigh reading too much into that kiss. She was halfway down the block when she turned around, ready to go back and ask Margo why she had kissed her in the first place but Maureen's call to her cell phone stopped her.

"Hi, Maureen," she said, standing on the sidewalk, staring at the Polar Bear sign.

"There you are. I was so worried when you didn't answer. I've been trying to get a hold of you for two days. I was ready to call the Aspen police." Maureen sounded anxious.

"I'm sorry, honey, but I've had the flu."

"Oh heavens, you're kidding. Are you still in bed?"

"No, I'm better. Just a little cough. I'm sorry you were worried."

"Worried isn't the word for it." Maureen gave a loud and relieved sigh.

"Anything going on at the office I should know about?"

"Nothing we can't handle. You just get yourself well. That flu can be devastating."

"I'm much better, Maureen. Really. What's going on?"

"Nothing major." Leigh could hear her rustling through paperwork. "Jeremy Payson has decided he wants pre-nups." Maureen rattled off several items but Leigh's mind wasn't on work. But on the feel of Margo's lips against her own, fever or no fever. What were her intentions? She had no idea but it was hard not to drown in the memory of it. "And there's the zoning commission meeting. You'll be here for that, right?" Maureen said in conclusion.

"Yes, absolutely." Leigh had almost forgotten about the commissioners meeting. That was very unlike her. "Wednesday, right?"

"No, Monday. I sent you the reminder. It was in the email with the building code revisions."

Where was my mind? I can't believe I forgot that.

"Yes, I remember now." That meant she would have to head back to Denver the day after tomorrow. She never thought she'd regret having to return home. It had nothing to do with the long drive or the mountain of work awaiting her at the office. It was quite something else.

She cast one last look at the sign hanging over the door to Margo's shop then headed to her car. She had work to do. Revisiting a momentary kiss wasn't going to help get that done. As much as she wanted to know Margo's motives, Leigh ignored her curiosity to concentrate on work.

Leigh spent the rest of the day immersed in contracts, proposals and emails. She occasionally stood at the door to the deck, watching the birds eat from her feeder, while her coffee reheated in the microwave. She allowed herself those precious few moments to relive lying in Margo's comforting arms. Why had Margo kissed her? Because she could? Because Leigh was vulnerable and Margo wanted to try out her moxie?

"You've got me way confused, mountain woman." She sipped her coffee as she went back to her desk to answer her cell phone. Leigh felt a flutter when she saw it was Margo's name on the screen. She couldn't hide a pleasant curiosity.

"Sorry about the customers. It got pretty crazy."

"That's okay. I didn't want to interrupt."

"I wanted to ask you something but you ran off before I got up the nerve." There was a nervous tightness in Margo's voice.

"What's that?" Leigh asked, smiling to herself at Margo's stammering.

"I know you have lots of work to do and all but if you had a little spare time I thought maybe you'd like to go out to dinner with me. I'll understand if you're busy and don't want to." Margo sounded like she was braced for rejection.

"Sure, I'd love to," Leigh said. Last week she might have accepted, knowing she had a long list of questions about the warehouse. That wasn't the case now. She was accepting for personal reasons, reasons not even clear in her own mind. "When?"

"Great. Tomorrow evening. I'll pick you up about six?" she asked cautiously.

"I can meet you someplace," Leigh offered although the idea of actually being picked up and taken out to dinner was a pleasant thought. It had been over a year since anyone offered to pick her up for a date. For that matter, it had been months since she had a date that didn't involve a briefcase and file folders.

"I'll pick you up. Do you like barbecue or Italian?" Margo asked, her voice now eager with anticipation.

"Whatever you and Lindsey like is fine with me."

"How about I surprise you then?"

"Sounds good to me."

"I'll be there around six. Got to go. Customers in the dressing rooms."

"See you tomorrow, Margo, and thanks. I'll look forward to it."

"'Bye, Leigh," she said softly and hung up.

Maybe the kiss did mean something after all.

Chapter 16

Leigh spent the day working, or at least trying to work. Margo's invitation to dinner had her mind too fragmented to concentrate. At five she went up to shower and change—she didn't know if Margo was punctual or not. There were a lot of things Leigh didn't know about Margo. She knew she was a hard-working mother of a cute well-behaved six-year-old. She was kind, honest, caring and, in spite of her flannel shirts and thermal long underwear, was an attractive woman with dazzling eyes and a melting smile. That was enough to accept a dinner date.

Leigh pulled on a black turtleneck sweater and gray dress slacks. She hung a gold chain around her neck and gold earrings that sparkled through the locks of her hair. There was a fresh dusting of snow on the driveway but she wore her tall dress boots anyway. Yes, Margo would probably be in jeans but Leigh wanted to look nice. She checked her looks in the bathroom mirror one last time before bouncing down the stairs to wait, confident in her professional attire. Six o'clock came and went. So did six thirty with no sign of Margo. Leigh paced the living room, checking her watch every few minutes. She was beginning to think she had been stood up when she heard the distant sound of an engine. She opened the front door as Margo's red pickup truck pulled into the drive.

"Hi," Margo said, climbing out. "Sorry I'm late. Last-minute very demanding customer." She smiled brightly, dissolving Leigh's anger. "So are you ready for some dinner?"

"Sure. I was beginning to think I misunderstood you."

"No, you weren't. You were beginning to think I stood you up. And I don't blame you. I just couldn't say no to a seven-hundred-dollar sale."

Margo followed Leigh inside while she got her coat and turned off the lights.

"Can I ask where we're going?" Leigh said, slipping into her gloves as she headed out to the truck.

"Grizzly's." Margo opened the passenger's side door, offering Leigh a hand up into the seat. "Careful. The step is slick."

Leigh took her hand just as she felt her foot slip slightly. Margo quickly moved to catch her, clutching her close.

"You should be wearing your snow boots, counselor," she said, their faces just inches apart. Margo took a whiff of Leigh's neck. "Hey, I like that. What is it?"

Leigh didn't pull away. She was mesmerized by the way the waning evening light danced in Margo's eyes.

"It's called Vanilla Magic," she said, her hand braced against Margo's chest. "Vanilla, lavender and eucalyptus body wash. I don't want to offend my clients so I don't wear perfume."

"I like it very much." She drank in another long sniff. "And you don't offend me at all." She smiled shyly then helped Leigh into the cab. She waited for her to get settled then closed the door.

"By the way, where's Lindsey tonight? At Wendy's?" Leigh expected her to be waiting in the truck, dressed in her favorite pink parka. Leigh had dropped a bedazzled elastic bracelet in her purse she thought Lindsey might like to have.

"She's at a sleepover. You like barbecue?" Margo said, steering through the ice ruts as she pulled away.

"I like about anything." Leigh grabbed the handle above the window as she was thrown back and forth in the seat. "Well, almost anything."

"How about squirrel?" Margo shifted through the gears as she reached the road.

"Ah, no. Not squirrel." She grimaced at the thought. "Or turtle or frog legs or mountain oysters. None of the rustic delicacies." *If that was her idea of culinary charm this was going to be an interesting evening.*

Margo hung her wrist over the steering wheel and chuckled. "Me neither."

"I'm so glad. Where is this Grizzly's? I guess I haven't been to it yet."

"Most tourists have never heard of it. Great food as long as you don't need marble floors and fancy chandeliers. The Hollywood crowd that comes to ski Aspen wouldn't like it. That okay with you?" Margo looked over at her expectantly.

"Sure. I don't need marble floors and fancy chandeliers." *If that's the case I bet Gwen has never been to Grizzly's.*

Instead of turning toward town, Margo turned south, away from the hustle and bustle of touristy downtown Aspen. It was a good ten minutes before she turned in to the parking lot next to a long wood-framed building nestled into a stand of tall pine trees. A blinking sign over the door read Grizzly's Den. The graveled parking lot was only partially plowed and filled with pickup trucks and SUVs. A row of three snowmobiles were parked next to the door.

"Don't judge a book by its cover, counselor," Margo said, seeming to notice the curious look on Leigh's face.

"Oh, I'm not." *Yes, I am.*

Margo took Leigh's arm, helping her over the ridges of snow. Inside was just what Leigh had imagined. Dim lighting, neon beer signs over the bar, beam posts and plank ceiling, wooden tables and chairs. What she didn't expect were the grizzly bear pelts, antique mining equipment and stuffed animal heads covering the walls. A wild turkey, its wings spread to nearly six feet wide, stared down at them as they entered as if ready to attack.

"Oh, my," Leigh gasped, startled at the mounted creature. "Is that real?"

"Yeah, isn't it magnificent?" Margo led the way to an available booth, waving at the man behind the cash register.

No wonder it's called Grizzly's, Leigh thought. That guy looks like Grizzly Adams.

"Hi, Margo," the waitress said cheerfully, setting two glasses of water on the table. "Do you need a menu?"

Leigh said yes the same moment Margo said no.

"Yeah, go ahead. Bring them, Noreen. This is her first time."

"Welcome to Grizzly's," she said politely.

The menu was a single sheet of paper, handwritten and photocopied. The choices were basic. Barbecued ribs or chicken, steak or hamburgers. From the orders being delivered to nearby tables, Leigh could see everything came as a large portion, with heaping side orders that included such things as french fries, hash browns, baked beans or potato salad. She had planned on ordering something healthy for dinner but Grizzly's didn't offer a lighter fare.

"What's good?" she asked, scanning the paper.

"Everything, but I come here for the barbecue," Margo said, pointing to the dinner special at the top of the page.

"Papa Bear portion is nine ribs, corn on the cob, fries and honey dipped rolls," Leigh read. "Mama Bear portion is six ribs. Baby Bear is three." Wow, that sounds good, she thought.

"What can I get you?" the waitress asked. She was dressed in jeans, cowboy boots and a blue polo shirt with a huge paw print on the back.

"Would you like me to order for us?" Margo asked without sounding pushy. "Or do you know what you'd like?"

"What are you having?" Leigh had no idea, although the platter of something going by looked and smelled delicious.

"We'll have two mama bears with sweet potato fries and cob corn. Dipping sauce on the side." She looked to Leigh for agreement. "Is that okay with you?"

"Ribs?" Leigh asked, her mouth already watering. "Yes, sounds good."

"And to drink?" the waitress asked, not taking notes.

"Two drafts," Margo said then thought better of it. "I'm sorry, counselor. Would you rather have ice tea or something?"

"Light beer is fine for me." Leigh wasn't much of a beer drinker. It made her belch.

"You won't like it," Margo whispered. "They carry Aspen Dark Lager on tap. It's really good with barbecue."

"Okay, I'll have that if you say so." It felt good to have someone looking out for her.

The waitress brought their drinks in frosted mugs along with a wooden bowl of pretzels. Margo took a long slow draw on her beer, her eyes on Leigh over the top of her mug.

"You look nice, counselor," she finally said.

"Thank you." Leigh blushed, not at the comment but at the way Margo's gaze seemed to undress her. "You know, you could call me Leigh. Counselor seems awfully formal. And we aren't in a courtroom."

"Aren't we? So you aren't still judging me?"

"Judging you? No. I'm not judging you. Why do you think that?"

"Maybe not now but admit it, you have been. From that first day on the side of the road in the blizzard, you have been making assumptions about me."

"I have not," she replied defensively. Margo raised an eyebrow. "Well, maybe a little," Leigh recanted. "But not anymore. I wouldn't have let you in my house while I was sick if I still was."

"Good point, counselor." She saluted with her mug. "And I probably owe you an apology for the way I behaved that day I caught you trespassing. I didn't mean to sound like such a bitch."

"I had it coming. I trespassed on private property and damaged your electrical system. I could have started a fire."

"I appreciate your not hounding me about selling it. I've had people who just wouldn't take no for an answer. I've had to practically throw them out of my store."

Damn, there goes my crack at bringing that up.

"How long have you owned it?"

"Awhile." She diverted her stare, playing with the pretzels in the bowl.

"What kind of plans do you have for it?" Leigh guessed she had something in mind for it, even if it was just a pipe dream.

Margo took a deep breath, as if preparing herself for an answer.

"Believe me, I'm not judging you, whatever it is," Leigh added.

"Aspen is a booming tourist spot. Condos are going for six figures that are no bigger than a pup tent. I could make big bucks turning it into high-end apartments but that's not what I want to do." She hesitated, scrunching her mouth and looking up, as if testing Leigh's reaction to what she was about to admit. "I know it sounds stupid but I want to turn it into low-income housing. I want to make one-and-two bedroom apartments for locals who can't afford the high prices a resort town creates. People like Wendy. Hell, she can barely afford her taxes, let alone repairs to that shit hole she's forced to live in. She's lived there for forty years because she can't afford anything else. When you have developers come in, buying up the prime real estate and turning it into luxury condos, it means there are fewer and fewer places locals can afford. The high demand for property has prices up so high most Aspen natives can't afford to live here."

"You mean like the three hundred dollar a night rentals overlooking Aspen Mountains," Leigh said, remember the cost of her hotel room.

"Exactly. Big city developers come up here waving big money around. It's hard to say no. Desperate people in desperate times. First thing you know an apartment building is torn down and a resort condominium goes up. We can't keep driving away the local residents. It affects our tax base, our education system and the employment reservoir."

Leigh was impressed. She didn't expect Margo to sound like a savvy economist but she seemed to have a keen business awareness of the real estate market in a resort environment. She also sounded passionate about her dream.

"Great goal, Margo. You mean renting only to locals who live here year round and work in Aspen?"

"Yes, or retirees on low fixed income." The more she talked the more excited she sounded. "I did some checking. The government offers financial assistance to developers willing to create low-income dwellings. That building could yield sixteen, maybe twenty units. It won't make me Midas but I could exist comfortably enough to take care of Lindsey and myself. Then she'd have it for the future. I'd create an owner's unit, two, maybe three bedrooms, couple bathrooms, best view of the mountains. Fireplace, maybe." Margo's eyes drifted off into space as she spoke, a contented smile on her face.

"Sounds like a nice place to live," Leigh said, watching Margo enjoy her vision. "Granite countertops I assume," she teased.

"You bet. Maybe a whirlpool tub for two."

"Wow, you have been giving this some thought."

"A few years ago I took an online extension class from the University of Colorado to learn how to do computer aided drafting. I wanted to know how to do those floor plans you see in magazines. I've got the whole thing mapped out right down to the elevators and laundry rooms. I know my plans aren't up to code or anything. I'd have to hire a contractor to do it right, but I wanted to have an idea of what it would look like."

"You'll need to have the zoning code checked." Leigh couldn't help but offer a little advice. This is the kind of thing she did, guiding her clients through the maze of governmental red tape and licensing.

"Yeah," she replied, heaving a sigh. She swirled the beer in her mug then took a sip, her thoughts seemingly miles away. "Someday maybe."

"Two Mama Bears," the waitress said, carrying a tray to the table. She set a platter in front of Leigh, watching for her reaction.

"Wow," Leigh declared at the huge pile of food. "And this is only the middle-size portion?"

The waitress tied a plastic bib around their necks as if that was part of the server's responsibility. A roll of brown paper towels stood on the table.

"Anything else, girls?" she asked, making room on the table for the dipping sauce and the basket of rolls.

"Anything else? I won't be able to finish this." Leigh touched her fingertip to one of the ribs and tasted it. "Oh, wow. That is good," she added dreamily then picked up her fork and began picking at the meat.

"You're not going to eat it like that, are you?" Margo asked, chewing on a bite of sweet potato.

"I thought so, why? What's wrong with the way I'm eating it, snowplow lady?" Leigh gave her a cocky grin.

Margo reached over and snatched the fork out of her hand. "You don't have anything on your plate that requires stabbing, counselor. Use your fingers. Just grab one and dig in." Margo picked up a rib and took a bite.

"I would if we were home but it's impossible to eat these without making a mess." Leigh stared down at the pile of glazed ribs, searching for a dry place to touch.

"Are you one of those prissy eaters? Everything has to be dainty and healthy? The different foods can't touch each other on the plate? And you only eat half of it then complain you're stuffed?"

"No." Leigh chuckled to herself. Margo had just described Gwen, Bev and the last two women Leigh had dated. "I'm afraid I'll get this all over me."

"So?" Margo took a bite, leaving a barbecue sauce smile across her mouth. She slowly ran her tongue over her lips, drinking it in. "It's good and it'll wash off."

Leigh looked around at the other tables. Many of the diners were elbow deep in barbecue ribs or chicken. A young couple in the corner were licking it off the other's fingers with seductive looks and giggles. Leigh never thought of barbecue as erotic food. Oysters, maybe. Chocolate-dipped strawberries. Candlelit steak dinner with an extraordinarily expensive red wine. Yes. Ripping gooey meat morsels from rib bones with her teeth, no. But there was something about Margo's tongue curled at the corner of her mouth, flicking off the last drop of sauce that completely captivated her. And Margo seemed to know it. She took another bite, repeating the sultry dance of her tongue over her upper lip.

"Yes, well," Leigh gasped, feeling a rush of libido. "I guess I can try one."

"Atta girl. Try dipping it in the sauce." She demonstrated.

Leigh held a rib between her index fingers, curling the rest of her fingers out of the way as she took a bite.

"Mmmmmm," she moaned, savoring the sweet flavor. "Oh, Margo!" she exclaimed, her eyes wide. "That's good."

"Told ya." She winked then dipped again, sucking the sauce off the end of the rib bone then grinned. She drank the last of her draft, leaving barbecue sauce fingerprints on the handle of the mug.

"Would you like mine? I'm not much of a beer drinker."

"No, thanks. I only drink one."

Leigh took another bigger bite, securing her grip on the rib and moaning softly. It was too good not to moan. She dipped and licked, moaning again.

Margo ate her dinner, watching and smiling as Leigh gobbled her way through the large ribs. Leigh gave up wiping her hands after each bite, surrendering to the animalistic style of eating.

"I bet Lindsey would like these?" Leigh said, remembering how the child gobbled down the chocolate cake.

"She can eat an entire Mama Bear order." Margo dropped her last bone in the bowl then licked her fingers before wiping them on a paper towel.

"I know it's none of my business and you can tell me to shut up but can I ask how you had her? Were you married at one time?"

"Me?" Margo gave a husky laugh. "Nope. Never been married. Never been with a man, either."

"So?" Leigh asked gently, easing her into an answer.

Margo wiped her mouth several times with the towel, rubbing hard at her cheeks to get the sauce off and seemingly to delay having to answer. Leigh sat quietly, waiting for her reply, suspecting she wouldn't get one.

"Lindsey isn't biologically mine," she finally admitted, keeping her attention on folding the dirty paper towel into a neat square. "I love her like she is but she isn't."

"Adopted?" Leigh asked warily.

Margo took a deep preparatory breath. "Yeah."

"Legally?" she added softly.

Margo's eyes rose to meet Leigh's but she didn't answer.

"An ex?" Leigh suggested.

Margo nodded once, her expression searching for Leigh's silent promise she'd keep this a secret.

"Is this ex still in the picture?"

Margo peremptorily signaled the waitress for the check, diverting herself from a response.

"Ready to go?" she asked, peeling off a section of paper towel from the roll and handing it to Leigh.

Leigh quickly wiped her hands then dug in her purse for her wallet, fully expecting to pay her half but Margo tossed her a stern look. Leigh didn't want to insult her and put her money away.

"That was excellent barbecue, Margo," Leigh said, allowing Margo to hold the door for her. "Thank you for including me into one of Aspen's little secrets."

"Next time we'll try the chicken."

Next time? She's already planning on a next time? What do I think about that? Hmmm. Yes, I can see a next time.

Margo opened the passenger's side door for Leigh, again offering her a hand as she maneuvered the ice-covered gravel in the darkened parking lot.

"Wait," Margo said, holding onto her hand and stepping closer.

Leigh felt her breath catch in her throat and a sudden twinge of anticipation. Margo was going to kiss her again. Right there in the parking lot, Margo Tosch was going to take her in her arms and kiss her. Leigh felt it with every fiber of her being and she could hardly wait. She could almost taste her soft lips, their warm suppleness devouring hers, demanding and controlling. Yes, Margo, she thought. Kiss me. Do it. I'll let you. Take me in your arms and kiss me. Leigh held her breath, turning her face up to Margo's as she moved closer, now just inches away.

"Hold still," Margo said, reaching up and touching Leigh's cheek.

Leigh wet her lips and closed her eyes, bracing herself against the open door.

"You've got barbecue sauce on your face." Margo wiped her thumb across her cheek. "There. All gone."

"Oh," Leigh said, feeling silly. "Thank you."

"What?"

"Nothing." Leigh climbed in and buckled the seat belt.

Margo waited for her to finish, then leaned in the door and whispered, "If I was going to kiss you, it wouldn't be in a parking lot." She gave her a determined look then closed the door.

Leigh was flustered, something she didn't often feel. She'd exposed her feelings to Margo and felt embarrassed for doing it. She couldn't blame this on the flu. She had feelings for this woman. Rudimentary, primitive feelings. No one had ever curled her toes by just climbing out of a truck. No one had ever taken her breath away by uttering her name. But Margo did. And all the education and degrees Leigh had earned couldn't hide that fact.

"So you plan to convert the warehouse to housing for low-income residents," she said, trying to find a subject that didn't make her crotch moist.

"Uh-huh." Margo seemed amused at her.

What is she smiling about? She can't know what I'm thinking. She can't. Not when I don't even know.

"Do you want to see the plans I've worked up? They aren't great but it'll give you an idea of what I've got in mind."

"Sure. I'd love to," Leigh said.

Margo headed into town.

Saturday night in downtown Aspen was a buzz of activity. Cars, pedestrians, twinkle lights, couples strolling the tree-lined sidewalks arm in arm. Even Aspen Mountain was speckled with lights. Margo pulled into the alley next to her store and parked in a spot marked Reserved. Leigh assumed the plans were on the computer she had seen in the back room of the Polar Bear but instead, Margo led the way up the stairs to her apartment.

"The floor plans are kind of crude but I think you'll get the idea," she said, trotting up the steps eagerly. "I concentrated the single-bedroom units on one floor so the elderly wouldn't have to put up with kids' noise. I made half of them with wider doorways and open living space so people with walkers and wheelchairs can get around."

"You've really given this a lot of thought," Leigh said, hurrying to keep up.

"Did you know eighty percent of women over seventy prefer bathtubs to showers?" She unlocked the door and flipped on the light.

"I didn't know that." Leigh smiled, watching the dedication on Margo's face as she explained her plans.

"I think I can petition the transit authority to add a bus stop on that end of Pinion." Margo dropped her coat on the chair as she headed to the desk in the living room. The computer was already on, a picture of Lindsey with a soccer ball as the desktop. Margo was bubbling with the details as she opened a series of diagrams. Leigh looked over her shoulder as she pointed out various features.

"I like the window placement," Leigh said, squinting at the screen. "Nice efficient kitchens, too."

"What do you think of this one?" Margo opened a two-bedroom unit with a small balcony off the living room.

"I like that. Is that on the south side?"

"You bet. They'll have a view of Ajax from the top floor. Those will be my top rentals. Everyone will want that view."

Leigh rested her hands on Margo's shoulders as she leaned in for a better look.

"I wouldn't mind a view like that."

"Sorry, counselor. I can't rent to you. Only low income," she teased.

"Damn. In that case I might have to quit my job." She squeezed her shoulders playfully.

"Naw, you don't have to. I'll let you look from my window." Margo spun in her chair and smiled up at her. "Anytime you want."

"I'll remember that. But why didn't you tell me you had these plans before when we were there? I would have understood. No, wait. Don't answer that. I know why. You didn't know me. For all you knew I was like Gwen. Out to get your property away from you at any cost."

"I knew you weren't like that."

Margo got up and went into the kitchen. "How about something to drink?"

"Sounds good. The barbecue was great but now I'm thirsty."

"Me, too." Margo squatted, digging in the back of the refrigerator and bringing out a bottle of wine. "Left over from the party," she said, holding it up like a trophy.

She poured two stemmed glasses and handed one to Leigh. "A toast to low-income housing." They clinked glasses then sipped.

"To your foresight and planning." They clinked again, this time sipping slowly, their eyes on each other over the rims of their glasses.

"Any more plans for me to see?" Leigh asked, needing a diversion from the flush she felt racing up her body.

"Nope, that's it." Margo opened the fireplace doors and applied a match to the logs already stacked for a fire. Within minutes it crackled to life with a soft glow. Margo snapped off the light on the desk and went to the window, sipping her wine and studying the street below. "Aspen is busy tonight. Lots of people in town."

Leigh stood by the fire, warming her back and watching Margo.

"Did I say something wrong when I mentioned Lindsey?" Leigh asked, the subject still on her mind. "I didn't mean to upset you."

"You didn't." Margo kept her eyes out the window. "Sometimes I almost forget she's not my flesh and blood."

Leigh could see Margo straighten her shoulders as if bracing herself against something she'd rather not think about.

"Margo, is there something I can do to help?"

"Nope," she replied lightheartedly. "We're fine."

Leigh came to the window, touching Margo's arm to offer reassurance. "Are you sure?"

"Yep." She looked over at Leigh. Her smile couldn't hide the glistening in her eyes that told Leigh something was wrong. Whatever it was, Margo wasn't ready to share it. Leigh could respect that. She refilled their wineglasses as Leigh stood studying the row of pictures above the fireplace.

"I've seen this photo before. This is the one of you in the poster downstairs, isn't it?" she asked, pointing to the skier cutting through deep powder.

"Uh-huh," she said, tossing another log on the fire. Then she brushed off her hands and closed the fireplace doors.

"You are one of those skiers who make people like me jealous."

"It's not hard to learn. I could teach you."

"Not me. Oh, no, not me." Leigh shuddered at the thought. "I'll watch you athletic types from the safety of the lodge."

"I could teach you," she repeated confidently.

"Thanks for the offer but I don't think so." Leigh sat down on the hearth, the fire warm against her back.

"Stand up." Margo set their wineglasses on the hearth then pulled Leigh to her feet. "First lesson." She moved Leigh to the middle of the room.

"Here? Now?" Leigh joked, allowing herself to be positioned.

"Sure. First put your feet shoulder width apart."

"Like this?" Leigh went along with it, assuming this was some kind of teasing.

"Yes. Now turn your toes inward, heels out." Leigh did, staggering a little in her high-heeled dress boots. "And now, bring your knees together as much as you can, pressing down with the inner edges of your feet."

"You're kidding, right?" Leigh giggled, the stout beer and glass of wine combining to make her a smidge giddy. "This can't be a ski position."

"Yes, it is. It's called a snowplow and it's how you stop. Tails out, tips in and press the inner edges into the snow. Basic braking technique." Margo squatted in front of her, tilting the insides of Leigh's boots toward the floor. "Keep your knees flexed. You can't do it stiff-legged."

"I thought I was flexed."

"Flex your knees. Not your back. You look like a swimmer on the starting block."

"I feel like a clown in the circus." Leigh giggled as she teetered back and forth in the stance.

"Don't stick your butt out so much." Margo couldn't keep from chuckling.

Leigh tucked her hips under but felt herself falling backward.

"Hang on there, Susie Chapstick." Margo grabbed her around the waist to keep her from falling. Leigh lunged forward, knocking Margo to the floor.

"Oops." Leigh caught her heel on the rug and fell on top of her, her right boob landing in Margo's face. Leigh quickly rolled off, blushing with embarrassment. "Sorry, Margo. I didn't mean to do that." She couldn't stop giggling.

"I was kind of hoping you did," Margo said, pulling a half grin as she lay flat on the floor. She tugged at Leigh's hand, keeping her from climbing to her feet. "You want to try it again?"

Leigh looked down at her. She wasn't sure if it came from the fireplace or from this woman lying prone before her but she felt a warm glow. Leigh could also see the imprint of Margo's nipples through her sweater. They looked like pencil erasers. She couldn't take her eyes off them.

"Um, no, I," she stammered, her breaths quickening. She tried to pull away but Margo squeezed her hand, easing her closer.

"Second lesson," Margo said softly, drawing Leigh's face to within inches.

"What's that?" Leigh found herself asking mindlessly.

"Never argue with your instructor." With that Margo laced her fingers around the back of Leigh's head and brought it down to meet her lips, kissing her gently.

Leigh heard a deep guttural groan. It was her own. Margo had found that animalistic need trapped inside Leigh and had released it. The taste of Margo's lips was a tonic for the mundane, workaholic life Leigh had draped around herself. Margo didn't wear a business suit or drive a luxury sedan. She didn't conduct conference calls or hold board meetings. But she had a magic touch Leigh was powerless to ignore.

"What are you doing?" Leigh whispered, gasping for breath.

"Third lesson, counselor," Margo replied, kissing her again as she rolled her over, covering Leigh's body with her own. Her hand drifted down Leigh's sweater, forming over one of her breasts. In an instant her hand was under the sweater, her fingers massaging Leigh's nipple.

"Oh, God, Margo," Leigh moaned. Her eyes rolled back and her breath caught in her throat. She clamped her hand over Margo's, holding it against her breast. "Don't do that unless you mean it."

"I mean it, sweetheart. I definitely mean it," she replied, massaging her palm over Leigh's swollen nipple.

Leigh looked into her eyes. She never thought she would say it or feel it, but she knew she would surrender unconditionally to this woman.

"Show me," she uttered.

Margo kissed her again, her tongue gliding into her mouth so gently it felt like warm velvet. Her fingers found the bra hook nestled between Leigh's breasts and released it then pushed up her sweater and took one of her nipples in her mouth. Leigh fumbled her hands up under Margo's sweater, searching for her bra hooks, but Margo stopped her, gently forcing her arms to the floor.

"No," she whispered, kissing down her neck. "Not this time. I want this to be all about you and just you. Let me make love to you." Her words floated through Leigh and warmed her more than the wine. No one had ever made her pleasure a priority. It was always reciprocal. She wasn't sure how to react but Margo's gentle touch and generous caresses soon showed her she had nothing to fear. Margo slipped Leigh's sweater over her head, her hands smothering and warming her skin as she moved from one nipple to the other.

"Whoa," Leigh moaned, closing her eyes and arching her back as she felt her nipples harden. "Those are definitely connected to something."

Margo reached over and dipped one finger in her wineglass then drew it around one of the erect nipples, leaving a red stain on it. "How about now?"

"Oh, yes," she could barely say. "That tingles."

Margo licked it off then did the same to the other one. She then kissed Leigh on the mouth, the sweet taste of wine on her tongue. Leigh hooked a leg over Margo's ankle, pulling herself closer. Leigh didn't know how or when it happened but she felt the zipper on her slacks open and Margo's hands guiding them down over her hips. Margo drew kisses down Leigh's stomach as she unzipped and peeled away her dress boots. All that was left was Leigh's panties, something her mind was already imagining Margo's fingers removing. But instead, Margo ran a fingertip along the elastic, teasing and tugging at it but leaving the lacy panties in place. Leigh felt herself arching, her body begging for the feel of Margo's hand inside her panties, probing and searching. But Margo moved up, massaging and playing with her breasts, molding, holding, sucking at them until Leigh ached with a need deep inside.

What are you waiting for? I'm ready. Take me. Please, take me.

Margo moved down her body, licking and kissing first one side then the other. Her hands stroked up and down on Leigh's legs, roaming tantalizingly closer and closer to her inner thigh. Leigh felt her insides pulsing, crying out to be touched. Margo slid down, positioning herself between Leigh's knees, her kisses and tongue now dancing over her knees and calves while her hands stroked the soft skin of her outer thighs.

Leigh could barely keep her hips on the floor as a fire began to smolder deep inside. She folded an arm over her eyes as she groaned with the expectation of what was to come and her need for it. Finally Margo gripped the waistband of Leigh's panties in her teeth and slowly peeled them down.

Leigh's defenses were gone. Any bashfulness she once felt had been replaced by lust, pure and simple. She wanted to feel Margo's mouth on her, her hands caressing places only a lover could find.

"Oh, please," she moaned, rolling her hips up to Margo's hot breath.

Margo didn't make her wait. She took her in, her tongue plunging deep into Leigh's sweetness. Margo seemed to know Leigh's body without being told. Her tongue drew a delicate path through every secret place, circling and stroking until Leigh was ready for her to move on, saving the best for last. Margo blew hot breath on Leigh's swollen nub, sending a shiver through her then took her in her mouth. Leigh drew a deep breath then groaned as her body shuddered. She reached for Margo, pulling her tighter against her clit as it began to throb.

"Don't stop, baby. Please don't stop," she gasped, her words gurgling up from the pit of her stomach.

Margo's tongue became hard, piercing through her, sending shock after shock. Leigh felt her legs begin to twitch uncontrollably, pulsing with each shockwave. She didn't think it was possible to feel anything more intense then Margo softened her tongue, sucking hard on her tenderness, tugging at it until Leigh could stand it no more and screamed out as an orgasm rolled through her, starting in her back and pushing its way up to her clit, erupting like a volcano.

"Yes, yes, yes," she screamed, unable to hold onto her dignity a moment longer.

Leigh had never felt an orgasm so deep and so profound. She had never experienced a second orgasm either. She often felt lucky to have one but as Margo continued to tease and suck, another began to build, just as intense as the first. Then another.

"Enough," Leigh finally gasped, barely able to breathe as her body twitched then fell limp on the floor.

Margo crawled up next to her, her strong arms folding around her, silently comforting her as she regained her senses. Leigh felt every last ounce of energy drain from her body. She snuggled into Margo's embrace as she released a long satisfied sigh.

"That was incredible," she whispered.

"You are incredible." Margo pressed her lips to Leigh's forehead.

Did Leigh hear a quiver in her voice? At this moment she was too relaxed and content to deal with it. If Margo was sorry for what they did, Leigh didn't want to know it, at least not now.

Chapter 17

"I'm really sorry, Leigh," Margo said, holding the passenger's side door for her.

"Don't worry about it. Really."

"I feel stupid taking you home so late at night. We're like teenagers sneaking in after curfew."

Leigh slid in then smiled up at her and said, "I don't. I had a wonderful time. And I understand completely. You have a job."

"I should have told Frank no when he called."

"Absolutely not. What kind of date would I be if I didn't respect your responsibilities? He wouldn't have called you this late if it wasn't important. Besides, I have work to do in the morning too."

"You're sure you don't mind?"

"For the third time, I don't mind. Now get in and take me home." She patted Margo's hand reassuringly.

Margo started the truck and headed through the deserted downtown streets.

"How about I make it up to you?" Leigh said coyly.

"You? Why would you be making anything up to me? I'm the one canceling the rest of our date."

Leigh just stared at her, a quirky grin growing across her face.

"Oh," Margo said, blushing bright red.

"I owe you big time, lady." Leigh cackled devilishly which made Margo blush all the more. She placed a hand on Margo's thigh. "You aren't so tough, mountain girl. I see your ears turning red."

"No, they aren't," she stammered, rubbing them.

"They are too." Leigh pulled her arm down, lacing her fingers through Margo's.

Margo looked down at their hands, her tanned fingers entwined with Leigh's pale ones, then back out the window.

"Does this bother you?" Leigh squeezed her hand, looking for a reaction.

"No," was all she said, her eyes riveted on the road.

That wasn't exactly the reaction Leigh expected. But she sounded almost indifferent. They had just spent two hours on the floor of Margo's apartment, wrapped in each other's arms, Leigh's naked body quivering and trembling at Margo's every touch. Now she couldn't care less if Leigh held her hand or not. The mixed signals were driving her crazy.

Leigh eased her grip on Margo's hand and shifted in the seat. When she did Margo pulled her hand away and hung it over the shifter knob.

"When does Lindsey get home?" Leigh asked, looking for a less sensitive subject.

"Sunday night. It's a weekend thing." She turned up White River Road, easing over the icy ruts. "Look, Leigh," Margo started, clearing her throat. "You don't owe me anything. You know." She shrugged.

Leigh knew exactly what she meant. Margo made love to

Leigh but wasn't looking for reciprocation. Or didn't want reciprocation.

"Are you dating someone, Margo?" Leigh felt foolish she hadn't thought of this sooner. She had seduced Margo. Not consciously but she obviously had. "You are. It's Adriana, isn't it?"

"I am not dating Adriana. We ski together. That's all."

"You don't have to hide it from me. It's okay. Really."

"I'm not dating her, counselor. You've seen us together because she is one of my students. She is way too young for me." She laughed. "And way not my type."

"But I saw you with her at Tink's. You had your arm around her, laughing and holding her."

"Oh, yeah, the night of the snowball fight. We were teasing her about her new ski boots. They look like frogs. You should see them. Ugliest things I ever saw. But we're not dating."

"And I saw you dancing with her at your party."

"I like to dance but she's just a student."

"What do you mean a student?"

"I met Adriana a couple years ago. Her folks paid for private ski lessons. She is good and could be great if she'd concentrate a little more and party a little less."

"You're an instructor?"

"Yes. I have been for about fifteen years."

"When you said you'd teach me I just thought you meant you knew how to ski and would show me. Wow, a ski instructor. I'm impressed, Margo."

"It's not that big a deal. There are a lot of us ex-ski bums who give private lessons. Helps pay the bills."

"Private lessons, huh? Maybe someday I'll take you up on that offer to teach me."

"When are you going back to Denver?"

"Early Monday morning. I've got a meeting I can't miss."

"Oh," Margo said, turning her attention back on the road.

"How would you like to come to the cabin for dinner tonight? Steak, baked potato, wine?" Leigh smiled her best flirting smile. "You have to eat you know."

"Okay." She grinned sheepishly. "If you promise not to make a big deal out of it."

"Oh, I promise." But Leigh knew she would. "Now, tell me why you and Gwen Foley are mortal enemies. It can't be just because you wouldn't let her sell your warehouse. There has to be more to it than that."

"You really want to know? Okay, I'll tell you. Yes, Gwen was dying to get her grubby little paws on my warehouse. She kept saying she knew the perfect price. She'd take care of everything."

"She's very good at what she does."

"Yeah, well, she also doesn't much care how she gets what she wants. When I said no, she invited me up to her place, for dinner and an apology, she said. But she did everything but apologize." Margo pulled a crooked grin. "That woman has quite a sexual repertoire."

"You mean she seduced you?" Leigh knew Gwen had many talents but not that.

"She tried. When I said no, she took it personally. Very personally. The way she tells it, I'm a sexually frustrated over-the-hill dyke who doesn't know what to do with a gorgeous pair of taa-taas."

"Why didn't you tell her you had plans for the warehouse? She would have understood."

"I didn't think it was any of her business. She should have taken no for an answer. You did."

"Well, I have to admit I was tempted to try again."

"I'm glad you didn't." Margo pulled up to the cabin.

"Thank you for dinner." She leaned over and kissed Margo before sliding out. "Drive carefully, snowplow girl. And by the way, you absolutely do know what to do with taa-taas. Very much so." She smiled and closed the door.

Margo waited until she was safely inside before pulling away. Leigh leaned back against the front door, her ear tuned to listen until the sound of Margo's truck faded into the night. She plugged her cell phone into the jack, slipped out of her clothes and into bed, sleeping naked for the first time in years. She wanted to imagine Margo's arms around her body, holding her, protecting her. She also wanted to imagine Margo's naked body lying next to her, the heavenly musk of their lovemaking filling the room. She could hardly wait for tomorrow. She hoped Margo felt the same.

The next morning Leigh awoke early and bounced down the stairs, ready for work and for her dinner date with Margo. She knew it wasn't going to be easy but she planned an hour or two at the computer before heading into town to the grocery store. She wanted everything just so for tonight. Only the best steak and the finest wine would do. While waiting for the coffeemaker to finish dripping she noticed a voice message on her cell phone. She felt a schoolgirl flutter when she saw it was from Margo and pressed the button to play it.

Hi, Leigh. It's Margo. Thanks for the dinner invitation. I appreciate it but I'm sorry, I need to cancel. And like I said, you don't owe me anything. Have a safe trip back to Denver. Drive carefully. Gotta go.

Leigh gathered the cell phone in her hands and pressed the button to replay the message, not certain what she heard. Margo's voice sounded unrepentant as if she had no remorse over canceling their dinner.

"Was my invitation to dinner that insignificant to you?" Leigh muttered, staring at the screen. "It wasn't to me."

She pressed the button to redial Margo's number, wanting more of an explanation, but canceled the call before it could go through. Margo isn't that interested, she thought. That's the reason for the mixed signals. She didn't need a rock to fall on her to see that. Last night was casual. And she wants to leave it at that.

Okay. Done.

Leigh tossed the phone on the counter and went to work at the computer. Just after three she packed her suitcase and headed back to Denver. She had no reason to stay another night and go back in the morning. She had work to do at the office, she told herself. And thank goodness. It would take her mind off Margo and what was left unfinished between them.

Chapter 18

It was Tuesday morning when Maureen tapped on Leigh's office door then opened it. She was a tall woman, several inches taller than Leigh. In her fifties, she dressed professionally, often in understated suits and dresses that she accented with a necklace here or a pin there. Today she wore a berry-colored pantsuit with a long strand of black and silver beads. An African-American woman with a smooth copper toffee complexion, she usually wore red lipstick, her signature color. Her hair was short and jet black but for a small patch of gray at each temple. Maureen was a quiet woman by nature. She was a calming and efficient force in Leigh's life, one Leigh had learned to rely on.

She stepped inside and said, "When you've got a minute, there's someone here to see you."

Leigh finished the sentence she was composing on the computer as she said, "Okay. Who is it?"

"Margo Tosch." Maureen said it curiously, watching Leigh for a reaction.

"Margo? Here?" Leigh sprang to her feet and followed Maureen into the outer office unable to hide a giddy anticipation.

Margo was standing at the corner of Maureen's desk fiddling with an azalea plant. She was dressed in slacks, ski sweater with the sleeves pushed back and down vest. At first Leigh assumed it was a social visit, perhaps an apology for canceling their date or perhaps a better explanation. But when Margo looked up Leigh knew something was wrong. There was no sparkle in her eyes and no dimpled grin. Just a deep furrow across her forehead and a frightened stare.

"Hello, Ms. Tosch," Leigh said with a bright smile, offering a handshake. "Nice to see you again. What brings you to Denver?"

"Have you got a minute?" she asked, swallowing hard. "I need to talk to you."

"Sure. Come on in my office." Leigh looked back at Maureen and gave her the hold-my-calls nod. "Can I get you some coffee? Tea?" Leigh asked, motioning Margo toward the chair at the end of her desk.

"No, thank you." Margo pulled a folded document from her inside vest pocket. "I've changed my mind. I want to sell the warehouse." She spread the papers open, smoothing the creases. "I don't need it."

Leigh had barely sat down. Margo's words took her completely off guard.

"You what? Why? I thought you wanted to convert it to apartments."

"No, I want to sell it. Right away." She pushed the document across for Leigh to see. "Here's the deed. The property tax statement and the survey report are in there too. It's all legal. I'm the sole owner. You said you had a buyer for it. I'm willing to accept a little less than market value for a cash purchase. You can call your buyer and tell them the deal's on. Maybe we can get things cleared up this afternoon."

Leigh almost chuckled at Margo's eagerness. Surely she didn't think selling commercial property was like buying a used car. And why now? Why sell it after all the plans and dreams she had made for it.

"Margo, I'm sorry but I don't understand. Why would you want to sell it? What happened to make you change your mind?"

"Nothing. Nothing happened. I just want to sell it." Margo bit down on her lip. "Go ahead. Call the buyer. I'll wait."

"First of all, I don't have a buyer."

"But you said you did." Margo sounded disappointed.

"My client is currently in negotiation over another piece of property in Steamboat Springs. She no longer has interest in Aspen property."

"Steamboat Springs? Why there? Aspen is a better investment. We have year-round tourism. Steamboat Springs doesn't," she argued. "This is prime location, Leigh. You saw it."

"I'll be glad to keep your property in mind but I'm sorry. I just don't have anyone looking for that kind of investment right now. Once we get past the holidays things might turn around."

"That's two months. I don't want to wait two months. I can cut my price. Thirty percent under market value. How's that?" Margo leaned forward in her chair as if expecting that to make a difference.

"Relax, Margo." Leigh studied Margo's face, wondering what had her so upset. "I don't have anyone ready to jump but I'm not sure this is a good idea anyway." Leigh leaned back in her desk chair, resting her elbows on the arms. "I think there is something you're not telling me. Why are you ready to sell your inheritance when a few days ago you were bubbling with enthusiasm over the prospects for the future?"

"Look, I want to sell it. That's all you need to know," she said sternly. "If you don't have a buyer, I'll find one someplace else. Gwen always wanted a crack at it. Maybe I'll let her list it."

"And lose over six percent to her commission?" Leigh didn't know what had happened but this was definitely not the Margo who held her in her arms and made love to her. This wasn't the happy-go-lucky mountain woman with the tender touch and gentle nature. "Margo, what's wrong? Tell me. Let me help. Do you need money? Is that it?"

"No, I need to sell my property," she said and launched herself to her feet and stormed out of Leigh's office.

"Margo, wait," Leigh said, hurrying after her. "Talk to me."

But Margo sprinted to the elevator, slipping inside just as the doors began to close.

"Damn it," Leigh said, arriving a moment too late. "Margo!" she called as the elevator started down. "Come back here." She rested her forehead against the closed doors, exasperated at herself for the way she handled that. "Margo, I want to help," she whispered. "Come back and talk to me."

"Ms. Insley," Maureen said softly, placing a hand on Leigh's shoulder.

Leigh looked up. The other secretaries were all staring at her as if she had just lost her mind. Bev had stepped out of her office and was glaring at her as well. Leigh straightened her posture, regaining her composure. She returned to her office and closed the door.

She remained cloistered in her office, hoping that if she threw herself into her work thoughts of Margo and whatever was bothering her wouldn't surface. Halfway through an afternoon meeting Leigh was so consumed with why Margo suddenly changed her mind about selling that she completely lost her train of thought, muttering something incomprehensible about construction licensing fees.

What did I say? Booty buildings? Oh, good grief. Get your brain back on business.

But that wasn't happening. She finally gave in and called Margo's cell, hoping to convince her to come back to the office or at least meet her for dinner. The call went to Margo's voice mail.

"Hi. It's me," she said, hoping she didn't sound too formal. "Margo, please call me. Let's talk about this. Maybe we could meet for dinner. Tell me where you're staying and I'll find a quiet place where we can talk. I truly want to help." Leigh wanted to use a term of endearment; baby, sweetheart, something, but it was clear Margo didn't share that attachment.

"Anything I can do?" Maureen asked with a benevolent look on her face. She stood at the corner of Leigh's desk.

"No," Leigh replied, placing the receiver on the cradle. "I'm finished with the Graham's Trust. Charlie can come in and sign it." She pushed the folder to the edge of the desk.

"That's not what I meant and you know it." Maureen picked up the folder and tucked it under her arm as if dismissing its importance. "What's going on? You haven't been yourself since that Margo Tosch was here this morning. Is everything okay?"

"Yes, everything is fine." She heaved a sigh then forced a smile up at Maureen. "But thanks for asking."

"She seems very nice." Maureen was fishing. "Is she one of your Aspen friends?"

"Margo owns the property Helen Vick was interested in but I think you already knew that."

"I thought you said she didn't want to sell it. Isn't that why we placed the offer on the vacant motel property in Steamboat Springs?"

"She won't tell me why but now she wants to sell it. And I have a feeling she doesn't completely agree with the reason. Maureen, you should see the plans she had for that building. She was like a kid with a new toy. She doesn't really want to sell it. I know she doesn't. But I'm afraid she's going to sign on the dotted line then there will be no turning back. Once she sells it, it'll be gone and with it, her dreams."

"Then why sell it?"

"I have no idea." She spun in her chair to gaze out the window at the snow-covered Rocky Mountains to the west of Denver. "But I sure wish she had told me."

"Maybe you should call her."

"I did." Leigh looked back at Maureen with a calculated frown. "Can you reschedule my appointments for the rest of the week?"

"Sure." Maureen studied her for a long moment. "What are you going to do?"

Leigh turned back to the desk and began shutting down her computer.

"I'm going to do what I wasn't smart enough to do today. Get Margo to tell me why. And if I can, help her."

"So you're going back to Aspen?" Maureen smiled curiously.

"Yes, I am." Leigh went to the closet and pulled out her briefcase, coat and purse. "Call me frivolous but right now this is more important than any merger or contract." She headed for the door.

"Leigh?" Maureen called, pressing the closet door closed. "Take all the time you need, okay? This will always be here when you're ready to come back."

"Thank you, honey." Leigh smiled back at her, feeling a sense of relief that someone understood. "I'll call you," she added then headed home to pack.

It was one hundred ninety miles from her house to her cabin in Aspen. Three and a half hours, assuming there was no blizzard waiting for her. Leigh didn't have time to worry about it. She wanted to be in Aspen first thing in the morning, knocking on Margo's door and ready to listen. And if she had to, use all her legal cunning to drag the truth out of her, stubborn mountain woman or not.

Leigh stopped at her townhouse and hurriedly tossed a few things in a suitcase then headed out of town. She had just entered Clear Creek Canyon west of Denver when Gwen's call came through on her cell.

"You're going to thank me, honey," Gwen said even before Leigh could respond. "And I mean big time thank you." She squealed happily then said, "I've got a nibble. It looks good, Leigh. Really good."

"You've got a buyer for the cabin?" Leigh didn't think that news would be disappointing but it was.

"I think we are really close. They like the view, the kitchen, the square footage. They wanted a garage but are willing to work around that. I reminded them they could always build one later."

"There might be room for one, I guess." Leigh had no idea why she was being defensive. Her cabin was perfect just the way it was. At least she thought so. "I'm on my way to Aspen. I'll talk with you about it tomorrow, Gwen. Okay?"

"You're on your way back already? I thought you just went back to Denver." Gwen sounded suspicious.

"I forgot something." *Why am I fibbing to Gwen? I don't owe her an explanation.* "Let me call you tomorrow. I think I'm losing the signal." *Another fib.*

"I'll try to have a formal offer worked up."

"Okay, 'bye." Leigh ended the call then activated the Bluetooth on her steering wheel. "Call Margo's cell," she said. The number rang but again went directly to her voice mail. "Call Margo's home." That too went to voice mail. "Call Polar Bear Shop."

"Hello, Polar Bear Apparel. Can I help you?"

"Hi, Karen," she said. "Does Margo happen to be there?" She knew she probably hadn't had time to get back to Aspen but asked anyway.

"No, sorry. I haven't seen her today. Did you try her cell?"

"Yes. It went through to voice mail." Leigh didn't want to give away the reason for the call. It was Margo's business, not Karen's. "Should she be in the store tomorrow morning?"

"I hope so. She's got inventory to do. End of the month stuff, you know."

"Okay, I'll try her then."

"Be sure and wear a bulletproof vest when you talk to her. She's been on a rampage for two days. She's got a bee up her ass about something."

"Oh? What about?" This is what Leigh wanted to hear.

"I have NO idea but whatever it is, she's been a bitch about it." Karen groaned woefully.

"But you have no idea why?" *Please, give me just a little hint. Something to go on.*

"Nope, not a clue. First I thought it was just her time of the month but that isn't Margo. Stuff like that doesn't bother her."

"Did something happen at work? Something with a customer?"

"Nope. Hey, Leigh, I gotta go. I've got three customers trying on ski pants. I better go supervise. Bye-bye."

That was no help, Leigh thought. But at least Margo should be back in Aspen at the store by morning.

Leigh spent the rest of the drive through the mountains wrestling with the possible reasons Margo had a change of heart. Weather and traffic had turned the three-and-a-half-hour trip into six hours. She pulled up to the cabin just after midnight. Exhausted, she unlocked the door and fell into bed without unpacking. For the first time in months she set the alarm. Normally she wouldn't need it but she didn't want to take any chances. Tomorrow she wanted to be up, dressed and in town when the Polar Bear opened. She slept in fits and starts. She was awake, dressed and sipping her second cup of coffee by six a.m.

It was a crisp twelve degrees as she hurried along the sidewalk. During her drive into town she couldn't help wonder why she had taken on the Margo Tosch crusade. After all, she didn't know much about her. Margo had made it quite clear she didn't need rescuing. She wasn't a fragile female. But there was something behind her sun-tanned complexion and wind-tossed hair that attracted Leigh. Something about her self-confidence. Her butchy tenderness. Her uncompromising dedication. And there was definitely something about her body and the way she kissed.

"Hi, Leigh," Karen called from the counter where she was visiting with two women. They seemed to be about Karen's age and from their smiles and gestures, Leigh guessed they all knew each other.

"Hi, Karen." Leigh made a quick scan of the store, looking for Margo before joining them.

"It was awesome," Karen said, continuing her conversation with the women. "Like one of those mushy romance novels. So next thing, I texted her to let her know I arrived at the hotel." She turned to Leigh and said, "I finally got to meet her." She gave a dreamy sigh.

"Jenny?" Leigh knew she wasn't going to be helpful until she finished telling her story. Leigh would just have to wait her out.

"Yes. I was soooo nervous. And the longer I had to wait the more nervous I got. By the time she texted me back I thought I was going to throw up. So, finally she sent me this text. She says, 'Are you ready to be nervous?'"

"What did you say back?" one of the women asked anxiously.

"I said yes, I already was nervous. Then she texts right back and said, well, open the door, woman. I did and she's standing there in the hall with this incredible smile on her face."

"Oh, wow," the woman said, drinking in the romance of the moment.

Karen released a long satisfied sigh and said, "She is ten times better looking in person than her picture."

"Really?" the younger woman asked, obviously living vicariously through Karen's story.

"She was amazing." Karen stared off into space, obviously reliving that moment.

"That's terrific, Karen," Leigh said, offering momentary encouragement so she could rein her back to reality. "Has Margo come down yet?"

"She left right before you walked in. I think she had an appointment somewhere."

"Do you know where?"

"No, but she'll be back pretty quick." Karen picked up a brown envelope from the counter. "She forgot this. Said it was important papers and not to let her forget them. Well, duh! She forgot them."

Leigh was dying to know what was inside the packet. Property deed? Was Margo meeting with Gwen after all?

"I could take them to her," Leigh offered innocuously, holding out her hand.

"I'd let you but I'm not sure where she went." Karen shrugged and dropped the envelope back on the counter. "She'll be back as soon as she realizes she forgot it."

"Yes, she will," Margo said, coming through the door, a scowl on her face that grew even deeper when she saw Leigh. "What are you doing here? Come to gloat that I didn't take your advice when you first offered it?" She snatched up the envelope and turned on her heels, retracing her steps out the door.

"No, that's not why I'm here," Leigh said, hurrying to catch up with her.

But Margo didn't hold the door or wait for her. She rounded to the driver's side of her truck, double-parked in front of the store.

"Margo, wait a minute. I need to talk to you."

"I don't have time," she said, slamming the door.

Leigh grabbed the passenger side door handle just as she was ready to pull away.

"What are you doing?" Margo demanded, stomping on the brake.

"I said we need to talk," Leigh replied, climbing in.

"Look, counselor, you had your chance. But I don't need your help. I can take care of this myself." Margo reached over and opened Leigh's door to let her out. "Now if you'll excuse me, I have an appointment." A car behind them honked impatiently.

Leigh pulled the door closed and said, "You're meeting with Gwen, aren't you?"

Margo roared around the corner.

"Where did you park? I'll drop you off."

"Does this have something to do with Lindsey?" Leigh asked, studying Margo for a reply. "Is that why you need the money?"

Margo's jaw muscles flexed, her eyes darting back and forth across traffic. Leigh reached over and touched her arm.

"Let me help, Margo. I can give you a loan if you need it."

"I don't want your money," Margo snapped. "I want to sell my property. If you don't have a buyer, I'll find one."

"So I'm good enough to fuck but not good enough to confide in?" Leigh knew that was cruel but it was justifiable if it cracked Margo's stubborn refusal to admit what was wrong.

"Look, I'm sorry, Leigh. I know we started something, but—"

"Yes, we did. What happened? What did I do, sweetheart? Why the cold shoulder?"

"You didn't do anything." That seemed to be all Margo was willing to offer.

"You have to give me more than that. I can't read the mixed messages you're sending. I'm trying, Margo. I really am but I don't know what you want from me."

"I don't want anything. You don't have a buyer for the warehouse. I don't want anything," Margo replied stiffly.

"I'm not talking about the warehouse. I'm talking about us. You and me."

"I don't have time for this, counselor. There's your car." She pointed across the street at Leigh's Lexus. "We'll talk later. I'll call you."

"No. We'll talk now. You'll tell me why you make love to me one day and cancel our date the next. And you'll tell me why you're pushing me aside like snow plowed to the curb. If you don't want to date me then tell me. Be honest. I have a right to know. Don't make me regret what we did."

Margo pulled to the curb and slammed the shifter into park.

"Okay, you want to know. I'll tell you." She turned an exasperated stare on Leigh. "Yes, I need to sell the warehouse. I need the money and I need it now." Margo pulled a twenty-dollar bill from her pocket and handed it to Leigh. "Here, take this."

"Why do I want that?" Leigh pushed it back at her.

"Take it, counselor. I want to hire you. This is your retainer." She tossed it on Leigh's lap. "Tell me how much more you charge."

"You don't have to pay me to be your lawyer. I want to help as a friend, if I can."

Margo looked out the window, scanning the horizon as if deciding if she could trust her. Leigh sat quietly, waiting for her explanation.

"Lindsey's mother's name is Elizabeth Breck. I met her through some mutual friends. She was this thirty-year-old perky little bundle of fire and energy. She could ski like a pro and was the life of every party. I fell for her instantly." Margo squinted out the window as if something painful just crossed her mind. "Elizabeth didn't want any kids. She said they tie you down. But I talked her into it. I said I'd take care of everything. I'd change the diapers and feed it. I'd pay for everything." She smiled reflectively. "I was sure once she had the baby she'd change her mind and become domestic and mothering. I figured her hormones would kick in."

"And they didn't?"

Margo shook her head. "We had only been together a few months when she agreed to be artificially inseminated. It was a rough pregnancy. She was sick a lot. Throwing up, couldn't eat. I felt really bad I had talked her into it."

"That wasn't your fault. Lots of women have one rough pregnancy then the next one goes just fine."

"Yeah, I told her that. She assured me there wasn't going to be a second one." Margo hesitated as if working herself up to what came next. "Lindsey was due the first week of November."

"I thought Lindsey's birthday is in October."

"It is. She was three weeks early. She only weighed five pounds." Margo's knuckles had turned white as she gripped the shifter knob. "Her blood sugar was real low too."

Leigh had an idea she knew where this was going but didn't want to mention it. She let Margo continue.

"I didn't know it but Elizabeth had been drinking while she was pregnant. Beer, wine, whatever she could get her hands on while I was at work. She said it was the only way she could deal with it. But it was more than that. Way more. I guess I was too blind to see Elizabeth for who she really was." Margo shook her head disgustedly. "She was an alcoholic. I just didn't see it. She's what they call a functioning alcoholic."

"Drinks but can still hold onto a job."

"Yeah. I thought I was in love with her. I thought a baby would make us a family. Lindsey was born with fetal alcohol syndrome. Her poor little body had the shakes. Her electrolytes were way out of whack. That little girl had to go through detox. I felt so helpless."

"Oh, Margo," Leigh gasped, squeezing her arm. "I had no idea."

"Elizabeth insisted Lindsey's condition had nothing to do with her or her drinking. We had a big argument. I knew I didn't love her. And she didn't love me. What's worse, she didn't love the baby either. So I offered to take over guardianship and raise her. Elizabeth agreed to let me raise Lindsey if I'd pay her rent. She wanted to move to Wyoming. So we wrote up a contract. I became Lindsey's mom."

"That's why all the extra jobs, right?"

"Yes."

"You do know it's illegal to sell a child? If she is relinquishing Lindsey's temporary guardianship to you, that's one thing, but she can't sell her to you."

"I know," Margo said, lowering her gaze. "But I couldn't allow Elizabeth to take that little girl. She wasn't a good mother. She came to see Lindsey a couple times when she was little. Then I didn't hear from her for several years other than she cashed my checks. That's where Lindsey was last weekend when I said she was at a sleepover. Elizabeth was in town and wanted to see her. She brought her a bunch of toys and video games. How could I say no?"

"What happened?"

"I guess Lindsey got homesick so Elizabeth cut the visit short. That's the day I canceled dinner with you. She dropped Lindsey off at the store, filthy. Her clothes were dirty. Her hair wasn't combed. She was hungry. The only thing Elizabeth fed her was a bologna sandwich and a candy bar. Lindsey hadn't even changed her clothes. She said Elizabeth told her she didn't have to wear clean clothes if she didn't want to."

"Wow, not a mother-of-the-year candidate."

"I told Elizabeth it would be a cold day in hell before I agreed to that again. That's when she went ballistic. She blames me for turning her daughter against her. So she wants full custody. That or a full settlement as she calls it." There was a pained look in Margo's eyes. "She's got me over a barrel, Leigh. She wants a lump sum settlement or she'll take Lindsey back to Wyoming. She knows what the warehouse property is worth. I made the mistake of telling her some of the offers I had on it."

"She wants half?" Leigh suggested.

"No, she wants it all. She said it was only fair for everything she went through to have her. She considers it a trade."

"That's so illegal, Margo," Leigh scoffed, barely able to contain herself.

"I should have never let her talk me into writing our own contract. I should have gone through an open adoption agency and done it right the first time. She holds all the cards. I have no parental rights. The sheriff could show up at my door and take Lindsey and I couldn't stop him. I'd have more rights if I were a foster parent. I've got one week to have a bill of sale and cash in hand."

"I can't let you do that. I'm a member of the Colorado Bar. I can't condone Elizabeth accepting money for her daughter. And I wouldn't want you to sell anyway, Margo. You have plans for your warehouse. Dreams for the future. How can you just toss them away like this? Let me help you."

"Who am I kidding? I was never going to build apartments. I've got no business being a landlord. Hell, I live in a second-floor storeroom over a store. I don't know anything about property management or government licensing."

"But I do. I'll show you," Leigh pleaded.

"I'm selling it. Elizabeth is not taking Lindsey from me. I may not be blood, but I'm her mother. I fed Lindsey her first bottle and I changed her first diaper. In my heart she's mine."

Margo's cell phone jingled in her pocket. It was Elizabeth.

"I'm not answering it," Margo said, staring at the screen.

"Tell her you have a buyer," Leigh said confidently.

"But..."

"Tell her you have a buyer," she insisted, fixing Margo with a demanding stare.

Margo hesitated then answered it and said, "Hello."

Leigh couldn't hear the other half of the conversation but it didn't take Margo long to interrupt and say, "I've got a buyer, Elizabeth. Yes, a very good price. It'll be enough." Leigh gave her a confident nod. "I'll call you later when I have the details. No, you don't need to know the buyer's name. I told you I'll take care of it." Margo ended the call, clutching the phone in her fist. "Okay, counselor, who are you going to get to buy it?"

"I need to make a couple phone calls. Promise me you won't do anything until you hear from me."

"Today?" There was an unmistakable tremble in Margo's voice.

"Yes. This afternoon. I promise you." Leigh leaned over and wrapped her arms around her shoulders. "I'm here to help you, Margo. She's not going to take Lindsey. We won't let her. She belongs with you."

"Thank you," she uttered, barely able to speak.

Leigh had offered comfort and advice to many a desperate client without allowing her own emotions to get in the way. But the tears pillowing in Margo's eyes touched her deeply. This was not just a friend. She was more, lots more. For now, personal feelings had to be set aside. Preserving a very special mother-daughter relationship was Leigh's number one priority. Worrying about her connection with Margo would have to come later.

Chapter 19

Leigh hurried back to the cabin and went right to work, not taking a break until her cell phone chimed.

"Are you in Aspen, Leigh?" Bev demanded, her call coming just as Leigh opened an online search page.

"Yes. I came in last night." Leigh pressed the print key then moved away from the desk as the printer began spitting out paper.

"Did you forget we're meeting with Diane Nelson's team today?"

"I didn't forget. I forwarded my recommendations to her office three days ago. Diane needs to settle. Maureen has the papers. I told Diane I suggest she sign this week." Leigh paced the living room, occasionally checking the computer for incoming email.

"What the hell's wrong with you? Where's that fighting spirit?"

"I'm saving it for cases we have a chance to win. You should know this isn't one of them."

"Admit it. You bailed on Diane. Pure and simple."

"I did not bail. If you take this baby to trial you can count me out. It'll be all yours." Leigh didn't have time to argue with her. She had Margo on her mind. As far as she was concerned, this case was closed.

"It's that mountain woman who came to the office the other day, isn't it? You're sleeping with her."

"Bev, I'm only going to say this once. Keep your nose out of my business and my bedroom."

"She's not good enough for you, Leigh."

Leigh drew a deep breath. She didn't want to do this. She didn't need to defend Margo. And she wasn't going to debate her private life with an accusatory ex.

"Is there anything else, Bev? I've got work to do."

"You've got work to do here too. I don't have time to take up the slack with your clients, Leigh. You need to get your head out of the clouds and back to reality."

"I beg your pardon," Leigh bristled. "First of all, at no time have I ever asked you to take up the slack with my clients. Just because I'm in Aspen has in no way compromised my clients. I don't have to clear my work schedule with you."

"This law firm is a team, Leigh. We are all in this together."

"I don't have time for this, Bev." Leigh gritted her teeth so hard she felt her jaw pop.

"You're slipping, Leigh. You're letting your personal life affect your professional efficiency. When that happens, clients suffer."

"Normally I wouldn't reply. But how dare you challenge my professionalism? I was writing mergers while you were still cramming for freshmen finals."

"I'm just saying maybe you need some time off. Time to refocus your career. Come back to Denver, Leigh. Take a vacation. Buy a new wardrobe. Color your hair. Do something to

clear your mind and recalibrate. Sell the damn cabin and forget
about Aspen."

"You're jealous." Leigh chuckled.

"Of what? Hell, I don't want a cabin in the freaking
mountains. Give me a beach house with blue waters and tropical
breezes any day," Bev scoffed.

"You're jealous of what I found in Aspen."

"Ha! That lumberjack-looking woman? Not hardly. I assure
you there is nothing about that woman to be jealous of."

"If you aren't jealous of Margo, you should be, Bev. You
definitely should be. She's got something you'll never have."

"What's that?" she said defensively.

"Me."

Leigh hung up without waiting for a reply. For the first
time since she came to Aspen three weeks ago, she felt a sense
of clarity. Margo meant more to her than she had been able to
admit. Declaring it brought everything into focus. She loved her
more than she thought she could ever love another person. Every
unpretentious, uncomplicated and charming thing about her.
From her windswept hair and denimed wardrobe to her dazzling
smile and soft touch, Margo Tosch had captured Leigh's heart—
completely and totally. There was no denying that. Ever.

"Hello," Leigh said, instinctively answering the incoming
call.

"Hi, honey. Great news." Gwen announced smugly, bringing
Leigh back from a happy image of Margo. "I've got a bona fide
offer in hand. If you're at the cabin I'll bring it up."

"Now?" Leigh wasn't in the mood for this. Fielding offers on
her cabin was the furthest thing from her mind.

"Yes. I think you're going to like this. It's not one hundred
percent but it's damn close. I told them it was going to take a
legitimate offer to make this fly and they took me seriously."

"Gwen, I've got something else I'm working on right now.
Could this wait? How about we get together Saturday?"

"Leigh, sweetheart, this is what we've been waiting for. Why
wait? Let's get pen to paper. What do you say?"

Two weeks ago Leigh would be on her way to Gwen's office
to discuss terms. But not now.

"Gwen, I'm not sure I'm going to sell after all. I'm so sorry but this just isn't a good time for me right now."

"WHAT?!!!" Gwen shrieked. "I've got an offer, Leigh. This isn't a joke. I've got a check in my hand for earnest money. These people are serious. They want the cabin. They want to be in by Thanksgiving so they can ski the holiday. Come on now. Let's think with our business brain here. This is what you wanted."

"I know it is. I know I told you I wanted to sell it but something has come up. I've changed my mind. I'm going to take it off the market."

"You can't do that," Gwen declared. "I've done my job and you owe it to me to field this offer."

"Gwen, I know you're upset and this comes at an awkward time for you but you know as well as I do I'm within my rights as seller to remove my listing at any time. I'm willing to reimburse the brokerage for advertising expenses but I would like an unconditional release."

"We don't offer unconditional releases, I'm sorry," Gwen replied indignantly.

"That's fine. Then a conditional release will work. I have no problem with that."

"You can't sell it or even list it for six months," she snarled.

"I'm fully aware of your brokerage's exclusivity clause. But this just isn't a good time for me to sell. I've got other things on my mind right now. Besides, you're the one who thought I should keep the cabin and learn to love Aspen."

"I busted my hump to get you a decent offer and this is how you repay me? Friends don't do that." Gwen had turned ice cold, as if whatever friendship they had was directly related to the sale of Leigh's cabin.

"I'm sorry you feel that way. I was hoping you'd understand and wish me well."

"Oh, I understand. It's that woman, isn't it? Margo. She's behind this. You slept with her so she'd let you sell her warehouse?"

"Gwen, I'd suggest you not go there. For the sake of our friendship, please don't."

"What friendship? You stabbed me in the back, Leigh.

Bev was right. You've changed. You're not the consummate professional you once were."

"You've talked to Bev about me?" Leigh couldn't help but laugh. Of course they had. Why else would Bev make such caustic accusations about Margo?

"Yes, we've talked. And we agree. Margo has you thinking with your crotch. Honey, wake up and smell the flowers. Margo Tosch isn't worth it. You deserve better."

"Stop right there. I don't want to hear another word about Margo. What gives you two the right to judge me? Who I choose to date or not date is none of your business. I'll tell you the same thing I told Bev. You're jealous of Margo and well you should be. She's got more sophistication and sincerity than you've ever had. I'll be in contact with Kathy Braden in the morning about removing my listing."

"And just exactly what am I supposed to do with this check for earnest money?" Gwen demanded caustically.

"Do you really want me to tell what you can do with it, Gwen?" Leigh hung up, adrenaline pounding in her chest.

Leigh didn't have time to dwell on Gwen or on Bev's small-mindedness. They just weren't worth the bother. How had she ever thought such people's opinion mattered? Only one person's opinion mattered right now.

"Leigh?" Margo said anxiously, picking up on the first ring. "What have you got?"

"Can I come over? I've got something to show you. I think you're going to like it."

"Sure. I'll be waiting."

Margo was waiting at the top of the stairs with the door open as Leigh started up, her briefcase strap over her shoulder.

"Have you got a buyer?" Margo asked nervously. "Who is it?"

"Calm down." Leigh smiled up at her as she climbed the last few steps, hoping to calm her anxiety. She placed a hand on Margo's chest as she slipped past, kissing her on the cheek. "Is Lindsey here?"

"No. Wendy took her shopping. She already suspects something is wrong. I don't want to upset her."

"You're a good mom, Margo." Leigh opened her briefcase and took out several packets of papers. "I did some research this afternoon and I think we can get this cleared up pretty easily."

"Who's the buyer? Someone local?"

"Margo, relax. Here, sit down." Leigh patted one of the stools at the kitchen counter.

"I don't want to sit down. Show me the contract. Where do I sign?" Margo asked, sifting through the papers."

"I don't have a buyer, Margo."

"What do you mean? You said you had good news."

"I do. I made a few phone calls and spoke with a friend at CDHS, Colorado Department of Human Services."

"You what?" Margo's nostrils flared as she slapped the counter. "Who told you to do that?"

"You did, by throwing that twenty-dollar bill in my lap and saying you wanted me to be your lawyer."

"That was a joke, Leigh. I didn't give you permission to go snooping into my private life."

"Who did you think I was going to call? I'm trying to get this mess untangled for you. This is what I do. Let me help."

"I appreciate the offer but if you don't have a buyer for my warehouse, I'll find one. This is my problem. I'll take care of it."

"Why are you being so stubborn? I'm a lawyer, Margo. Nothing you tell me goes any further than right here in this room. We have attorney-client privilege. What are you afraid of anyway?"

"You can keep the twenty bucks. But I don't need a lawyer." Margo stuffed the papers back in Leigh's briefcase and draped it over her shoulder.

"You don't have to sell the warehouse. I wouldn't let you pay Elizabeth for custody of Lindsey anyway. It's against the law. What I can do is help you become Lindsey's legal guardian and if you want, her legally adopted mother. You have a hell of a good case."

"No," Margo said, opening the door as if expecting Leigh to leave.

"Don't you want legal rights to your daughter?"

"Please, I'll take care of this." Margo sank her hand in her jeans pocket and nodded toward the door.

"You're actually going to sell the warehouse and your dreams for you and Lindsey's future?"

Margo diverted her gaze as if too ashamed to look Leigh in the eye.

"If you give in to her now, what's to stop Elizabeth from doing it again in the future? How do you know she won't drain you of every last dime you have?"

"I don't care," Margo said. "If that's what it takes to keep Lindsey safe, she can have it all. Lindsey is more important to me than all the money in the world. Don't you understand that?"

"Yes, I understand that," Leigh said softly, looking up into Margo's eyes. "And that's why I want to help. Margo, listen to me. Elizabeth is an unfit mother. I can prove it in court. Her alcoholism during pregnancy proves it."

"That was six years ago."

"You said she came to see Lindsey when she was younger but not recently. Do you know where she was during that time? I'll tell you. She has four DUI arrests and served two separate jail terms on drunk driving charges. She can't keep a job. She's living with a couple of alcoholic druggies and spending the rent money you send her on booze. The authorities know all about her."

"She told me she's working for some dude ranch near Laramie."

"I'm sorry, honey, but Elizabeth is a drunk. If you give her the money for the warehouse I guarantee it will be gone in six months. The Laramie County Sheriff faxed me her rap sheet. Her next DUI arrest will put her behind bars for a long time. Alcoholics will say whatever you want to hear. Let me set up a meeting with her. She'll have no choice but relinquish guardianship to you. We can petition the court for legal custody and adoption. There will be a permanency hearing but we can demonstrate you have established a safe, healthy and loving environment from day one. For all intents and purposes, you have been and are Lindsey's mother. It's not about just the birth-mother anymore. It's about what's in the best interest of the child." Leigh stroked Margo's arm reassuringly. "They would never give Lindsey to Elizabeth. Believe me. It won't happen."

Margo stared at her, a million thoughts obviously churning in the back of her mind. She finally closed the door and went to the window, resting her hand on the frame as she looked out at the sunset.

"Let me take care of this for you," Leigh said, following her. "Elizabeth has no choice but to agree."

"There's something I haven't told you," Margo said, her eyes drifting across the horizon.

"What?" Leigh couldn't imagine there was anything else. The secrets were out. Margo's life had been stripped bare. And for that, Leigh was sorry. "What is it, sweetheart?"

"What if I told you there was something about me, something in my past you couldn't accept?"

"What do you mean? I accept you for who you are. I love you for who you are. There, I said it. I love you." Leigh stepped closer, slipping her hand into Margo's.

Margo looked down at their hands and said, "But you won't, not after I tell you." She heaved a great sigh and pulled away. "I didn't want to tell you, Leigh."

"You can tell me anything, Margo. Whatever it is, I'll understand." When Margo hesitated, Leigh added, "Why don't we wait. I'll take care of this situation with Elizabeth and we can talk about this later. How's that?"

Margo shook her head.

"Sure. One thing at a time."

"I can't let you meet with Elizabeth."

"Why not? This is a slam dunk, sweetie. She can't win. Even though your contract isn't legal, it demonstrates her intent to profit from the sale of a minor."

"It has nothing to do with the contract." Margo stiffened as Leigh moved closer.

"Would you like another lawyer? Is that it? Someone else to meet with her? I don't mind. This is probably considered a conflict of interest anyway. I'll be glad to step aside."

"Yes," she said then swallowed and said, "No. I don't want anyone else. You're the only one I trust."

"Then what is it?"

"There is something about me. Something I didn't want you to know but if you meet with Elizabeth it's going to come out. I know it is."

"I know everything there is to know about you," Leigh replied softly, swimming in Margo's big brown eyes. "Everything I need to know. The rest we'll figure out along the way."

"There is one thing I haven't told you because I'm ashamed of it. But something I have to tell you. It has to come from me. No one else." Margo drew a deep breath then looked at Leigh with a pained expression. "I did time, Leigh. I'm a convicted felon."

"For what?" Leigh chuckled. "Parking tickets?" She couldn't imagine Margo ever doing anything illegal. She had never met a kinder, gentler woman.

"Breaking and entering. And grand theft."

"Margo, that's not funny."

"I did six months of a six-year sentence. I could make excuses but the fact is I have a criminal record." Margo looked into Leigh's eyes, desperately searching for understanding. "I'm sorry. I just didn't know how to tell you. You're the most wonderful woman I've ever met. I love you so hard I can't think straight. How do I tell you I'm a convict?"

"You're serious."

Margo nodded.

"What was it you stole?" Leigh asked, almost afraid to hear the answer.

"Does it really matter?"

"It matters that you are completely honest with me. If I'm to understand this I have to know everything. What did you steal?" Leigh insisted.

"Six thousand dollars worth of ski equipment."

Leigh sat down on the couch, trying to reconcile Margo's words.

"I know what you're thinking, Leigh."

"No, you don't," she said quietly.

"You're disappointed. You feel betrayed. And I don't blame you."

"That's not what I'm thinking." Leigh swallowed back the quiver she felt rise in her voice. "This isn't about disappointment. It's about trust, Margo. If you truly love me why didn't you trust me enough to tell me this before?"

"And risk losing you too?"

"I can deal with about anything so long as you're honest with me."

Margo sat down on the couch next to Leigh and took her hand.

"You're right. And I'm sorry."

"No more secrets. I have a right to know the whole truth."

"Okay. I'm not proud of it but I'll tell you. It happened in Calgary during the qualifying for the Olympic ski team." Margo looked down, digging the toe of her boot into the nap of the rug. "I was twenty-two. I had a shot at making the U.S Women's Downhill team if I could put together two decent runs. My dad's company had begun manufacturing ski bindings, the mechanism that holds the boot to the skis. I was working with him to develop a lightweight binding that had good edge control. A binding that would allow a steep angle without releasing too soon. We didn't always see eye-to-eye but I knew if I could qualify for the team using Tosch and Tackett bindings it would legitimize the name. Ski racers will pay about anything for equipment that could shave a tenth of a second off their time. So I told him I'd use them. They were new and experimental but the potential financial gain was enormous. He talked four other skiers into using them too. I tried to talk him out of it. I thought we needed more testing but the word got out I was skiing titanium bindings and they wanted a crack at them too."

"I thought your dad manufactured lift equipment."

"He did. Tosch and Tackett chain brakes and cable feeders were big business. The company didn't need to branch out. It was successful just the way it was. But he wanted more. That poster of me skiing, the one hanging in the store, was for Tosch and Tackett bindings. I cut the ad off the bottom. By the time those posters came out, I was sitting in jail waiting for my preliminary hearing." Margo hung her head.

"What happened?"

"I skied a practice downhill run the day before the qualifying heat just to be sure I had the ramp angles the way I wanted them. That's the way the boot sits in the binding. I knew something was wrong as soon as I made the first turn. The bindings were supposed to be stiff but they didn't feel right. So I leaned them over, way over. Far enough so they should have released. But they didn't."

"You mean if you had fallen, the bindings wouldn't have released your boots?"

"Exactly. Anyone using those bindings could have potentially broken a leg or even both legs. It could have been career-ending."

"Maybe it was just that pair of bindings. Surely the other skiers tested their own equipment."

"We'd used them for several days. They liked the stiff action. It gave good control in the turns. And no one noticed anything wrong because no one fell."

"Then maybe they were all right."

"I'll never know if they would have performed correctly or not. I couldn't take that chance. I broke into the storage room and stole the skis with the Tosch and Tackett bindings on them. I didn't want anyone to know I was targeting just those so I took a couple other sets of skis too. I thought the team could replace the missing skis before the qualifying runs and no one would know. I didn't count on security cameras."

"You stole the skis on the outside chance they might fail."

"I didn't see I had a choice."

"Why didn't you just tell them you suspected the bindings were bad?"

"My dad asked me not to. He said I made a mistake that was going to cost him his business. If Tosch and Tackett bindings were thought to be substandard, he was afraid of losing the contracts for lift equipment. He assured me there was nothing wrong with the bindings. So I let everyone think I stole the skis because I was afraid I wouldn't make the team."

"My God, Margo. How could your own father ask you to take the fall for his shoddy equipment?"

"A million dollar contract, that's how. And he didn't ask me to steal them. I did that all on my own. Maybe he was right. Maybe there was nothing wrong with them."

"Did you test them?"

Margo shook her head. "Not until years later, after dad died."

"And?" Leigh asked expectantly. "Did they release?"

Margo stared at her and slowly shook her head.

"Why didn't you test them right away? Prove to him you were right."

"I didn't need to prove anything. In my mind, I did the right thing. It doesn't matter anymore. He's gone. The business is only a memory. But that's why I can't let you meet with Elizabeth. She'll use this against me. I know she will. No court is going to give a child to a convicted felon. If Elizabeth is an unfit mother, they'll take Lindsey from me. I'd sell the warehouse before I let them put her in foster care."

"Family courts allow a preference where one parent can demonstrate they have been the child's primary caretaker. You have established an emotional bond with Lindsey. They won't break that bond. You're her mommy. You have always been her mommy," Leigh said, placing her hand on Margo's. "Let me do this for you. Let me handle this the right way."

"I can't lose her, Leigh," Margo looked away as tears filled her eyes. "I'm scared shitless I'm going to lose my daughter."

"It won't happen, sweetheart. We won't let it," Leigh said, folding her arms around her. "I promise. Please, let me help."

Margo agreed. She called Elizabeth and made an appointment for Leigh to meet with her at Archie's Café on the edge of town in one hour, ostensibly to discuss the sale of the warehouse. Leigh gave Margo a reassuring kiss and promised to call the moment the meeting was over then headed across town.

Elizabeth was late—thirty-five minutes late. Leigh wasn't surprised, not with what Margo had said about the woman. But if she wasn't going to show up, Leigh would like to know.

"More coffee, ma'am," a waitress offered, ready to fill Leigh's cup.

"No, thank you. I've had plenty," she said, covering the cup with her hand.

Leigh checked her watch. She'd give Elizabeth ten more

minutes. Who was she kidding? She'd wait as long as it took. This wasn't about Leigh. It was about Margo. Leigh would do whatever it took to keep Elizabeth from reclaiming Lindsey, even if it meant waiting all night.

Her cell phone jingled in her purse. She was tempted to ignore it, assuming it was Maureen with a question or an update. She could always check in with her later. But to her surprise it was Margo sending a text.

How's it going?

Leigh suspected Margo was pacing the floor in nervous anticipation awaiting word about the meeting with Elizabeth.

Still waiting. I'll let you know.

Margo replied immediately.

She hasn't shown up?!?!?!

Before Leigh could reply a woman came through the door. There was no mistaking this was Elizabeth. She was just as Margo had described her. Five foot four, petite features, athletic body, shoulder length blond hair and a charismatic spring in her step. There was no doubt Lindsey was this woman's child. What Margo had failed to describe were the telltale wrinkles and dark circles from her years of alcohol abuse.

Leigh quickly sent Margo a text.

Just arrived. Later, sweetheart.

"Elizabeth?" Leigh stood up and extended her hand.

"Leigh, right?" She smiled pleasantly though disingenuously. She slid in the booth across from Leigh, pushed the napkin holder and catsup bottle out of her way and folded her hands on the table. "Sorry I'm late. You know how it is." She laughed. "God, I don't know whether I'm coming or going these days. Work, work, work."

"Would you like something? Coke? Coffee?" Leigh didn't ask where she was working. That would be confrontational. She knew she probably wasn't working anywhere.

"Coffee, I guess. Although it isn't very good here." She looked around anxiously as if she had been waiting hours for service. "Black coffee," she announced as the waitress approached. She stirred two teaspoons of sugar into the cup as soon as the waitress placed it on the table. "So, you're buying the warehouse?"

Elizabeth's question was steeped with self-confidence, as if she was prepared to close the deal for Margo.

"No, I'm not the buyer." Leigh studied her expression, looking for a reaction. "Margo isn't selling the warehouse, Elizabeth."

"That's ridiculous. I just talked to her this afternoon. She's selling it. She told me so," she said, discounting Leigh's statement.

"No, she isn't. She's decided not to sell it. Not now, not ever."

Elizabeth laughed nervously. "Look, I talked to her this afternoon. She's selling it. So don't tell me she isn't 'cause I *know* she is. What do you know about it anyway? Who are you?" she snarled.

"I'm a friend of Margo's. She asked me to pass a message on to you."

"What message?" she snapped.

Leigh kept a calm demeanor, hoping Elizabeth would do the same.

"Margo has decided selling the warehouse isn't in her best interest right now." Before Leigh could finish Elizabeth interrupted.

"I told you I talked to her this afternoon. She's selling it. She doesn't have a choice." Elizabeth's eyes narrowed venomously, her nostrils flaring.

"She does have a choice."

"What the hell does this have to do with you anyway?"

"I'm a friend, a close friend who cares deeply about her and doesn't want her to get hurt." Leigh knew better than to divulge her personal feelings for Margo. They were none of Elizabeth's business.

"If you're that good a friend go tell her to get on the stick and find a buyer for that worthless piece of crap property. And now."

"Elizabeth, the reason I offered to meet with you is to explain why Margo isn't selling the warehouse. I'm sure we can discuss this calmly, like two adults."

"Margo owes me money," she said smugly. "She owes me big time and I have the IOU."

"Did you bring it with you?"

"Yes."

Leigh held out her hand, waiting while Elizabeth fumbled in the bottom of her purse.

"I'm sure I put it in here. I know I did. But I've got one."

"Do you remember exactly what it said?"

"I don't remember the exact wording, legal mumbo-jumbo." She chuckled pompously. "They write that crap so no one but a lawyer can understand it."

"So it was a legal document? Duly notarized and recorded?"

"Sure it was."

Leigh pulled a folded letter from her purse and opened it, scanning down the page.

"I presume you mean this." She held the letter up for Elizabeth to see. "This is a photocopy of the document Margo has, the agreement you made, accepting payments in return for allowing Margo to retain guardianship of your daughter, Lindsey."

Elizabeth snatched the letter from Leigh's hand. She read it then tossed it back across the table.

"That's not all of it. There's more. Where's the other page? It says how she promised to pay me. And believe me it was way more than that old warehouse is worth. But I'm not greedy. I told Margo I'd settle for whatever she gets for it. That's only fair."

"How much do you consider fair?" Leigh asked, refolding the paper into her purse.

"She knows."

"Maybe I should ask how much you consider a fair price for Lindsey." Leigh rolled her eyes up to Elizabeth. "That's what you're doing, isn't it? Selling your daughter?"

"NO! She owes me. She promised," Elizabeth said through gritted teeth. "She owes me big time. She wanted that kid. Now she's going to pay me or she'll be sorry. I know my rights. She can bring on the blood tests but I'm that kid's biological mother." She held out her wrist as if offering a blood sample. "Bring on the needles. I dare you. That kid's mine."

"Margo doesn't dispute that. Yes, you are Lindsey's mother. Absolutely."

"You bet your ass I am." Elizabeth gloated.

Leigh took a deep breath, swallowing back her contempt for this woman. She knew better than to argue with a drunk. She couldn't win.

"I know what Margo's doing," Elizabeth said in an accusatory tone. "She's trying to scare me off. Well, it won't work. Either she pays up or I'm taking the kid back to Cheyenne and she'll play hell ever seeing her again. You go back and tell her that." She pointed a sinister finger at Leigh. "I know stuff about Margo. If she doesn't want it spread all over this town, you go tell her to get off her ass and get my money and fast."

"Okay," Leigh said, placing a five-dollar bill under her coffee cup. She pulled on her gloves, strung her purse strap over her shoulder and stood up. "I'll tell her."

"You do that." Elizabeth had a victorious albeit sarcastic glint in her eye.

Leigh looked down at the woman. She had seen this before. An alcoholic fortified with a false bravado who actually believed what she was saying. She had wrapped herself in a thick blanket of self-righteous indignation and a false sense of security. Leigh could tell her the bullying and blackmail with Lindsey as the bargaining chip was over. She'd never see another dollar from Margo. But nothing could be gained from it. She wasn't going to pick up that rope and play tug of war with this woman.

Leigh leaned down, looked Elizabeth in the eye and said, "Give it your best shot, girlie." With that, Leigh walked out.

Chapter 20

"Leigh, over here," Margo called from her place along the rope barricade. It had just begun to snow as Leigh made her way through the crowd.

"Did I miss her?" she asked, looking up the hill.

"She's next." Margo pointed to the pink-clad skier waiting at the staging area.

"Is she nervous?"

"No. She said she wasn't." Margo kept her eyes on the skier as if they were glued there.

"Are you?" Leigh asked, reading the worried look on Margo's face.

"Hell, yes." She laughed.

"She'll do fine. She's got your athletic talent." Leigh hooked her hand through Margo's arm. "And thank you."

"For what?"

"Exchanging the tire chains for me. I think I'll leave that kind of thing to you."

"My pleasure," Margo said with a chuckle.

"And I have good news."

"Let's hear it. I could use some good news."

"The prosecutor's office called. They caught the two punks who broke into my cabin."

"That is good news. Who was it?"

"They were brothers. Their father works for the security system company I used to use. He was positive his little darlings couldn't possibly have done anything like that but the DNA collected at the scene said otherwise. The two scuzzbags ejaculated in my underwear drawer. I call that the ultimate humiliation. It seems Jason and Joel had dropped out of college and were supporting a very nasty drug habit daddy didn't know anything about."

"You're pressing charges, aren't you?" Margo suggested sternly.

"You better believe it. And speaking of court decisions..." Leigh suggested, rubbing Margo's arm softly.

"We haven't heard yet, if that's what you mean." Margo turned her attention back up the hill. "It's taking forever."

"Our next competitor is six-year-old Lindsey Tosch," the public address announcer said. "Skier, take your mark."

"Bend your knees and pole the turns, baby," Margo muttered anxiously.

"When did Elnora say you might hear something? Any idea?" Leigh asked, watching for Lindsey to start.

"No. And I don't understand why you couldn't have been our attorney."

"I told you, I'm a corporate lawyer. Elnora specializes in family law. Some of the laws have changed and I wanted to be sure we didn't overlook anything. She's one of the best."

"If you say so," Margo said as a horn sounded. "Here she comes."

"Come on, Lindsey," Leigh shouted, clapping encouragement.

Lindsey pushed off, her pink helmet bobbing along as she

started toward the first set of flags. Margo watched intently, her body language imitating Lindsey's actions through the turns.

"Little more speed, baby," Margo urged. "That's it. Keep your hands out front."

The crowd, mostly parents and siblings of other skiers, cheered and applauded as she sailed by, a determined look on her face and her blond ponytail flying behind.

"Way to go, Lindsey," Margo shouted as she crossed the finish line.

"Forty-one point two seconds," the announced said. "That puts Lindsey in first place."

"Yeah!!!" Leigh cheered, jumping up and down and tugging at Margo's sleeve. "She's in first place."

Margo and Leigh hurried down the slope to where Lindsey was standing in her skis. Margo greeted her with a hug, lifting her off the ground.

"Way to go, short stuff," Margo exclaimed.

"Did you see me, Leigh?" Lindsey asked eagerly, her cheeks as pink as her helmet.

"Yes, I did and you were great," Leigh said, hugging her as well. "I'm so impressed. I wish I could do that."

"Can I have some hot chocolate? Katy and I want to get some at the snack bar." She didn't seem impressed at being in first place.

"Sure," Margo said, unhooking Lindsey's bindings and safety straps. She handed her some money, enough for both girls. "Come right back, okay?"

"We will." The two girls tromped off toward the snack bar, hand-in-hand.

"I think that's great she won," Leigh said, smiling in their direction. "We should do something special to celebrate."

"I don't want to burst your bubble, counselor, but she's in first place because she's only the second skier to come down the course. There are sixteen more skiers in her division."

"Oh." Leigh snickered. "But at least she's first for now."

Margo beamed with pride as Lindsey's name appeared on the scoreboard above the official's table. She hooked Lindsey's skis and poles together and hoisted them over her shoulder.

"Want some hot chocolate, counselor?" Margo asked, her hand against the small of Leigh's back.

"I'd love some." Leigh nonchalantly hooked her hand through Margo's arm as they walked along.

"By the way, how did your big merger thing go?"

"It went well. All settled. Everyone is happy."

"Good. I was beginning to think you wouldn't make it back for Lindsey's race."

"I wouldn't miss it."

"Can I watch the rest of the race with Katy?" Lindsey asked, carrying her hot chocolate in two hands. "Katy's mom said I can watch with them."

"Okay." Margo wiped a whipped cream smear off her upper lip. "Behave yourself," she added.

"I will," Lindsey headed across the slope with her friend.

"Hey, Lu-Lu," Margo called.

"Huh?" she said, looking back.

"I love you, kiddo."

"I love you too, Mommy," she replied then waved.

"I assume you heard Elizabeth put up quite a stink," Margo said after Lindsey had gone.

"Yes, Elnora told me. She said Elizabeth was fighting for Lindsey all the way."

"I'm a little nervous about that. The judge seemed very sympathetic to her story." Margo shook her head disgustedly.

"It'll be okay. You know what they say, the wheels of justice turn slowly but they do turn. We just have to wait it out."

Margo and Leigh sat sipping hot chocolate and visiting about anything Leigh thought would take her mind off Lindsey and the impending court ruling while Lindsey played with her friends and watched the other racers.

"When do you have to be back in Denver?" Margo asked cautiously.

"I'm not sure. It kind of depends."

"On what?"

"On whether I have any clients in Aspen who need my services."

"I didn't know you had clients in Aspen."

"Aspen is a very lucrative market. Lots of business opportunities in the area. Lots of corporate dealings taking shape. Great place for a branch office." Leigh raised her eyebrows.

"Oh, really?" Margo smiled coyly at her.

"I heard there might be a bright development opportunity on the horizon that could use some pro bono legal advice." Leigh winked.

"Could be." Margo slid her fingers across the bench to where Leigh's hand was resting. "Maybe we could work out a trade."

"What did you have in mind?"

"Legal advice in trade for private ski lessons." Margo laced her gloved fingers through Leigh's.

"You wouldn't happen to know anyone willing to give private lessons, would you?"

"I think we can work something out."

"It might take a long time. I'm not used to the snow like some of you mountain women."

"That's okay. I'm prepared to dedicate years to it," Margo said, holding Leigh's gaze in a captivating smile.

"Mommy," Lindsey said, rushing over to them with a disappointed look on her face. "I didn't win."

"I'm sorry, baby, but that's okay." Margo extended an arm and gathered her in. "I'm very proud of you anyway. You did a great job."

"You absolutely did, Lindsey. I'm proud of you too," Leigh added. "I bet you do better next time. Tell you what. How about I take us to Grizzly's for barbecue?"

"Oh, boy," she squealed eagerly. "Can I have ribs?"

"You bet you can," Leigh said, kissing Lindsey on the cheek. "Maybe we can talk Mommy into driving us." She grinned up at Margo.

Margo returned a coy smile and said, "I'd be glad to."

On the way through town, they stopped by the Polar Bear. While Lindsey ran upstairs to change out of her ski clothes, Margo checked in with Karen. The youth ski races meant a busy day for thermal socks, stocking caps and insulated gloves.

"It's a good thing you ordered extra liner socks. I can't keep up with the demand for them. Kids are wearing the adult sizes like tights. Who knew?" Karen said, restocking the display.

Margo looked up and gasped as a sheriff's car pulled up out front. Leigh hadn't noticed the car at first but she did notice the horrified look on Margo's face as she said, "Oh, shit."

"Hey, Margo," a uniformed officer said, coming through the door.

"Hi, John," she said, a worried expression on her face.

He scanned the store as if looking for something or someone.

"Hello, Sheriff. Can we help you with something?" Leigh said, extending her hand to the man. "I'm Leigh Insley, Margo's attorney."

"This is for you," he said, handing a folded stack of papers to Margo. "The county clerk's office sent me over with it."

"What is it?" Margo asked suspiciously. She stared at the papers but didn't take them.

The door opened and Lindsey came bubbling through it. "I'm ready," she said, tugging a stocking cap down snug.

"Come over here, Lindsey," Margo said, moving to collect her. She picked Lindsey up and held her in her arms. Leigh took the folded papers from the sheriff and opened them, scanning down through the pages. The more she read the tighter Margo held onto Lindsey.

"What does it say?" Margo asked, tightly braced for bad news.

"What's wrong, Mommy?" Lindsey asked. "Aren't we going to Grizzly's?"

Leigh finally looked up and said, "Yes, Lindsey, we certainly are going to Grizzly's. You and me and your mommy." She smiled at Margo then released a satisfied sigh. "She's all yours, sweetheart. Forever and ever."

Margo looked over at Leigh, tears streaming down her face. She finally drew a deep breath and buried her face in Lindsey's coat, crying sobs of relief. Leigh ran to her, wrapping her arms around the two of them.

"Thank you," Margo said through her tears. She set Lindsey down and gathered Leigh in her arms, kissing her passionately. "I love you, counselor. Can you forgive me for being stupid?"

"There's nothing to forgive. I'm yours forever and ever, too," Leigh said then kissed her back.

**Publications from
Bella Books, Inc.
Women. Books. Even Better Together.
P.O. Box 10543
Tallahassee, FL 32302
Phone: 800-729-4992
www.bellabooks.com**

CALM BEFORE THE STORM by Peggy J. Herring. Colonel Marcel Robicheaux doesn't tell and so far no one official has asked, but the amorous pursuit by Jordan McGowen has her worried for both her career and her honor.
978-0-9677753-1-9

THE WILD ONE by Lyn Denison. Rachel Weston is busy keeping home and head together after the death of her husband. Her kids need her and what she doesn't need is the confusion that Quinn Farrelly creates in her body and heart.
978-0-9677753-4-0

LESSONS IN MURDER by Claire McNab. There's a corpse in the school with a neat hole in the head and a Black & Decker drill alongside. Which teacher should Inspector Carol Ashton suspect? Unfortunately, the alluring Sybil Quade is at the top of the list. First in this highly lauded series.
978-1-931513-65-4

WHEN AN ECHO RETURNS by Linda Kay Silva. The bayou where Echo Branson found her sanity has been swept clean by a hurricane—or at least they thought. Then an evil washed up by the storm comes looking for them all, one-by-one. Second in series.
978-1-59493-225-0

DEADLY INTERSECTIONS by Ann Roberts. Everyone is lying, including her own father and her girlfriend. Leaving matters to the professionals is supposed to be easier! Third in series with *PAID IN FULL* and *WHITE OFFERINGS*.
978-1-59493-224-3

SUBSTITUTE FOR LOVE by Karin Kallmaker. No substitutes, ever again! But then Holly's heart, body and soul are captured by Reyna... Reyna with no last name and a secret life that hides a terrible bargain, one written in family blood.
978-1-931513-62-3

MAKING UP FOR LOST TIME by Karin Kallmaker. Take one Next Home Network Star and add one Little White Lie to equal mayhem in little Mendocino and a recipe for sizzling romance. This lighthearted, steamy story is a feast for the senses in a kitchen that is way too hot.
978-1-931513-61-6

2ND FIDDLE by Kate Calloway. Cassidy James's first case left her with a broken heart. At least this new case is fighting the good fight, and she can throw all her passion and energy into it.
978-1-59493-200-7

HUNTING THE WITCH by Ellen Hart. The woman she loves — used to love — offers her help, and Jane Lawless finds it hard to say no. She needs TLC for recent injuries and who better than a doctor? But Julia's jittery demeanor awakens Jane's curiosity. And Jane has never been able to resist a mystery. #9 in series and Lammy-winner.
978-1-59493-206-9

FAÇADES by Alex Marcoux. Everything Anastasia ever wanted — she has it. Sidney is the woman who helped her get it. But keeping it will require a price — the unnamed passion that simmers between them.
978-1-59493-239-7

ELENA UNDONE by Nicole Conn. The risks. The passion. The devastating choices. The ultimate rewards. Nicole Conn rocked the lesbian cinema world with *Claire of the Moon* and has rocked it again with *Elena Undone*. This is the book that tells it all...
978-1-59493-254-0

WHISPERS IN THE WIND by Frankie J. Jones. It began as a camping trip, then a simple hike. Dixon Hayes and Elizabeth Colter uncover an intriguing cave on their hike, changing their world, perhaps irrevocably.
978-1-59493-037-9

WEDDING BELL BLUES by Julia Watts. She'll do anything to save what's left of her family. Anything. It didn't seem like a bad plan...at first. Hailed by readers as Lammy-winner Julia Watts' funniest novel.
978-1-59493-199-4

WILDFIRE by Lynn James. From the moment botanist Devon McKinney meets ranger Elaine Thomas the chemistry is undeniable. Sharing—and protecting—a mountain for the length of their short assignments leads to unexpected passion in this sizzling romance by newcomer Lynn James.
978-1-59493-191-8

LEAVING L.A. by Kate Christie. Eleanor Chapin is on the way to the rest of her life when Tessa Flanagan offers her a lucrative summer job caring for Tessa's daughter Laya. It's only temporary and everyone expects Eleanor to be leaving L.A...
978-1-59493-221-2

SOMETHING TO BELIEVE by Robbi McCoy. When Lauren and Cassie meet on a once-in-a-lifetime river journey through China their feelings are innocent...at first. Ten years later, nothing—and everything—has changed. From Golden Crown winner Robbi McCoy.
978-1-59493-214-4

DEVIL'S ROCK by Gerri Hill. Deputy Andrea Sullivan and Agent Cameron Ross vow to bring a killer to justice. The killer has other plans. Gerri Hill pens another intriguing blend of mystery and romance in this page-turning thriller.
978-1-59493-218-2

SHADOW POINT by Amy Briant. Madison McPeake has just been not-quite fired, told her brother is dead and discovered she has to pick up a five-year old niece she's never met. After she makes it to Shadow Point it seems like someone—or something—doesn't want her to leave. Romance sizzles in this ghost story from Amy Briant.
978-1-59493-216-8

JUKEBOX by Gina Daggett. Debutantes in love. With each other. Two young women chafe at the constraints of parents and society with a friendship that could be more, if they can break free. Gina Daggett is best known as "Lipstick" of the columnist duo Lipstick & Dipstick.
978-1-59493-212-0

BLIND BET by Tracey Richardson. The stakes are high when Ellen Turcotte and Courtney Langford meet at the blackjack tables. Lady Luck has been smiling on Courtney but Ellen is a wild card she may not be able to handle.
978-1-59493-211-3